THE TERROR

by

Jonas Saul

PUBLISHED BY:
Imagine Press Inc.
Ebook ISBN: 978-1-927404-47-8
Paperback ISBN: 978-1-998047-42-0
Hardcover ISBN: 978-1-998047-43-7

The Terror
Copyright © 2017 by Jonas Saul

All rights reserved. No part of this publication may be reproduced, stored in a retrieval system, or transmitted in any form or by any means (electronic, mechanical, photocopying, recording, or otherwise) without the publisher's prior written permission.

This is a work of fiction. The characters, organizations, and events portrayed in this novel are either products of the author's imagination or are used fictitiously. References to real people, events, establishments, organizations, or locations are intended only to provide a sense of authenticity and are used fictitiously. Any resemblance to actual events, places, organizations, or persons, living or dead, is entirely coincidental.

Imagine Press Inc. does not have control over, or any responsibility for, any author or third-party websites referred to in or on this book.

The Sarah Roberts Series

Dark Visions (One)
The Warning (Two)
The Crypt (Three)
The Hostage (Four)
The Victim (Five)
The Enigma (Six)
The Vigilante (Seven)
The Rogue (Eight)
Killing Sarah (Nine)
The Antagonist (Ten)
The Redeemed (Eleven)
The Haunted (Twelve)
The Unlucky (Thirteen)
The Abandoned (Fourteen)
The Cartel (Fifteen)
Losing Sarah (Sixteen)
The Pact (Seventeen)
The Terror (Eighteen)
The Chase (Nineteen)
The Betrayal (Twenty)
Sarah's Return (Twenty-One)
The Hunt (Twenty-Two)
The Delivery (Twenty-Three)
The Trap (Twenty-Four)
The Ultimatum (Twenty-Five)
The Depraved (Twenty-Six)
The Condemned (Twenty-Seven)
Payback (Twenty-Eight)
The Unknown (Twenty-Nine)
Wrath (Thirty)
The Damned (Thirty-One)
The Game (Thirty-Two)

The Decoy (Thirty-Three)
The Disappearance (Thirty-Four)
The Whole Truth (Thirty-Five)
Alex (Thirty-Six)
Parkman (Thirty-Seven)
Darwin (Thirty-Eight)
Aaron (Thirty-Nine)
Remains To Be Seen (Forty)

The Jake Wood Novels

The Immortal Gene (Book One)
The Immortal Target (Book Two)

Standalone Novels

'Til Death Do Us Part
The Drowning
The Woman in the Woods
The Threat
The Specter
The Mafia Trilogy
A Murder in Time
Frequency of the Dead

Co-Authored Novels

Collision Course (Written with Gary Ponzo)
There Will Be Blood (Written with Rania Stone)
The Soulless (Written with Rania Stone)

Short Story Collections

Twisted Fate (Tales of Horror)

Twists of Fate (Tales of Hope)

Chapter 1

Two innocent people would die in twenty minutes, and Sarah Roberts could do nothing about it. The ability to avert their deaths was beyond her control. After everything she had done to prepare for this moment, it was coming, and those lives would be taken.

Sarah was well aware of her limitations, and they disgusted her. Her job—Vivian's job, really—was to see the future incident and do something about it. But sometimes, changing fate wasn't in the cards. Sometimes, the Roberts sisters were *not* supposed to save a life.

Sarah hadn't informed the dozens of emergency personnel assembled in the previous twenty-four hours that their efforts were hopeless. They had worked tirelessly to save the two people destined to die. The Royal Canadian Mounted Police were conducting a full-scale search of local buildings for the device Sarah had described. The bomb squad had been brought in from Vancouver—a four-hour drive—and had spent several hours evacuating buildings, working with city planners, and utilizing any tidbits of information Sarah could offer to locate and remove the threat. Neighboring cities had sent key personnel to Kelowna, hoping they could stop this.

All this took place at Sarah's word. Whether the authorities believed in the paranormal or not, it was abundantly clear that enough of them believed in Sarah. Or maybe they were just desperate. Kelowna had recently been hit by two bombs that killed five people. To date, the investigation had led nowhere. Police had found no connection between the people who had died. The bomb material used was similar—something homemade by an amateur—but that alone had turned into a dead end.

This prompted Officer Stephen Lee to call Parkman and ask if Sarah would come and lend a hand. They hoped she could tell them if they should expect more bombs in the city. And if so, where and when?

That answer wasn't always easy. Sarah had determined that another was coming, but she couldn't tell where the bomb was at any given moment. It seemed to move from place to place. This was most peculiar. Why was it moving? Could someone be wearing the device? Vivian had assured her the device would detonate at the corner of Bernard and Ellis.

Sarah checked her watch. Eighteen minutes left. Acts of terror had seized this summer vacation city during July, one of the busiest months of the year. Bernard Avenue had been blocked off at the intersection with Ellis Street in the heart of downtown Kelowna. The usually bustling core, streaming with vacationers and locals alike on its recently widened sidewalk, was about to be marred by blood.

Someone slapped Sarah's arm, breaking her trance.

She turned, scowling.

"You good?" Parkman asked.

Her face softened, then dissolved into a half smile. "Yeah. No. Not really."

The bank across the street was empty. The vape shops closed. Retail stores had been vacated early on the opposite corner, and shoppers and staff were told to go home for the day.

"You've done a great job organizing this," Parkman said. "Take pride that it's only two people and not a dozen bystanders or more. Lives were saved today because you were here."

She had told Parkman, her trusted confidant, everything. He'd traveled with her to Kelowna to make sure she received a warm reception after what she had done on her previous visit to the city. Antagonizing a member of the RCMP until the man was murdered might be a wound several of his fellow officers weren't prepared to heal quite yet—even if that cop was a horrible, law-breaking man who was killed by his cannibalistic wife. Certain people wouldn't take too kindly to having Sarah Roberts *working* with the police now, as some thought she was complicit in the murder of a cop.

"If you weren't here and that bomb went off in," Parkman glanced at his cell phone, "eleven minutes, a lot of people would die." His free hand landed softly on her shoulder. "You're doing the right thing."

An officer in full tactical gear came out of a building across the road. Sarah watched him speak into his lapel mic, then trudge along the sidewalk to the next building. A few feet to her left, three officers talked to a city planner about the sewer system under the streets, but they were out of time to navigate them. There was nothing left for anyone to do.

Sarah faced Parkman. "We're out of time. Vivian's asleep or some shit. I'm not hearing anything new from the other side." His hand was still on her shoulder. She brought hers up and clamped onto his wrist, head tilted, eyes closed, listening. "I detect nothing," she whispered. "Feel nothing. All I have is the bomb. Two people dead. It's moving right now. Coming closer." She opened her eyes and stared into Parkman's face. "I'm sorry. I wish I could tell them more—" Sarah stopped talking as a distant voice echoed in her head. She glanced at the sidewalk, not looking at anything in particular. She focused on that echo, listening to it, the hot summer sun beating on the back of her neck.

"Sarah?" Parkman's voice was soft, calm.

"One sec," she snapped.

The voice came again. Gibberish, saying nothing discernible. She shook her head as if to dislodge the voice, then glanced upward.

"What is it?" Parkman asked, any patience he might have held melting away.

"Thought I heard something." She was thankful when Parkman didn't ask for more.

She released his wrist and faced the office building across the street. In the front window of the building on the second floor, a man stood watching her. Sarah stared back. Their eyes locked. He was well-dressed and appeared to be in his early fifties. He held up his right hand at shoulder height and moved it in an odd circular motion.

"Parkman?"

"Yeah?"

"How much time left?"

There was a pause, then, "Just over six minutes."

"Has everyone been evacuated from nearby buildings?"

"Of course. They believe in what you can do, Sarah. They're listening. Everyone's in position and ready."

"Then why is there a man in that building with no body armor?"

Parkman moved closer. "Where?" he asked. "What building?"

Sarah pointed. "That one."

As she pointed, the man backed away and was lost from sight.

"I don't see anyone," Parkman said, a hand above his eyes to shield the sun.

"Parkman, we need Officer Lee to have someone clear that building." The thought they would be too late sent a shiver through her. "Hurry. That building will sustain damage."

Parkman bolted away from her and joined the three officers and the city planner ten feet away, hastily explaining what Sarah saw. Officer Lee shouted into a radio for a team to evacuate the B.C. Health Services building immediately.

Less than a minute later, two bomb squad team members, covered in thick gear, disappeared through the front of the building.

Sarah shielded her eyes and stared up at the window on the second floor again.

The man in the black suit reappeared, his right hand moving just as before. He wasn't waving. It was like he was trying to tell her something with his hand. She stepped closer, yellow police tape pressing into her thighs.

What was he trying to say? She stared, his presence magnetic, drawing her to him.

"Sarah?" Parkman shouted beside her.

His voice was so sudden she jumped.

"What?"

"It's time to pull back. We're down to a couple of minutes."

Sarah scanned the second-floor window. The man was gone. Something was wrong. The bomb was still mobile, but it wasn't here yet. Was someone carrying it? A suicide bomber in Kelowna? It seemed unlikely but possible.

Or was the man in the suit the bomber? Something didn't match up with that. She was certain the man was not connected to what would happen. He had been trying to tell her something.

Someone clutched her forearm.

"Ma'am, you're going to have to step back."

One of Lee's officers gestured for her to follow him to where they would be concealed from the explosion. He'd been introduced to her earlier, but she forgot his name.

Head down, Sarah followed the cop, her mind racing through possibilities and scenarios. Did she just send two bomb squad members into the building that would be destroyed, thereby killing them? If so, the RCMP wouldn't just want her out of the city, they would blame her for their deaths.

They reached the containment area with one minute to spare.

A car horn blared in the distance.

Sarah looked up. Her heart raced in her throat, pulsing in her ears. If she was going to save anyone, the time was now. There was something about that horn. Something that made sense to her intuitive side.

"That's it," she whispered.

"What's it?" Parkman asked, stepping closer to her.

Two uniformed officers eased in to listen.

"The bomb," she said, her voice hardened, deeper. "It's here."

Sarah dropped low to avoid being grabbed by anyone and ran back outside.

Chapter 2

JOHN HAMPTON WAS NOT ready to settle down. The suburban life, the barbecue parties, and the social events weren't in his nature. They had never been. He knew that at twenty-six years old, but his twenty-four-year-old girlfriend didn't.

"Look, Susan, I have nothing against your friends, but they're *yours*, not mine."

Susan, in the seat beside him, crossed her arms. "The point of having them come over to our new place is so they can become your friends, too." She stared out the window to her right.

This was her routine. At the beginning of every fight, she performed her ritual. Close down. Lockout. Let no one in. John had met Susan's mother and knew it was something she had taught her.

John rubbed the inside of his palms on the steering wheel as he tightened his grip to calm the rising anger, trying to formulate a response. Susan had seemed on edge lately, blowing a gasket for no reason. His father always told him to avoid arguing with his better half. "They always end up winning," his dad would say. "Pick your battles, then stand up for your beliefs." It seemed he was picking too many battles lately, which led him to dangerous territory. Maybe he wasn't the right man for Susan.

Or maybe she wasn't the right woman for him?

It'd been a week since they'd moved in together, and today was no different from any other day of being around each other constantly. If this week was any indication of where they were headed, the destination was quite bleak indeed.

"Susan, it's okay if we have different friends." John snuck a peek at her, then looked back at the road as they approached a red light. He waited another breath, then added, "Isn't it?"

"You know it is," she snapped without facing him. "But Nancy and Jim have been in my life since we were kids. I just thought you'd be willing—"

"Willing?" he cut her off. It was his turn to be angry. She always forced her will upon him. First, it was where the garbage container in the kitchen had to be put. Then what drawer the cutlery had to be placed in? He always had it beside the stove to grab easily when cooking. Susan even took the painting of the Greek house out of the kitchen and placed it in storage until *she* could find a suitable wall to rehang it on. Susan had become a controlling bitch, and he was tired of it. Pick his battles or not; he wasn't willing to walk away from this one.

"You know what, Susan, fuck it," he said loudly as the

light changed to green, and he hit the accelerator harder than he wanted. "Bring Jim and Nancy over. See if I care. I'll *try* to be nice, but you already know Jim and I won't get along."

He signaled to turn left onto Ellis Street and waited at the light, hands clenched even tighter on the wheel, eyes locked straight ahead. Susan breathed in and out audibly like she was trying to keep tears at bay.

Tears of manipulation, he thought. *Fuck her. I'm done. This isn't a relationship. This is a constant battle.*

They were supposed to pick up Nancy and Jim downtown, then take them to their new place. He almost laughed at the thought.

"Maybe moving in together was a mistake," Susan whispered, her voice monotone, clipped. It didn't match the rapid breathing, seething little girl beside him.

The verbal sucker punch staggered John's own breathing, and he looked at her. *A mistake? Really?* She disgusted him now. Small and fragile, she hunched down in the passenger seat of his minivan, shooting her mouth off to cut him emotionally. He wanted her out of his van. He wanted her out of his life. But how? It would take months. They'd just taken up residence together. Moved all their stuff into one place. Consolidated their finances. That had been *her* plan. Lock him down in every way, then act out however she chooses.

A mistake? Well, fuck you.

John Hampton wouldn't be played like that.

A car horn honked somewhere.

John blinked and looked forward. The light was green. Cars on the other side were being rerouted for some reason. He was clear to turn left.

John mashed the pedal down. The van shot forward. He

crossed through the intersection and aimed for the curb on the right, pulled up alongside it, then jammed on the brakes.

"Get out!" he shouted. Blood rushed to his face, heating his cheeks. "Get out of my van. Now! I'm done with you."

Susan recoiled against the door at the sudden burst of anger but didn't reach for the door.

"*A mistake.*" He mocked her voice, albeit a whinier version. "Yeah," he bobbed his head, the words hoarse and loud, "a real fucking mistake." He shot his arm out and pointed at the sidewalk. "Get the fuck out!"

If it was possible, Susan shrunk lower in her seat and shook her head. She wasn't getting out. She was refusing his command in his own vehicle. At least the van was his. They hadn't shared that yet.

How dare she try to fuck with me?

"Fine," he shouted at the top of his lungs. He slapped the horn, then held it for several seconds. "Stay the fuck right where you are, then. We'll get into trouble together."

Without checking his blind spot, he slammed the pedal down. The van shot forward. At the next set of lights, a police cruiser was parked on the side of the road, its lights rotating slowly. Two red sawhorses blocked the road. As John drew closer, he read the words stenciled across them.

Police Line Do Not Cross.

"Don't, John," Susan said, barely loud enough to be heard over the revving engine. "You always have to make a scene," she shouted, louder now. "Just don't."

Susan wouldn't tell him what to do anymore.

John tried to maneuver around the sawhorses but couldn't. One of them bounced off the front bumper and shot sideways, the crack of wood like a slap across someone's fleshy cheek.

"Stop the van," Susan said beside him, her voice broken, gone to tears. "Stop! I want out."

Someone shouted outside the van. John paid them no attention. Susan, his girlfriend, his lovely woman, the bitch that always had to control his life, control everything, was willing to walk away. She was willing to leave.

He slammed on the brakes. They rocked forward, then slammed back into their seats as the van came to a complete stop.

"Get the fuck out!" He tried to lunge across her but got tangled up in his seatbelt and banged his shoulder into her left forearm. She cried out in pain while using her good hand to open the door.

At the same second, Susan spilled sideways from the van, her face a mask of wet redness, and someone slapped the window beside John's head.

Startled, he whipped around so fast a wave of dizziness came over him.

A pretty blonde girl—more woman than girl—stared at him with a frantic expression. She tried his locked door.

Susan's friend, Nancy. It had to be.

"Open up, John!" the woman yelled as she pounded on the window like a lunatic. "Get out of the van."

Of course, Nancy would know his name.

Nancy eased away from the window, then backed up quickly as a small contingency of police officers ran toward her.

"You will die if you stay in the van." The woman's face changed to a look of panic. "Get out now while you still have a chance." As she moved farther from the van, her lips formed the words, *I'm sorry.*

In that brief second, John couldn't believe that Susan had set him up that well. Why would Nancy be saying she was sorry? Susan had played him the entire time. She was trying to *force* him to meet her friends. But to what end? Why was it so damn important? And what would Nancy have to apologize for?

John had been given a glimpse of how protective Susan's friends were. That Nancy would run up to the van as Susan jumped out and tried John's door, pounding on the window, yelling at him to get out, only told him that Susan could keep her friends. He didn't need them. And he certainly didn't need her.

"Fuck all y'all."

The passenger door remained open. The street was oddly empty. Not a soul to be seen. Susan was gone. It was over.

A smile cut his lips sideways.

"Good riddance, bitch." John hit the gas. "Fuck you to glory hell, whore bitch."

Then John was no more.

Chapter 3

SARAH CONTINUED MOVING AWAY from the van after mouthing the words, *I'm sorry.* Several officers held her arms as they guided her back to safety.

The van's engine revved. It shot forward, then lifted off the ground as something exploded in the rear of the van. The shock wave knocked Sarah's entourage to the sidewalk. She shook her head, trying to clear the dull ringing in her ears. The red van rolled forward until it butted up against the building beside the Scotia Bank. Flames licked up and out of the rear windows that had been blown out.

The B.C. Health Services building would have a burn mark unless the fire department got into action fast enough.

Sarah rolled to her side and managed to clamber to her feet. The three uniformed men beside her also stood. She closed her eyes and listened. Vivian was trying to tell her something. It was important. The plea in Vivian's voice was evident around the ringing in her head.

What is it? Sarah shouted internally.

Her sister's words came through loud and clear.

"Get down," Sarah yelled as she bent over and waved her arms. "There's another bomb."

No one moved. Not a single person responded, their hearing jeopardized by the blast. Officers on the street watched as the van burned while others kept back from the heat of the flames. A firetruck barreled along Bernard Avenue, making its way to the burning minivan.

A stinging drop of sweat fell into her right eye. She had to blink it away, then rub her eye. This was madness. Being deafened by the first blast would kill so many more as they converged on the van to extinguish the flames licking out the back when the second blast came.

In thirty seconds, another bomb would take the doors off the van.

Sarah grabbed the cop beside her, spun him around, snatched the gun from his holster, then shoved him away from her. He pivoted quickly and lunged for the gun, clinging onto her wrist, his mouth emitting some kind of shout, but she couldn't hear him over the ringing in her own ears.

She pulled her hand out of his grip easily enough. After a quick step back to make room, she raised the weapon and clicked off the safety.

The firetruck's siren broke through the ringing in her ears. Sound was returning, and that truck was getting too close.

At any moment, she expected a bullet for her efforts. Stealing a cop's gun and lowering it to aim at the firetruck was enough for another officer to shoot her. She only hoped she was too quick for any of them to respond.

She aimed at the approaching vehicle and fired into the large, square grill. The driver reacted instantly by spinning the wheel and heading toward the opening that turned onto Ellis Street to his left, away from the burning red van.

Six seconds ...

Wild with panic to keep people away from the van, Sarah screamed and jumped into the middle of the street.

Five seconds ...

From the corner of her eye, she saw Parkman trying to pull Officer Lee's arms off him. Another cop jumped in, subduing Parkman, his face a mask of fear and anguish.

Several uniformed officers lined the sidewalks, weapons trained on Sarah. A brave cop stepped toward her, arms extended, empty palms facing her, his mouth working. It looked like he was saying, *calm down.*

They didn't want to shoot her. She knew this intuitively. She was an invited guest. She had known about the bomb. She was Officer Lee's pet project, and no one wanted to kill that.

But aiming the gun at a cop was a surefire way to get shot herself, regardless. In the highly anti-cop environment society had taken on, the police weren't taking any chances.

Four seconds ...

In retrospect, this might have been a mistake. Stealing an officer's weapon would have consequences. Aiming it at a cop, dire ones.

"There's another bomb in the van," she shouted, her voice distinctly different because she only heard it internally. "Stay back."

The van was close. Too close to her.

Three seconds ...

Vivian's whisper, a caress in her inner ear. A welcoming, comforting voice. She needed to get away from the van. The urge to hold her ground for a few more seconds warred with the urge to run at full tilt toward safety.

The prophecy said a man and a woman would die in the blast. But the girl got out of the van in time. The man didn't. Sarah had stood at the driver's side door, banging on the window. She'd looked inside. Only John had remained in the vehicle.

Two seconds ...

Her heart fluttered in her chest as if someone had reached under her rib cage and squeezed it with their hands.

A woman would die, too.

She was the only woman standing close to the van.

Vivian?

A cop lunged at Sarah, scrambling for the weapon. Sarah reacted by dropping the gun and jumping back in the same instant.

One second. Run!

Sarah jumped, twisted her body while still in the air, and, as if in a slow-motion movie reel, landed on her left foot, her right sweeping in a wide arc. She connected with the cop's shin, altering his trajectory.

At the exact second the cop hit the ground awkwardly and tumbled into a roll on the concrete, Sarah was already leaping away off her good foot.

She made it three steps before she dove for the ground.

The second blast came, bigger than the first.

From her perspective, the ground seemed to take forever to reach her. She landed on her right shoulder, took the hit hard, and rolled four times before coming to a stop. The ringing in her ears increased as she lifted her head and grunted.

The shock wave had prolonged her dive, thrusting her fifteen feet past where she had been standing with the cop. His unconscious face had black patches on the cheeks and forehead, but his chest still moved.

She lowered her head and focused on getting to her feet. Bent over, hands on her knees, trying to collect her breath and slow her heart, someone stepped up to her.

Parkman.

His hand rested on her back.

He knew why she stole the weapon and discharged it at the firetruck. He knew it was to warn people away, to save people who couldn't hear her pleas.

A thankless job. A dangerous job.

She straightened up and wrapped an arm around his shoulder. He offered her a subtle nod, then led her back to the command station where Lee awaited them.

Firetrucks were coming in again, and the threat to their safety was eliminated. Two officers surrounded the two paramedics tending to the brave cop who had come at Sarah.

Lee was saying something, but Sarah couldn't hear him. She looked away and watched as crew after crew of emergency personnel stepped in to do their jobs. They were the real heroes here. They donned their uniforms every day and did this sort of thing for strangers.

The only difference was they were bound to appear in scenes after calamity. Sarah, on the other hand, appeared before the calamity. But what good was that if she couldn't do a better job and stop the chaos from happening in the first place?

She allowed Parkman to lead her inside, where a paramedic checked her over with a small flashlight. He did something with cotton swabs in her ears. Cops came and went, some offering her looks of gratitude, others snarls of anger. She wasn't well-liked in these parts. Stealing a weapon and shooting into a firetruck wouldn't win her any points with the RCMP.

Shuffling sounds, clicking, and fabric rustling came to her. Voices made it down her ear canals.

Then Officer Lee was in front of her. He jerked his head to the side and walked away.

"C'mon, Sarah," Parkman shouted beside her. "Lee wants to talk."

She allowed herself to be led by Parkman, her right shoulder still aching.

A man and a woman would die.

But only the man died, as far as she knew. Did she save the woman? Could she, even after Vivian said it was in their blueprint? Lives were planned before people came here to live their lives out. Sarah wasn't authorized—nor was Vivian —to alter a person's blueprint. Only when death wasn't in the cards could Sarah step in and stop it. Free will allows people to act in any way they want. But when that free will not only impinges on others but hurts them, or worse, kills them, causing far-reaching consequences, then Vivian and Sarah could step in as was part of Sarah's new understanding.

When Vivian said the bomb was coming and a man and a woman would die in the blast and Sarah could not save those two, Sarah believed her. Telling her where the bomb would detonate saved dozens of lives because the police had cleared the street. According to Vivian, that had to be good enough.

Lee led them through a clothing store that had been converted to a rudimentary command post. At the back of the employee lunch room, he cleared out two officers, pointed for Parkman and Sarah to enter, then slammed the door behind him.

"What the fuck was that?" Lee shouted, his white blonde hair mussed from exhaustion. His glasses slipped down the sweat on his nose, and he pushed them back up. He held a hand to his side as if it ached.

Sarah didn't have to read his lips anymore. Her hearing was coming back enough that Lee's shouting was discernible.

"What was what?" she asked. Her mouth suddenly dry, she glanced around for a water cooler or a sink. A small fridge sat on a table in the corner. She walked over to it, found a bottle of water inside, and drank half in one go.

"You almost done?" Lee asked.

"Hey," Parkman cautioned, a hand raised, voice tinged with aggression. "Take it easy. I saw what happened, too. Sarah saved lives today. Lighten up here."

"She stole a fucking gun," Lee screamed, a thick vein pulsing down the center of his forehead. "A cop's *gun!* She could've been killed out there."

"But she wasn't, was she?" Parkman shouted back, taking a step toward Lee.

Lee blinked in surprise at Parkman's aggression.

"You may want to rethink your position here," Lee said, his voice a notch lower.

"That's where you're wrong, Lee. It's you who needs to rethink what you've done here."

Lee crossed his arms. "How's that?"

Parkman pointed at Sarah. "You invited her here to stop that madness." He pointed toward the door. "And she did just that. Did you stop to think why she took that gun when no one could hear her warning them off?" Parkman waved his finger back and forth while shaking his head. "Sarah's no idiot. She knew the second bomb was coming. And when no one could hear her, she did the next best thing at great risk—infinite risk—to herself." Now he pointed back at Sarah. "She saved lives at her own risk because that's what Sarah does. She does not need a lecture on her actions after the fact."

Parkman stepped back, took a deep breath, and turned away from Lee. He walked to the lunchroom wall, placed an open-palmed hand on it, and leaned into the wall.

Sarah downed the rest of the water as Lee, arms still crossed, faced her, seemingly unfazed by Parkman's outburst.

"Sarah?" Lee said.

"Yeah?" She had collected herself, calmed her heart rate, and felt cold in the air-conditioned back room after coming in from the outside covered in sweat.

"You gonna play a little nicer when helping the authorities in the future?"

"I do what I have to. If I can play nice, I will. If not, I won't."

"Who decides?" Lee asked.

"Certainly not you. At least not where I'm concerned. And I hope you don't let anyone ever decide for you how you will act in any given situation. I can't be placed in a box, Lee."

"What I meant was, am I talking to you or Vivian?"

"One and the same." She capped the water bottle and

tossed it in the recycle bin.

Lee stole a glance at Parkman, who was now leaning his back against the wall, arms crossed. Sarah knew it bothered him to shout at Lee, but Parkman had to be riled up after seeing what Sarah had just done and how close she was to being killed by the people she was there to save.

"Sarah?" Lee said. "Do you know why you weren't shot when you aimed the gun at that firetruck?"

She shrugged. "Luck?"

"I called out the order to not fire at you. I waved them off. I ordered my men to stand down."

"So I have you to thank for saving my life? Is that it?" She walked closer to him. "Look, I'm not trying to be a prick here. I'm just doing what I do, and at the time, getting that gun and warning people away from the van was the best I could come up with. At the second it popped into my head," she tapped her temple, "another thought came to me from Vivian. She said I would be okay. That understanding was like a comfort blanket for me. So I went with it, and here I am. All okay."

Lee uncrossed his arms and opened his mouth to say something, but a knock on the door stopped him. He half turned toward the door.

"Yes?" he shouted.

"Officer Corey Hallagan, sir," a man's muffled voice came through the door.

"Open it," Lee called.

The door opened, and a tall, barrel-chested RCMP cop in uniform stepped just inside the door, hand still on the knob.

"I came to report that we had two casualties, sir."

"Two?" Lee said.

"Two?" Sarah whispered to herself.

Parkman pushed off the wall.

"The driver of the vehicle, John Hampton, was identified by his girlfriend, Susan. And Officer Mary Stein with the Vancouver Bomb Squad."

"How was she close enough to the van?" Lee asked.

The tension in the room thickened. An officer was killed. That would not bode well for Sarah. She was here to save people. By blocking off the intersection, they saved members of the public. But somehow, through Sarah's actions, one of the authorities had been killed. A woman. That would instill deeper sympathies.

"After the first explosion, the minivan rolled until it rested against the B.C. Health Services building. Moments before the van arrived, two bomb squad members were sent into the building looking for a man in a black suit that apparently was not evacuated. According to Officer Stein's partner, the man in the black suit was not found." Officer Hallagan stared at Sarah. "The building was empty, sir. Officer Stein was exiting the building when the second bomb exploded five feet from her." Hallagan turned his eyes back on Lee. "Even with all her gear, she didn't make it, sir."

Lee's hands hung at his sides. He stared at the floor. Parkman watched him, then exchanged a glance with Sarah.

She had sent them into that building on a wild goose chase. But she had seen that man on the second floor. It wasn't imagined. He'd motioned to her with his hand in an odd fashion.

Lee glanced over his shoulder to look at Sarah. She could almost read his mind. Not safe for Sarah in Kelowna anymore. She needed to leave. Not show her face on the street.

Lee turned back to Hallagan. "Anything else?"

"Nothing, sir."

"Shut the door, then."

Hallagan stole another look at Sarah, paused momentarily, then eased out of the room and closed the door. A second later, the latch clicked.

"What now?" Parkman asked.

Lee wiped his face with both hands. "I don't know," came the muffled reply. He shook his head and walked toward the door. "We have to deal with an officer's death now. Think about where you want to go, what you will do."

"What?" Parkman frowned. "What's that supposed to mean?"

Lee stopped at the door. "They're going to blame Sarah for Stein's death. Say she sent those bomb squad officers into that building. They found nothing. If what Hallagan's saying proves correct—shit, man, they're probably already doing that as we speak. She needs to leave Kelowna."

"We just got here. You've got a real problem on your hands. Sarah can help." Parkman faced her. "Right?"

"Help?" Sarah said. She started toward the two men at the door. "Not just help. I can fix this. I can stop it. I just don't know how yet."

"I think we're too late for that," Lee said. "We'll have to rely on old-fashioned police work."

He turned the knob and pulled on the door. It slammed shut half a second later as Parkman slapped his right hand on it, barring his exit.

"What the hell do you think you're doing?" Lee barked.

"We're not through here. If you're throwing us out, then

you get us out of town. This is on you."

Vivian whispered in Sarah's head. Sarah looked away from the two men, a blank stare on her face as she listened to her sister whisper the words she might have had to write on a piece of paper years ago when she was an automatic writer. Vivian got Sarah to understand what she needed to do and hated the thought of it at the same time.

"Is there any other way?" Sarah asked out loud. "Are you sure it has to be done like that?"

Both men looked at her as Vivian answered.

"Shit," Sarah whispered under her breath. "Thought so." She checked her watch, then met Lee's eyes. "Sometimes I hate my job."

She crossed the space between her and Lee in seconds, raised her leg, and brought it down on the back of his knee. Lee dropped to the floor with a small yip. He fumbled with Sarah in an attempt to push her away from him, but she easily smacked his hands away. She unclipped his car keys from his belt loop and relieved him of his weapon before he could grasp her, then stepped back out of his reach.

"What the fuck are you doing?" Lee shouted as he scrambled back to his feet. "You'll end up in prison for this."

Sarah had backed away, his keys already in her pocket, his gun held loosely at her side.

"Sarah?" Parkman asked, his voice soft, caring. "What is this?"

"Another bomb." She looked at her watch. "Eight minutes. This time the bomber is delivering it himself."

"Then tell *me*," Lee pleaded. "We'll go together."

"There's no time. I see it detonating. Coffee shop. Seventeen dead. I don't want another cop close to this one. I can't have that on my conscience." She clicked the safety off on Lee's weapon. "Now. Step aside."

Lee moved in front of the door.

"I thought so," Sarah muttered. "By blocking that door, you're telling me that you're more important than those people who will die in just over seven minutes. Your ego is bruised." Sarah moved closer. Parkman edged back. "I'm here to save lives," she shouted. "Get the fuck out of the way, or you will be hurt. Is that what you want, a free trip to the hospital?"

"Sarah," Parkman cautioned. "Go easy."

Lee's confidence wavered. He started to move, then didn't.

She came in low, dropped her left fist into his sternum, and elbowed his cheek with her right arm as he bent toward her from the impact of the first blow. As Lee grabbed for her, she kicked his feet out from under him.

She slid the gun into her waistband and wrenched the door open.

"Sarah?" Parkman shouted. "I'll come."

"Not this time," she shouted as she ran through the clothing store and onto the sidewalk. "Keep him off me."

Seven minutes ...

"Too close," she railed at Vivian.

A paramedic's bag sat on the ground, blocking her exit. She jumped it and ran for Lee's unmarked cruiser twenty feet away. She dropped inside, started it, and squealed away from the emergency vehicles lining the street.

In her rearview mirror, Lee came running out of the clothing store, pointing at his car, his mouth wide as he shouted something. Before she turned the next corner, it was clear other officers were running for their vehicles to give chase.

Sarah took the corner, the back tires screaming for purchase, then dropped the accelerator and gunned the engine. Before she hit the next streetlight, she'd flicked on the siren and the small, rounded lights in the corners of the windows.

Maybe this time, she could grab the guy setting all these bombs around the city and end this thing before he killed more people.

Maybe.

Chapter 4

SARAH RAN TWO RED lights with the use of the siren. At one point, as she approached the intersection of Harvey and Spall, she had to drive in the opposing lane as traffic was too tight to squeeze through. As she neared the mall, she turned the siren and lights off to avoid warning the perp she was coming.

With a minute and a half to spare, she parked in front of a large drug store where she left the car, driver's side door wide open. Three seconds were wasted in front of the automatic doors as they slid apart slowly. When she entered the mall, a rugged-looking guy leaving the mall almost collided with her. She spun off his shoulder and scanned faces in the immediate area. The perp was close. He was among the people at the entrance. The bomb was in a backpack to her right sitting in a chair in the coffee shop that was part of a large bookstore. Because it was common practice for patrons to leave a bag in a chair while in line for a coffee, the bomber felt his backpack would go unnoticed—at least until the bomb detonated, then everyone would notice.

But the bomber—the unidentified subject, the perp—wasn't in the line. He wasn't even in the coffee shop anymore. He had left through the bookstore's mall entrance and was just now leaving the building. She had no image to go on, no idea what he looked like. All she heard from the other side was that the guy was dead already, which made no sense.

Dead already? How?

Vivian remained quiet.

Fifty-five seconds left.

Police sirens wailed outside the building, catching the attention of shoppers who slowed their pace and tried to catch a glimpse of what was happening on the other side of the entrance.

Sarah ignored the racket outside and entered the coffee shop attached to the bookstore. Just over half a minute left. She was shocked to see the place was nearly full. Half a dozen people lined up to order beverages. Five employees crowded behind the counter, busily running around preparing drinks while two girls worked the tills. Six people waited for coffees to be served at the far right. At least a dozen people were sitting at tables. Some were on laptops, some reading, and others chatting with one another.

Sarah walked into the center of the coffee shop and yelled one word.

"Bomb!"

Heads turned toward her, but no one reacted. No one got

up to leave. She read their faces. Precious seconds ticked by. There was obvious distrust of some lunatic among them, ranting in a coffee shop. It was like they expected a punchline to a joke. Punked came to mind. But nothing else happened. No one moved.

She scanned the chairs until her eyes locked on the black backpack on a wooden chair. It would explode in twenty seconds, and the coffee shop patrons simply stared at her.

She lunged for the bag, withdrew Lee's gun, raised it to the ceiling, and fired a round.

That got the patrons moving.

People ducked. A woman screamed. Someone spilled their coffee, then shot up from their seat, knocking the chair back a few feet. Another woman snatched her teenage daughters and ran for the bookstore's aisles. The employees ducked behind the counter, but not far enough that they couldn't peek above its edge. The coffee shop became a chaotic brew of spilled coffee, frantic moves, and exasperated grunts in the pandemonium.

While people ran away from her, Sarah clutched the top of the backpack gingerly and lifted it off the seat.

She faced the counter. "Get out of the back room," she shouted. "All employees exit the building." She started toward the counter. "Get out!" she shouted at the top of her voice.

Through the plate glass window to her right, a smattering of police officers entered the mall, running for the entrance to the bookstore. Sarah fired her weapon again. The employees weren't leaving fast enough, and she wanted to halt the officers' approach.

After slipping behind the counter, she jostled past two

baristas on her way to the back room.

Only a dozen seconds remained.

"Anyone left back there?" Sarah asked.

A dark-haired woman in a green apron with a rather large piercing on her lower lip shook her head violently back and forth.

"Empty," she said, her voice broken with nerves.

Sarah opened the door to the back room, saw it was empty, then set the backpack down to rest against a large silver fridge.

Five seconds.

In panic mode, barely able to catch her breath, she turned around and leaped over the counter, then ran toward the waiting line of police officers hoping she would get enough room between her and the bomb.

"Run," she shouted at the men blocking her way.

Her words got through to the assembled men. Their line wavered and then broke. But it was too late.

The explosion sent a shockwave outward. Sarah was thrust forward just as she was about to enter the mall. Knocked off her feet for the second time that day, she was thrust into a discount rack of books, making contact with her already sore right shoulder. The rack shook with the impact but didn't move out of the way. Instead, it knocked Sarah to the carpet, where she covered her head to avoid flying debris.

The magazine rack was the closest to the explosion, which sent hundreds of shredded magazines into the air. Ripped and torn pieces of glossy paper slowly dropped from above.

Sarah sprawled on the floor, exhausted, eyes closed as she tried to reach her sister. It was over for now. No more bombs in the near future. She thought she understood something Vivian had said earlier about the bomber having one more bomb, something like a landmine, but it wasn't set to be detonated for days. Vivian kept mentioning that the guy was dead already, but she wasn't clarifying what that meant.

If the guy was dead, who delivered this bomb twenty minutes ago?

Sarah received no answer.

In her mind's eye, the area where Vivian offered her picture clues and voice instructions, Sarah saw the international symbol for poison. A skull with two bones crossed below it centered in a triangle.

What's that, Vivian?

She perceived that Vivian would tell her soon.

My future's looking great, she thought.

Another image fluttered into her consciousness. One word.

Sharpshooter.

Sarah opened her eyes and stared at the bookstore's ceiling.

Explain some of this, Vivian. I'm dealing with a sharpshooter now? A sniper?

Someone grabbed her arms and flipped her onto her stomach. Pain flared in her right arm. She groaned as someone jammed a knee into the small of her back.

"Hey," she shouted, but the word was muffled by the carpet. "Take it the fuck easy."

"You're under arrest, Sarah Roberts. Stop squirming, bitch."

"Get the fuck off me," she shouted when she could turn her head enough that she wasn't eating the carpet.

Cold metal clamped over her wrists painfully, wrenching her sore arm back even farther.

Strong hands gripped her, then lifted her upright. She was half carried, half dragged out into the mall, where a large crowd had gathered to watch the drama unfold.

She studied the crowd in search of a sharpshooter. Was she a target now? Was the perp watching her as the police dragged her to their cruiser?

Several people were being tended to as the glass separating the coffee shop from the mall had blown outward, cutting passersby. Other than minor wounds, the bomb caused significant damage to the back of the coffee shop and little damage to the front.

Two men with their girlfriends clapped by the doors as Sarah was taken outside. They had seen what Sarah had done.

"Thanks," one of the men said. "That was brave."

Sarah nodded their way.

As always, it was the authorities who got in her way. It was the authorities who misunderstood her. If she had taken the time to talk to Lee and convince him to come along and try to save the people at the coffee shop, they wouldn't have made it. According to Vivian, the only method to successfully save people from the coffee shop explosion was exactly what Sarah had done. But why hadn't Vivian given her more warning, more time?

There were two bombs, after all, not just in the minivan. That was one. The other was in the coffee shop. Half an hour earlier, both bombs were en route to their location. Vivian must've simply misread or misunderstood that there were two bombs in the van, and that was it. Once the van exploded, she saw the other device still on the move.

It made sense, but Sarah didn't like it. There had to be a better way to communicate, a better way to stop the guy. Weren't they closer, more in tune with each other, since the pact they'd made in Denmark?

Just tell me who he is, Sarah said as she was shoved into the back seat of a cruiser. *We'll pick the guy up and be done with it. I want to get back to Toronto.*

Can't, Vivian whispered. *Because he's dead.*

So I'm looking for a ghost?

No ...

You're not making any sense, Vivian.

Because. Vivian paused. *I'm being blocked.*

Blocked? Sarah stared out the cruiser's window, seeing nothing. *Blocked how?*

The police car pulled away from the curb and headed back toward downtown.

Vivian? What do you mean by blocked?

A minute passed without an answer.

Vivian? Sarah waited. Then shouted, *Vivian!*

She received no answer.

Chapter 5

Thirio watched the police officers attack the girl. They held her down, then slapped cuffs on her. He watched as they hauled her to her feet and led her outside to a waiting cruiser. The RCMP was doing its job. The RCMP always got their man, or in this case, their *wo*man.

At least he still had the bomb downtown. That unsuspecting couple delivered it to a popular intersection where it would cause the most damage. But that wasn't the only reason he wanted it to blow at the corner of Bernard and Ellis. No, he had his reasons, and the mounting death toll would illuminate his purpose.

But this woman was something else entirely. How did she know about the backpack or what chair it would be on? How could she know how much time was on the detonation clock?

If she hadn't entered the mall in such a dramatic fashion,

he would've been in his truck and already driving away from the mall when the device exploded.

When she ran through the sliding doors, she almost bumped into him. The look on her face, the determination, made him stop and watch her. She ran for the coffee shop and stopped a few feet from the backpack. When she yelled about the bomb, then fired a gun, he knew exactly what she was up to. But how could she have known? It was virtually impossible. Unless he learned who she was and how she knew, he would go insane. Someone was bugging him, watching him. Had to be the case.

The more important question was her identity. He needed to know who she was.

Thirio had too many questions that were going to have to wait. Now wasn't the time to stand around. The police were talking to people who had witnessed the event. They were asking for everyone to stick around and talk to them. Maybe someone saw who left that backpack in the chair at the coffee shop.

The chance that some snot-nosed kid might turn to him and point was a risk he wasn't prepared to take.

He slipped sideways between a woman and her husband, then moved down the hall to his left that led to the public washrooms. Before entering the men's room, he turned left and entered the back hallway of the mall, where retailers walked their garbage to a central bin or took deliveries at the backs of their stores. He followed the corridor toward the exit. Seconds later, he left the building and started across the parking lot toward his work truck as the sun beat down on the back of his neck. He felt its warmth between his shoulder blades as his black collar shirt attracted the heat.

Whoever that woman was, he hoped he didn't meet her again. She had thwarted his plan. How she had figured it out was beyond him. What he had planned next could never be stopped. No Wonder Woman could get in his way again, especially since she was carted away by the cops and driven off the premises handcuffed and in the back seat of a cruiser.

Thirio hopped up in his truck, turned it on, and let the air conditioning cool the sweat from his brow. He frowned as he recalled the planning stages of the coffee shop attack. There was no way anyone could have seen him at any planning stage. Nothing he did caused alarm. The device was set to a timer he initiated in the truck before entering the mall. The device was gently placed inside the backpack two hours before in a secluded area. He drove to Kelowna from Penticton, about an hour's ride, parked at the mall, and entered the coffee shop. No one observed a thing. As far as he could tell, no one looked at him wrong or suspiciously. If they had, wouldn't the police have nabbed him before he left the mall?

That's where it didn't make any sense. Unless that blonde girl was psychic, there was no way she could've known about him or his plan. If she knew what he was up to, she would've done something about it when she was manhandled toward the cruiser not five feet away from him.

The girl didn't even look at him.

Then how could she know about the bomb? And by her actions, how could she have known about the timer?

Utterly impossible.

Yet, somehow, she'd known.

Thirio put the truck in gear and started out of the mall parking lot. The Penticton site was burned. The city of

Kamloops was burned. He turned onto Harvey Avenue toward Vernon. The half-hour drive would give him time to think as he prepared to start his money-making scheme one more time before the denouement.

He would continue with his plans. They would never catch him. He was as elusive as D.B. Cooper or Jack the Ripper. He was as sly and as cunning. But most importantly, he was as dead as those men were, so they would never catch him. The authorities couldn't catch a dead man.

Nor could a psychic blonde girl.

Chapter 6

Another interview room, another police interrogation. This time, the interview room wasn't numbered. It was in a separate building from the police station because Sarah was to be interviewed by British Columbia's Serious Crimes Unit. They explained to her that they had this office outside the police station as these guys worked provincially, not municipally.

There was no traditional two-way glass. Only a digital recorder and a dome lens camera were above the door. The small room was no bigger than an average four-piece bathroom in an average-sized house. One desk, two chairs. Sarah's chair rested against the back wall beside the small table. The interviewer's chair was to her right, still empty.

At least an hour passed before the door clicked open, but Sarah was grateful for the break. It gave her a chance to rest. After massaging her wrists where the cuffs had bit in, she dozed off during her time alone. Her nerves frayed after two close calls with explosives, the quiet time was a welcome reprieve. Even Vivian was absent, leaving Sarah to ruminate over her next step. She wasn't a bomb disposal type of girl. She preferred roving street gangs or guys in back alleys with knives to bombs that could tear her apart before she had a chance to blink. That made the last few hours a test of faith. Even though Vivian was a truth-teller, what if she got the exact second of detonation wrong? Trusting her sister wasn't the issue when self-preservation kicked in. The urge to avoid that backpack stuffed with a bomb at the coffee shop was felt in every limb. Either live with the countless dead or wounded on her conscience or deal with the device in a cool-headed fashion.

And this was the thanks she got. Stuck in a small room by herself without a single glass of water or a cup of coffee. It would give her a large lump of pleasure to tell Officer Stephen Lee that she was done.

"Find the perp on your own time," she mumbled. "Fuck you guys."

But she couldn't do that. She came here to find the home-grown terrorist at the behest of Officer Stephen Lee, and she wouldn't stop until the unidentified subject—perp—was arrested or killed.

Isn't he already dead, Vivian?

The door handle clicked. Sarah opened her eyes, blinked twice, then sat up, wincing when her sore shoulder smarted. A female cop in an ironed blue shirt and red tie stepped into the room and closed the door. She held a blue binder in her left hand.

Sarah rubbed her eyes, paused, then rubbed them again.

"Ah, damn," Sarah murmured.

"What's that?" the woman asked.

"I thought if I rubbed my eyes hard enough, you'd disappear."

The woman ignored her, adjusted her shirt at the belt line, then moved closer. At the desk, she opened the blue binder, pulled out a pen from the back, and sat. The chair scraped annoyingly across the floor.

"Coffee?" Sarah asked.

The woman stopped flipping through pages in the binder and addressed her.

"Maybe we got off on the wrong foot," the woman said.

Sarah shrugged and shook her head. "Don't think we even got off yet, let alone on the wrong foot." She placed her right arm on the table's edge and leaned closer to the woman. "Doesn't that sound creepy to you? Got off on the wrong foot? How could you say such a thing?"

The woman blinked twice and leaned back. "You're here to answer a few questions—"

"Where's my Miranda?" Sarah wagged a finger back and forth. "No Miranda, no case. Tsk, tsk, tsk."

The woman set the pen down on the binder. "This is Canada. We don't Mirandize our citizens during an arrest. We follow the Canadian Charter of Rights and Freedoms. It recognizes the right to counsel—as early as possible. Even though you may clam up, we may continue to question you. You're not under arrest, though. Even if you were, I understood the officers at the mall explained this when they cuffed you."

Sarah huffed. "That's their story."

"Is it true?"

"They tried to give me your version of Miranda by calling me a bitch, but didn't continue with the female-bashing name-calling."

"You're here as a guest of Officer Stephen Lee. According to witnesses, you saved the day at several locations in Kelowna today. I'm not here to give you a hard time. Just ask a few questions."

Sarah sat back in her chair and picked at a damaged fingernail tip. "I didn't save the day. Two people died."

"I've been brought in to learn what you know, as this is a province-wide case now."

Sarah frowned. "Province-wide?" She met the woman's eyes. "How's that?"

"The minivan that exploded downtown today came from Penticton. The woman who'd jumped out at the intersection gave us a good description of where they were and who sold them the chairs."

"The chairs?" Sarah asked, suddenly feeling out of the loop. "What chairs?"

The woman picked up the pen, clicked a button on the tape recorder, and met Sarah's eyes again.

"State your first and last name, please. Speak clearly."

"Without being advised of my rights?" Sarah acted affronted, a shocked expression on her face. "How about a lawyer? What kind of police system are you guys running here?"

"Look, you're not a suspect. You're not even a person of interest. I merely have questions that may be used in a court of law at a later date regarding other suspected parties. Other than information, this has nothing to do with you personally."

"If it has nothing to do with me, why do you need my

name? In fact, why do you need me at all?"

The woman grunted. "Lee said you might prove to be difficult."

"Lee said that? Suddenly he's the expert on me? I've known him all of five hours. And what about your name? Who are you?"

"I'm Corporal Nan Hammock with the Southeast District Major Crime Unit. Would you *please* answer my questions?"

Sarah eased back in her chair, then slouched until her head rested against the wall.

"I'll negotiate with you," Sarah muttered.

"Negotiate? What?" Hammock appeared surprised. "How?"

"Because you could've been nicer about all this. We don't need to be here in such a controlled environment. Leaving me in this room for an hour without a coffee or an offer of a washroom break was disrespectful. You guys forget whose side I'm on." She pushed herself forward and leaned across the desk. To Nan's credit, the woman didn't move away. "I've always been treated as less than by the authorities because I haven't *earned* a badge. I won't hold it against you. So, yeah, I want to negotiate. Or you get nothing from me except a big fuck you, and I walk out of here. Now, interested in making a deal with me?"

Corporal Hammock tapped the pen on the binder. Her mouth held back a smile as if Sarah was telling her a joke and Hammock was trying hard not to laugh. "Go ahead. What are your terms?"

"Get me a large coffee. Black. Come back with it still piping hot. That gives you one question, one answer. After that, we exchange information. I'll answer one of your questions after you answer one of mine. It goes on like that until one of us is satisfied. Or, as you put it earlier, until one of us gets off. Wrong foot and all."

"No deal." Hammock locked the pen onto the paper in the binder. "I'll get you the coffee." She rose from her chair and started for the door. "When I return, we'll take thirty minutes to get through my questions and be done with it. Coffee. Then questions. But I won't answer yours. I'm not bound to."

Sarah watched as Hammock left the room, then shut her eyes and leaned back in the chair.

"We're in for a long night then, Hammock."

Vivian, you got anything for me?

Vivian remained silent.

Chapter 7

"WHAT THE FUCK IS this?" Parkman asked.

Lee tossed a folder onto his desk and placed both hands on his hips. His face had reddened after reading some of what was in the folder.

"There's nothing I can do," Lee said. "It's been handed off to the provincial task force. Even I.H.I.T. wants a piece of this."

"I.H.I.T.?"

"The Integrated Homicide Investigation Team."

"Where the hell do you guys come up with these names?" Parkman plopped down on the small sofa in Lee's office. "Look, I don't care who is involved. This is no way to treat Sarah. You saw what she did. You were there. Fuck all the rest of it. Stealing guns. Shooting at fire trucks. Storming a coffee shop and scaring people. She saved lives today. Dozens of lives. She shouldn't be stuck in some room being questioned like a suspect. She should be in here telling us our next move."

Lee turned and stared out his office window. His shoulders hitched. He adjusted his glasses. Parkman gave him the time he needed. If he didn't fix this somehow, Sarah would fix it, and no one would like what Sarah did—no one.

"Parkman, maybe this was a mistake. You know, bringing her to Kelowna." Lee turned to face him. "I know what she did, but—" Someone knocked on his door. He turned toward it and shouted, "What?"

The door opened, and a woman wearing a red tie stepped inside.

"Hammock, I thought you were talking to Sarah?" Lee asked.

"I was. And now I'm getting her a coffee. I just thought I'd let you know it's not going well."

Parkman chuckled.

Hammock looked his way.

"Ignore him," Lee said. "What do you mean, not well?"

"She's refusing to answer any of my questions unless I answer hers."

"Then answer hers."

"But sir, some of the questions she may raise aren't something I'm able to divulge—"

"Don't you understand?" Lee said as he stepped up to his desk and set both clenched fists on its top. "Sarah will give you nothing if that's what she decides to do. So do it her way."

"It's the only way," Parkman added, his mouth in a half smile.

Hammock glanced at Parkman, then back to Lee.

"Am I authorized to bring another officer along?" Hammock asked.

"For what?" Lee asked.

"Intimidation. We could threaten to arrest her on weapons charges. Assaulting a peace officer. A whole slew of other charges could get her talking."

"You do that," Parkman said, rising from the sofa, "and Sarah will eat you guys for breakfast. And hey, Lee, fuck you if you try that shit. We came as guests. She saved lives. Bring her in here. Talk to her yourself. You'll get the answers you need. Do anything else, and you'll be stunted. Or fucked. Or both." Parkman's voice held an edge of hardness that he was sure Lee would take as a warning.

Hammock went to say something, but Lee held up a hand. "Shh," he said to her. "Parkman's right. Get Sarah that coffee, then bring her in here."

Hammock was clearly vexed. "But sir—"

"I don't care about I.H.I.T. or your team or anyone else. Sarah came to Kelowna because I invited her here. I'll deal with her and the fallout thereafter. It's on me."

Hammock looked from Parkman to Lee, then back to Parkman. In a huff, she retreated from the room, turned at the door, and disappeared down the corridor.

"That seemed to go well, don't you think?" Parkman asked.

"Fuck you, Parkman." Lee ran a hand through his hair. "No, really, fuck you."

Parkman smiled as he dropped back onto the sofa. That's what he loved about Sarah. Her ability to get under people's skin by just being herself.

"Hey, Lee. Call Hammock and get a coffee for me, too."

"Get it yourself," Lee grumbled as he dropped behind his desk chair. "And get me one while you're at it."

"Fuck you, Lee."

Their eyes met. They smiled at each other.

Everything would work out after all.

At least, he hoped so.

Chapter 8

Corporal Hammock entered the small room, handed Sarah a coffee, then walked back to the open door where she waited, her fingers tapping gently on the door's frame.

"What now?" Sarah asked. She wrapped her hands around the warm coffee cup. "No questions?" She studied Hammock's face a moment longer. "You appear perplexed. Are you not happy with me?" She went to sip from the cup, then stopped, the cup suspended by her mouth. Her eyes met Hammock's over the cup's lid. "You're being pulled from the case. We're done here, that's it, isn't it? That's why you're waiting for me at the door?"

"You're to come to Officer Lee's office. He'll talk to you there."

Sarah tried not to smile but couldn't restrain herself as she rose to her feet, stretched, and took her first sip from the cup. "Someone didn't like what you were doing in here, eh?"

Hammock maintained a stony expression. Sarah stopped at the door mere inches from Hammock. "Let me tell you a little secret. I'm not here to bother you. I'm here to catch the bad guys." She offered Hammock a pensive expression. "Don't worry. I'll be out of Kelowna in less than a week. You'll never see me again."

"Is that a promise? Or a premonition?"

"Both."

Hammock walked down the corridor toward the elevators. Sarah followed, sipping her coffee, already waking up from the aroma.

Minutes later, Hammock knocked on a door with Officer Lee's name engraved on a plaque to the right of the door.

"Come in," someone shouted from the inside.

Hammock opened the door and moved aside to let Sarah enter.

"Corporal Hammock," Lee said.

Sarah took in the room, then headed toward the sofa where Parkman was getting to his feet.

"We need two more coffees in here," Lee said.

Parkman wrapped his arms around Sarah. She involuntarily winced when he touched her sore shoulder.

"That's not my job," Hammock protested.

"Just get the fucking coffees already."

Sarah glanced back at Hammock. The woman genuinely looked pissed off.

Lee held his hand up in a calming gesture. "I'm sorry. It's been a long day. The paperwork alone will take a week, and we need to talk to Sarah. Could you please, with sugar on top, bring us two more coffees?"

"Take your sugar on top and shove it up your ass."

Hammock backed out of the room and slammed the door.

"Wonder what got her so riled up?" Lee said as he turned to face Sarah. "Wouldn't have been you, would it?"

"I try not to have that effect on people. Sometimes it just comes out." Sarah sat beside Parkman.

No one spoke for a full minute. Sarah placed her cup on the small table in front of the sofa, then eased back and rubbed her face. Fatigue was also part of the job, and right now, she wanted to sleep for fifteen hours.

"Lee," she said.

"Yeah?"

"I've always had trouble with the people I try to help."

Lee pulled his office chair out and plopped down in it. "Shouldn't be that way." A moment of silence filled the room. "But I understand," he added.

"You guys are accountable to bosses who are accountable to the public. I'm not. We're on two different trains heading in the same direction. Sometimes it's advantageous for us to cross paths."

"Agreed."

"But when we do, I'm asked to do it your way—"

"It's not my way," Lee cut in.

"I know. I'm talking about doing it by the book or whatever you guys call it here. That doesn't work for me. Assaulting you and taking your car and your weapon saved lives. Doing it any other way would not have saved lives. I saw that in the blink of an eye. It became an instant understanding for me, thanks to my sister. Regardless of the consequences, I did what I had to do, and I'd do it again."

"I know that now. Parkman explained."

"You have to ask yourself if you're prepared for the

fallout of having me here. Or maybe the question is, what's worse? Your homegrown terrorist running loose, or my collateral damage and your terrorist is dealt with?"

They exchanged a glance. Lee turned to Parkman, then swiveled his chair to face his window. Sarah waited.

"I want you here," Lee said after a long pause. "I just wish you could be calmer about things. Do what you have to do in a quiet, safe manner."

"You're looking for Kermit the Frog or Barney the purple dinosaur then. You will never get calm and quiet out of me. That's not how this psychic thing works. Sometimes I'm told what to do with only minutes to spare. Then I'm given an understanding of how to do that very thing. It's rarely quiet. Or calm."

She almost forgot her coffee. After two more sips, the phone on the desk rang.

Lee picked it up. "Lee here." He paused, stared at the ceiling momentarily, nodded, and said, "I understand, sir." Then he gently placed the receiver back.

"What?" Parkman asked. "That call wasn't good, was it?"

"No, not good," Sarah said. "That was his boss."

Lee nodded and fidgeted with something in his lap.

"Your boss told you to debrief me, then send me on my way, didn't he?" Sarah asked.

Lee raised his head and nodded. "He said you weren't needed in Kelowna. We already have one dead officer from the bomb squad. He asked me how many more cops will die while you're here."

"Bit unfair, wouldn't you say?" Parkman said.

"Tell them I'll leave." Sarah raised her coffee above her

head. "As soon as we stop this guy." She lowered the coffee. "In the interim, Parkman and I will stay low and feed you information."

"Just tell me you're leaving," Lee said. "I'll report that. It saves me a lot of bullshit. Then you can do what every free citizen does from wherever you are. Come and go as you, please. Keep in touch with me, though. I'll follow up on any lead you give me."

"That debriefing? Was that what Corporal Hammock was trying to do?"

Lee nodded.

"Tell me about the couple in the red minivan."

Lee looked flustered. "What's there to tell? The girl was being interviewed as a potential suicide bomber who got scared and changed her mind. She jumped from the van—"

"It wasn't her," Sarah cut in. "She didn't know about the bombs."

"We know that now."

"What about the chairs?"

Lee raised his eyebrows in surprise but didn't question how she knew about the chairs. "The fire marshal, as well as the bomb squad, are still on the scene. They've found fragments of a recliner in the back of the van. Apparently," Lee leaned forward and adjusted his glasses to read something on a document on his desk. "Apparently, John and Susan had answered an ad in one of those online buy and sell websites. They drove to Penticton to pick up a piece of discounted furniture for their new home. They recently moved in together. Unbeknownst to them, the seller was our perp. What they picked up was a bomb stashed deep inside their new recliner." He lowered his glasses and sat back.

"They were the unwitting delivery system for the bomber."

Sarah leaned forward. "Can she ID the seller?"

"Yes. Barely. John, her boyfriend, did the deal and the money exchange. Susan waited in the van. She only saw the perp once when he helped John load the recliner. And her view was limited as it was through the mirror on the passenger door. But she said she saw enough that if she were to see him again, she'd be able to identify him."

Sarah clasped her hands together, cracked several knuckles, then sat back. She steepled her fingers and listened for Vivian.

"The Penticton location won't matter," she said. "The perp left it and won't return as he now knows that place is burned."

Lee nodded. "My boss sent a crew down anyway. They'll scan the place for prints, hair fibers, anything they can find."

"Was it a house?" Parkman asked.

Lee shook his head. "No. It was an empty storage unit rented with a fake ID."

"The unsub delivered the backpack to the coffee shop in the bookstore himself," Sarah said. "He watched me toss the device into the back room."

"What?" Parkman snapped. "He was there?"

She nodded slowly. "I almost bumped into him but didn't know it was him until after I'd dealt with the bomb."

"Why not?"

She turned to look at Parkman. "There was a timing issue regarding the backpack."

"Right," he nodded. "Understood. Do you recall anything about him?"

She shook her head.

"Anything from Vivian?" he asked.

She shook her head again.

"Okay." Parkman glanced at Lee. "That's confusing."

"Vivian's being blocked at times. Never happened like this before."

Both men stared at her. They were probably waiting for a better explanation. Something compelled Sarah to push off the sofa and walk to the window beside Lee's desk. This feeling, a certain drive from within to head to the window, didn't come from her. In the few seconds, it took to cross the floor, the room around her dimmed briefly. Sound diminished, and darkness clouded her peripheral vision.

Drawn to the window was more of a calling, a yearning, and not something precipitated by Vivian. This was different. Utterly opposite, in fact. At the window, she looked down at the sprawling city of Kelowna and wondered what compelled her to do so. Why here? Why now? What was out there? The nature of her reasoning to walk to the window was so foreign she didn't want either man in the room to notice the change in her.

"Any idea why she's being blocked?" Lee asked. He sounded like he was talking through a large tube. His voice contained an odd echo to it now.

Time passed as Sarah stared out the window. Then Lee and Parkman were talking again. "Our unsub has no conscience. He is the worst kind of killer because he feels nothing. He met the people that would deliver his bomb to Kelowna for him knowing they would die. What did it matter if they saw his face?"

Sarah spun from the window. "Which means Susan could be in trouble. She's seen his face. Can you keep her survival out of the papers until this is over?"

Lee shook his head. "Already too late."

"Shit," Parkman muttered.

"What about you, Sarah?" Lee asked.

"Me?" Had he noticed the sudden change in her? "What about me?"

"You said our unsub saw you at the mall. He'll hear Susan lived. Our unsub will have put it all together by tomorrow, if not sooner. He'll know who you are and what you've done to sabotage his progress."

"And?" Sarah asked.

"And it lends one to think that your safety could also be at risk."

"I'll be fine." Sarah fought the internal urge to be at the window. She moved toward the middle of the office, where she stood momentarily, listening for her sister.

"But if Vivian's being blocked," Parkman added. "How can you be sure you'll be fine?"

Sarah ignored Parkman's comment. She didn't want to dwell on her personal safety as it was pointless. She was staying on until this was done, whether or not she was safe. This guy had to be stopped. Whatever compelled her to be at the window in the first place rose tenfold. Obediently, she walked back to the window and looked at the street below.

"Lee, listen to me," Sarah said, keeping her voice even.

"I'm listening."

"This guy has to be stopped." She waited. When no one spoke, she added, "But your people want me out."

"I know. I will try to reason with them—"

"Don't."

"Sarah?" Parkman said from the sofa.

It suddenly occurred to her she hadn't seen a toothpick in his mouth for at least two days, which was a strange thought considering what they were dealing with.

On the street below, nothing appeared out of the ordinary. A man walked along the sidewalk on the other side. Something drew her eyes to him. She watched as he stopped, head bent slightly downward in thought. Then, after a moment's pause, he turned and looked up at her. His right hand rose, and he gestured like he was trying to tell her something.

Just like the guy in the suit on the second floor of the medical services building.

Sarah frowned as she watched the man. Could he see her at the second-floor office window? Wouldn't there be a glare as the sun set in the west?

The arm gesture was the same, repeated over and over. It looked like he was trying to spell out a word or give her a number of some kind.

"Sarah?" Lee said behind her.

She studied the man on the street, focusing on the message.

"Sarah?" Parkman said from behind her, his hand on her shoulder. "You okay?"

She edged sideways, looked at Parkman, then pointed at the man on the sidewalk.

"Can you read what he's trying to say?" she asked.

Parkman peered out the office window, following her fingertip. He looked at her, then back outside.

"Who are you pointing at?" he asked.

Sarah stared down at the street below. "That man on the sidewalk, right there—"

The man was gone.

"I don't see anyone on the sidewalk, Sarah. A block back, there's a woman pushing a stroller. She's walking with a man. But that's it."

The gesturing man was gone. But not just gone. He'd vanished as if he wasn't there in the first place.

She rubbed her eyes when a chill shook her body.

Vivian? Do you want to explain what that was?

From left to right, the sidewalk was relatively empty, with only a few people walking its length. No one resembled the gesturing man.

Parkman's hand on her shoulder applied pressure. He tried to turn her away from the window. The expression on his face was one of concern.

"C'mon," he whispered. "Come sit down."

Sarah took one more look out the window, then followed Parkman to the sofa.

"You okay?" he asked softly.

She nodded as she dropped down on the cushion hard. The urge to be at the window had disappeared. Whatever had compelled her to stand and walk across the room was gone.

"You don't look okay."

She inhaled a deep breath, then released it.

"I'm fine," she whispered. "Let it go for now."

Parkman waited a heartbeat, then nodded.

"You were telling me not to reason with my superiors," Lee said. "But Sarah, if I don't, you will have to leave."

She sat on the edge of the sofa as Vivian entered her thoughts. A wave of information flooded her. She got more than she wanted all at once.

"Whoa," she murmured.

"Whoa, what?" Parkman asked, his concern for her renewed.

She met his eyes and studied his face a moment. He'd aged in recent years. He was a good-looking man who had chosen her instead of a regular job and a girlfriend. Their exploits together didn't allow him to have a normal existence. But that was something he knew and accepted, and she loved that about him.

According to Vivian, they had to part ways for this fight in Kelowna. She didn't like it, but Parkman would be safe in Kelowna with the authorities.

The emotions she struggled with were entwined with the knowledge Vivian imparted to her. Sarah now understood what she had to do and how to go about it.

"Lee," she said as she turned to face him. "Don't reason with your superiors. Just tell them who I am and what I have done in the past. Explain my mission here. With my help, I can stop this guy."

"I can do that," he said, both hands flat on the desktop. "But after what happened today, it'll be a hard sell."

"There's poison coming."

"Poison?" Lee sat forward. "What are you talking about?"

"When I know more, you will. Keep your cell phone on. I'm also being told something about a sharpshooter. I don't know what that means yet, but it has something to do with our unsub."

"Like he's ex-military or SWAT? Maybe a sniper?"

Sarah shrugged. Vivian was gone. The man on the sidewalk was gone. She came back into herself, feeling grounded.

"Wish I could tell you more. It'll come in time."

"Is that it?" Lee asked.

"Walk a day in my shoes." She let that sink in. "See how misunderstood I am. See what I go through." A wave of empathy resonated from Parkman. The look in his eyes said he understood. That was why he had chosen this life with her. He was her angel, her savior. She wouldn't be who she was without him. "This fight your boss is putting up to oust me is a painful waste of time. It's stupid, too. They're doing it ass-backward. If I stay on, the casualty rate will be minimal. If I leave, hundreds more will die, which will be on your team's head."

Lee looked down at the floor. Parkman stared off into space.

Sarah continued, "It's like using an entire bottle of No Tears Shampoo on a baby to get them to stop crying. What might make sense on the surface is absolutely ludicrous. Regardless of what you or your bosses do, I am staying until this perp is caught or killed because I'm the only one who can stop him. I'm in a unique position to do that."

"How so?" Lee asked, his voice subdued as if Sarah's words had cut him to the quick. Lee believed in her. That's why she was here in the first place. But he was on the losing side.

Sarah rolled the idea around in her head. How could she tell them without sounding insane herself? She looked from Parkman to Lee and back to Parkman.

"This is the strangest thing I've ever dealt with. Until I know more, I'm a little lost."

"We're listening," Parkman said.

"I'm hearing from my sister that the man we're looking

for is *dead*."

"Dead?" Lee stammered. "As in dead right now?"

Sarah nodded. "Yeah, like dead dead."

"Then how is he doing what he's doing? Are you saying we're hunting a ghost?"

"No, not a ghost," Parkman said. "A man everyone thinks is dead."

Sarah grabbed his arm. "That's it. At least, I think so. He must've faked his own death. If we had a name, it would come up in the system as dead. That has to be it."

"Almost impossible to fake your own death today, though," Lee said. "Technology is too advanced. And we would need a body for a death certificate nine times out of ten."

Sarah nodded. "As far as I understand, there was a body." She shrugged. "Maybe there wasn't. However he did it, he was efficient because I'm hearing he's dead, yet our unsub is actively setting bombs off in your city. What Parkman says makes the most sense."

"Leave that with me." Lee swung his chair around and tapped on his computer keyboard. "I'll have someone look into suspicious deaths in Kelowna and the surrounding area. Is there anything else?"

"There is." Sarah pushed off the sofa and walked across to Lee's desk. "I need you to do something for me."

"What?"

"Call your son, Nicholas. Make amends."

Lee shot back in his chair. "My son?" The look on his face was surprise mixed with confusion. "How did you know about …" He trailed off.

"Lee, it's important," she added.

"But why? How does my son have anything to do with this case?"

"He's connected. That's all I can say right now. Just call him. Make amends."

Lee got to his feet and stared at Sarah. She wondered how much to tell him. Their family estrangement had lasted a decade. Making them talk again because a terrorist was killing people in Kelowna didn't feel like the right reason, but it was necessary. Their lives—and death—depended on it.

"Sarah." Lee's tone suggested anger. "Tell me how he's connected."

"He met the perp."

"What?" Lee shouted. "He knows who is doing this? How's that? I don't believe it."

"I didn't say he knows the person. I said he *met* the perp. I don't even know how yet. And I'm sure Nicholas—"

"Nick. Just Nick."

"I'm sure Nick doesn't know the man he met is the terrorist. All I'm getting is we stop this guy through your son. You make the call. I'll give you more as we go."

"That's not good enough. He'll never talk to me."

"Then we really are done here." Sarah started for the door.

"Wait," Lee called after her. "You can't just walk out after saying something like that." His voice filled with emotion. "Tell me more about my son."

"I can't. I don't have more."

"Then I'll have him picked up by the police and interrogated."

"Won't work. He doesn't know who the perp is. All I said

was that he had met him. Once you've reconnected with him, I'll know more about their meeting. Then we go to the next step." Sarah stopped at the door. "We do anything else, it backfires."

Lee seemed to think about things a moment. He lowered back into his chair, then tapped his fingers on the top of the desk. "Okay, let's say I do reconnect with Nick. Then we discover what we need from him. What then? He feels used by his dad?"

"No, Lee. You have your son back. That's what, then. It's a win-win."

Officer Lee's glazed over. "I still don't see the need—"

"It's about family, Lee. That's what I'm getting at here. This whole thing is about family. Your family. The perp's family. Somehow it's all connected."

Lee walked from behind his desk. "Is my son involved in what's happening to my city? Do you see him breaking the law?"

"No." Sarah waved at Parkman. "Come on. I need dinner and a soft bed. Let's find a hotel and a nice restaurant by the airport."

Parkman got up off the sofa. "By the airport?"

"Yeah, I want to give the image that we're leaving."

"I still don't see how my son is involved," Lee muttered to himself.

Sarah opened the office door. "You will. Eventually. But you have to do what I've asked. Make amends. Talk to him. Plan a dinner or something. A way to catch up, socialize. But make the call tomorrow morning. Meet him within a day or two."

"Then what?" Lee asked.

"Then I'll tell you more. Oh, and one more thing to remember."

"What's that?" Lee asked.

"Humanity has an odd way of learning lessons through death."

"What's that supposed to mean?" He turned to Parkman. "Is that some kind of veiled threat?"

"Just listen." She held up a hand. "Small lessons like fixing the water supply after people drank it and died. Cleaning parsley or cilantro after people in a fast food restaurant catch E. coli. All the way up to large lessons like the Holocaust, which gave rise to our anti-genocide laws. That's the way humans are. Instead of thinking about how fast cars can go and implementing seatbelts decades ago, we wait until there are countless deaths in car accidents, then implement them and make a law to force people to wear them. There are still cars on the road in some countries where seatbelts weren't even installed." She cleared her throat. "All I'm saying is, don't let this be one of those times. Don't *learn* that I might've been able to help after a hundred—or more— Kelowna citizens are dead. Find a way to let me help and save those lives. Don't learn this lesson through the death of others as so many others are determined to do."

"Is that what you're seeing? Over a hundred dead before this ends?"

"Without my help, double that number and then some."

Lee mumbled several expletives to himself as Sarah stepped out of the office and started down the corridor. Parkman's footfalls hurried to catch up to her.

They entered the elevator, but before the doors closed, Lee's voice boomed throughout the building.

"Would someone bring me a fucking coffee!"

The elevator doors shut.

"Parkman, you need a toothpick," Sarah said. "I don't recognize this guy beside me."

He didn't smile.

Chapter 9

THIRIO SAT IN A back corner of a coffee shop just off the highway that ran through the center of Vernon, about a half-hour drive from Kelowna. His first appointment wasn't for another hour. He would use that time to drink coffee and catch up on what happened yesterday.

The newspapers covered the carnage of the two explosive devices at separate locations in Kelowna. People were scared. The authorities appealed to the public to take precautions. Watch for peculiar activity. Report anything suspicious to the police. Their investigation was ongoing. Witnesses were being interviewed. Someone claimed to have seen the man who dropped the backpack at the bookstore's coffee shop.

He stabbed the iPad with his finger to close the news article. It took two tries, his anger making him miss the small button.

He tapped his legs up and down, almost in rhythm with his tripping heart rate. What the hell had happened? A witness can place him at the scene? That bomb was supposed to kill any potential witnesses in the coffee shop. He hadn't cared who saw him as they were not supposed to live to tell about it. But that girl stepped in and wrecked everything.

Who the fuck is that girl?

The morning news reported two deaths at the site where the minivan exploded. The driver and a bomb disposal expert had died. But how? The bomb went off at one of the busiest intersections in Kelowna.

He stared out the window, fury rising inside him like a tsunami. Everything he had planned. All his careful deductions and now this. His previous bombs had worked perfectly. No one could stop him because he had planned his chaos to be random events. The implicit nature of randomness, ignoring all rules of order and expectation, allowed him the freedom to do what he pleased, when he pleased, without fear of being stopped by any authority figure. But somehow, someone had stepped in. And that someone had stopped yesterday's events from having their maximum casualty rate. It also slowed his end goal.

All this meant was more people had to die in a shorter period to right the balance.

More people had to die.

How could it be possible for someone to know his plans? He'd read that a woman had been brought in to help the police with their investigation. This woman was known to the police to have special abilities. The name rolled around in his head.

Sarah Roberts.

How could that woman stop him? How could she know his plans? According to one website, Sarah Roberts had told the authorities about the bomb in the van. That was how they'd been able to clear the area in time to avoid further casualties.

After Thirio sold those chairs to the man and woman in the red minivan in Penticton yesterday, he had tracked the device hidden inside the chair by GPS as he followed a kilometer behind the van. At Ellis Street, Thirio watched as John turned for the downtown area, then continued toward the bookstore coffee shop. Two bombs were in separate parts of the city within a half hour of each other. It was his last two devices, too, except for the big bang he had planned for the end.

What if Sarah stepped in again? If she knew about yesterday's bombs, could she know about him? Could she know where he was at any given time?

He looked around the inside of the coffee shop. Only three people sat in chairs. It was quieter than he expected at this hour, but that was probably because a coffee shop was blown up yesterday in nearby Kelowna. People may avoid these kinds of places for a while. At least until the bomber was caught.

He turned his iPad sideways and searched for any more news on yesterday's events in Kelowna. After frantically covering every article on Google, he hit his Alien Blue application and opened Reddit. He read more about the woman who stopped the attacks in Kelowna. Sarah Roberts was a renowned psychic vigilante. One article talked about how ballsy that was considering what she had done to the RCMP the last time she was in Kelowna. The writer suggested Sarah was here by personal invite of a member of the RCMP.

He googled her name, then hit the first link and started reading. Ten minutes later, he came up for air, staring blankly out the window.

With Sarah Roberts in Kelowna, he had to consider that she would try to stop him. She could show up any time. Her online presence was enormous. Sarah had just cracked open a case in Toronto. She had shut down a computer hacker who left no trail. Before that, she was in Denmark, Las Vegas, and Mexico. Page after page was dedicated to her exploits. Even books on Amazon that Sarah herself had supposedly written detailed her crime-fight adventures.

Several websites were dedicated to her. One called her *Immortal*. Because she could talk to the other side, nothing could kill her. She was too valuable for the other side to ever let anything happen to her.

He checked Google Images for a picture of her face. He knew it when he saw her face—the woman who ran past him into the mall yesterday. She had grabbed the backpack, cleared the coffee shop, and tossed the device in the backroom, which made all the sense in the world. She was psychic. Whether he believed in that sort of thing or not, her actions made it real. That was the only explanation. It was how she knew about his devices when no one else could have. It was how she knew about him.

Thirio was the reason Sarah Roberts was here. And she was coming for him. Then why hadn't she just told the police his name and where he was? What was stopping her?

He set the iPad cover in place and slipped it into his duffel bag. He felt sick. Sarah could ruin everything. He hadn't accounted for her. On the other hand, if Sarah were dead, the threat would disappear.

He thought back to what he had concluded moments before: more people had to die in random acts of madness.

That would be on Sarah.

He got to his feet and started for the door. Sarah would know within the hour who she was dealing with. The police would know who they were dealing with. He would complete his mission one way or another, and the people who were supposed to pay for what they had done to him would pay one hell of a steep price.

Two people rose from their table and opened the coffee shop door to leave just as he approached it. The man smiled and held the door for him. He shook his head, then nodded as if to say thanks.

The door closed.

He stood at the glass and stared out at the half-empty parking lot. With his thumb and finger, he locked the bolt on the door and flipped the button on the neon open sign.

As he turned around, he pulled his gun from his waistband and aimed it at the only customer left.

"Get up and walk to the back of the store," he ordered.

The customer looked up from his novel, jerked his head back when he saw the gun, and nearly fell out of his chair.

"Hey, mister, I got no beef with you—"

"Get on your feet," Thirio shouted and jabbed the gun in the air. "Now."

The man got up so fast he knocked his chair over. Hands raised at shoulder height, he stumbled toward the back. The male employee came out of the back washroom, a mop in his hands. He set the mop in a bucket, squeezed the water out, then looked up as they approached.

Thirio adjusted the weapon's aim until the barrel was squarely on the employee's chest, then squeezed the trigger.

The report inside the small establishment was deafening. The employee's uniform shook with the impact of the bullet. He released the handle of the mop as he was shoved backward into the ladies' room door.

The customer dropped to the floor and covered his head, mumbling something about not wanting to die. The employee slid down the length of the door, a look of panic on his face, a line of blood trailing behind his head.

The man raised his weapon and fired into the employee's body again.

Then again.

Chapter 10

Sarah finished packing her overnight bag, then headed to the small table by the bed and grabbed the hotel pad and pen. She quickly jotted down a note telling Parkman to hide behind a blue spruce tree and about the murder of two police officers—per Vivian—which made no sense to her, ripped the paper off the pad, and slipped it in her back pocket.

Parkman would knock on her door within minutes. They were supposed to leave the city after all. Lee's boss had called back late last night. According to Kelowna's mayor, the police were well-equipped to handle criminals in their city. They did not want a psychic vigilante on staff. She was a civilian and had no formal training in law enforcement. Therefore she couldn't be used in any ongoing investigation. Officer Lee called an hour ago, at seven in the morning, to tell Parkman to get Sarah out of Kelowna for her own good. He expressed gratitude for what she had done for them, but his hands were tied. Her part in this task was complete.

Room service had brought a coffee with two croissants after Parkman had given her the news. She'd eaten the croissants before packing. Now she took the coffee and sat by the large window overlooking the airport across the street.

She ruminated on how Vivian could be blocked from her. If whatever was blocking them was malicious, what was its purpose? How could it block them without Vivian knowing about it? There were so many questions but little in the way of answers. After her understanding with Vivian when Sarah endured a near-death experience in Denmark, she thought the days of little or no information were over. It almost seemed that every time they went two steps forward, something knocked them back a step.

What she really wanted to know was who was the man in the B.C. Medical Services building? Or the man on the sidewalk below Lee's office window? Could they be the same man? And what was the message he kept gesturing with his hand? Most importantly, how could Parkman not see him?

Something very strange was happening in Kelowna. Whatever it was, a lot of people were going to die. Because of that, Sarah had no intention of leaving.

Someone knocked on the door. Sarah got up to open it, almost stumbling over her own suitcase.

"Parkman," she said as she stepped aside to let him in. "You got toothpicks?"

He nodded, a toothpick dangling from the side of his mouth. "I grabbed enough to do me until I get home."

Sarah headed back to the chair by the window. "We're not going home."

Parkman let go of the door, and it closed on its own. After a moment, Parkman sat on the edge of the unmade bed.

"We're not?" he asked. "Even after what Lee said?"

"There's been another murder."

The toothpick slipped from his lips, hit the corner of the bed, and tumbled to the floor. "What?" he managed to say. "When?"

"This morning." She faced him. "I just learned about it."

"Did Lee call you?"

She frowned, then grimaced. "No."

"Oh, right. Okay, I understand." Parkman got to his feet. "Where?"

"In another city."

"Another city? How will they connect it to the Kelowna terrorist?"

"They will."

Another knock on the door.

"Who is it?" Parkman shouted.

"Police," a man shouted through the door. "We're here to escort you to the airport."

"One sec." Parkman moved to stand in front of her chair. "Looks like we need to leave."

"Agreed," Sarah said. "Be compliant." She smiled. "Do as they say."

She headed for the door, opened it a crack, whispered something, then closed it.

"What did you say?" Parkman asked.

"To give us a few more minutes. They can wait in the hall while we use the bathroom."

"You knew I had to go?" he asked.

She nodded. "It's that new understanding Vivian and I

have. Basic information that she possesses simply transfers to me via some kind of intelligence tether. In one respect, it's maddening. In another, I'm grateful. I knew when you'd knock. I saw those four officers walking toward my door. I know you have to piss pretty bad right now, so I bought you some time."

"Wow, that's impressive." He started moving toward the bathroom. "I don't even know this new Sarah."

"Me neither."

The bathroom door shut.

Sarah opened the zipper on Parkman's suitcase, retrieved the note from her pocket she'd written earlier with the hotel pad, and slipped it inside Parkman's case. Then she zipped up the bag.

She was standing by the door when he stepped out of the bathroom.

"Ready?" she asked with a smile, hoping Parkman wouldn't detect her sadness.

"All ready," he said. "Although, I'm a little confused. We're leaving, but we're not. Right?"

"Something like that." Sarah opened the door, then leaned back so only he could hear her. "Just do what they say. It'll all work out."

They followed the four officers to a waiting SUV at the front of the hotel. Something about the four men was off. She searched for Vivian, but she was gone again.

The driver of the SUV drove quickly and parked in front of departures. All six of them exited the vehicle and entered the airport. No one said a word the entire time. The officers didn't want them here. It was obvious how they felt in the expressions on their faces. But not just that, Sarah saw something below the surface, especially with one man.

The older RCMP man handed Parkman two boarding passes.

"You're all set," he said, his tone clipped, lips tight. He pointed toward the security area. "Clear security first. Then head to your gate. You won't need to come back."

"We've done this before," Sarah said. She stopped moving as Vivian made an appearance. She listened to what she had to say. "What do you mean when you say we don't need to return?"

The man swung toward her. "I wasn't talking to you," he snapped. The other three officers eased in closer to Sarah, crowding Parkman out.

Sarah offered the man a wry smile as she stepped inside his space. She had to look up to meet his eyes. "Was this the same attitude you showed Samantha last week when you shouted at her to move out? Or what about Vicky? Too bad she didn't press charges for the beating you gave her three years ago, eh, Officer Tom Mason? If she had, we wouldn't be speaking right now because you'd be out of a job."

The senior officer glared at her, his face tight and gaining a reddish hue. He moved nose to nose with her. Rage oozed from his pores, exciting Sarah for what was to come. She wouldn't be bullied, and when she was, there was no greater revenge than having that person pay for their actions.

"How about it, Officer Mason?" Sarah turned to the man on her right. "Officer Brent Waters, you remember Vicky, right? You helped cover it up."

"That's enough, Sarah," Parkman cautioned from behind Mason. "Let's just leave." He tried to squeeze his way inside the officers' inner circle, but the men tightened their ring.

"C'mon, guys," he added. "Let it go. She's only taunting you."

"Hey, Officer Waters, wait a second." Sarah raised her hand for silence. After two heartbeats, her eyes closed while listening, and she glanced back up at Mason. "Officer Brent Waters. Vicky came to you for help, and you threatened her into silence." Sarah looked at each officer's face in turn. "All of you are common thugs." She stepped back as Parkman pulled on her sleeve.

She snatched her arm out of his grip.

"Officer Jeff Calder." She studied the man to her left. "What have we here? A man who has planted evidence on several occasions to get your informants off the street because they got too wise and knew too much about you. Like where you buy your personal stash."

Calder grabbed Sarah's arm just under the shoulder and jerked on it.

"Listen here, you little bitch," Calder snapped. "Don't meddle where it's not safe. You seem to know way too much."

"Hey," Parkman shouted. "Take it easy. Let the girl go."

Calder held on a moment longer, then released his grip by shoving her away. She bumped into Mason, who stood his ground. It was like bumping into a padded wall.

"We done here?" Mason asked. "Or do you have any more cute parlor tricks for us?"

Sarah took her time to look into the eyes of all four men, pausing slightly on Parkman's face, then ending on the last of the four, Officer Simon Amparo.

"Simon, you're new," she said. "Two years on the force and still on the straight and narrow. Maybe that's why you're with these guys. So you can be trained on the subtleties of police work. There's a fine line between doing the right thing and doing the thing right."

Parkman shoved his way inside the inner circle. "We're leaving. And don't try to stop us."

He wrapped an arm around her and pushed past Calder and Mason. Mason grabbed Sarah's wrist and wrenched her back toward him. Parkman's arm slipped off Sarah's shoulder. Mason moved to block Parkman with his body.

"What you just did here," Mason said, "was threaten four police officers—"

"No. I did not." Sarah pushed into him, but Mason was around two hundred pounds of solid male form. Her arm brushed against the holster on his belt, hidden under his light jacket. "What I did was tell the truth. That little tiny word, *truth*, is what hurts. It's biting into your gonads as we speak. Pain causes you to lash out."

"I'll lash out all right. So hard you will always know my name as synonymous with pain."

"You threatening *me* now?" Sarah asked.

"Roberts bitch," Mason nearly growled. "Get on that fucking plane and never return to my city." Small pieces of spittle landed on her cheek, cooling instantly. Arms, shoulders, guts, all crammed around her, locking her in place.

Vivian whispered through it all, and Sarah listened.

"Mason, tell me something."

His grip tightened in reply, her hand cooling as circulation was reduced to her lower arm.

"Do you want to kill me?" she asked. "For the murder of Barry Ashford? You were friends, right?"

He pulled her in close, then appeared to hug her, his

mouth edging close to her right ear.

"For my dear friend Barry Ashford, I will rip you limb from limb, tear your eyes out, and piss in your fucking skull, you worthless whore of Satan." He pulled away from her slightly. "So yes, you could say that."

His grip released. Parkman slipped inside the group again. Several people had gathered to watch the ensemble.

"Show's over," Mason shouted. "Keep moving."

"I see it now," Sarah mumbled to herself. "Your arm. Broken. On your dashcam. I see everything." After nodding in confirmation of the new data she had just received, she felt marginally better. "Do you believe in God, Mason?"

"Fuck you, Sarah."

"You're going to meet him."

"That's enough taunting, Sarah," Parkman said as he moved between them.

The four officers stepped away. Parkman gently nudged Sarah the other way. She glanced over her shoulder. "When I see you again, Mason, walk the other way."

"Sarah, come on," Parkman persisted.

"Leave here," Sarah shouted back at them. "Leave here and forget about me. It's the only way to keep breathing."

She offered the four men one last sarcastic smile and turned around to walk with Parkman.

"What was that all about?" Parkman asked, his voice an octave higher than usual. "Did you have to do that?"

"They sent those four guys to drive us to the airport because they volunteered to get *the bitch*—their words—out of Kelowna. You saw the hate Mason had for me. He was Ashford's best friend. He wants me dead for what happened to his old partner, even though Ashford's wife killed him."

"Yeah, but pissing him off usually leads to trouble we don't want."

"Once we're through security, I'll tell you why that happened."

Parkman raised one eyebrow as he pulled off his belt and slipped out of his shoes to place them on the conveyer belt. Once their bags were on the belt, Parkman and Sarah walked through the body scanner.

At their gate, Parkman sat down across from her, elbows on knees, and rolled his hand twice in a give-it-up gesture. "Come on, Sarah," he said, calmer now. "Out with it. Why did that verbal scuffle just take place?"

"Because we're not leaving Kelowna, and those men will be back to pick us up. At one point, several of them will have a question of conscience, and I want them to choose my side. Before what just took place, they would not choose my side. All I did was create leverage."

"But what if their decision is against you and leads to your death? Then what? You wouldn't be around to get them into trouble."

Sarah leaned forward. "The time will come, and the decision will be made. If it's against me, it won't be my death they're concerned about. It will be theirs."

Chapter 11

OFFICER STEPHEN LEE STARED at the clock on his desk. He'd been there since six in the morning, writing one report after another. It was almost eight. Sarah and Parkman would be at the airport by now. His son, Nick, would be awake with his family as they got ready for whatever it was they did during the summer months.

Nick had two young girls, four years old and a six-month-old baby. Lee had never met them but stayed up-to-date on his son's family when he could through Facebook. He loved Nick's wife's name, June Sumner. Sumner reminded him of a character in a Greg Iles novel he'd read years ago.

The decades-old spat had been a misunderstanding. The family dispute fueled several fights and ultimately led to an estrangement. It had been so long that Lee couldn't remember the exact reason for the dispute. It had something to do with Lee's wife—Nick's mother—before she died.

Nick had gone to the right schools but dropped out early and became a salesman. Nick and his mother didn't get along well for the last year of her life. She died before he could get to see her one last time. During the grief Lee endured at losing his wife, Nick had been distant. That chasm increased over the years from phone calls at Christmas and birthdays to just Christmas and no calls for at least six years.

Lee had tried a couple of times, but Nick didn't return his messages. Maybe Lee reminded him of the law enforcement job his mother had attempted to force upon him years ago. Was there guilt behind that memory? How had Nick not listened to her final wishes in his mother's dying days?

As confusing as Sarah's directive to contact Nick was, Lee had no idea what to say to his son when he finally made that call. He picked up the phone, hovered a finger over the buttons, then set the phone down again.

What would he say?

He picked it up and dialed Nick's number. He had to do it. He trusted Sarah. He wouldn't have had her come to Kelowna if he didn't trust her. And if Nick had met their unsub at some time in the recent past, he was definitely someone they needed to speak to.

The phone rang at the other end.

He leaned back in his chair and let the chair spin away from the desk, his stomach doing small flips.

On the fourth ring, he placed a hand on his stomach to calm it. Someone picked up. A child cried in the background.

"Hello?" a woman answered. "Just tell me Nick's okay."

"Hello?" Lee said, sitting forward.

"I have call display," the woman said. "You're calling

from the RCMP. Is it about Nick?"

"No, no, it's not Nick. Well, maybe. I'm Stephen, Nick's father."

He was sure he heard an intake of breath on the other end of the line. There was a long enough pause. He was about to ask if she was still there when she spoke.

"Nick's father?" she whispered. "Is this for real?"

"Yes," Lee said. He placed his free hand on his forehead and closed his eyes. "It's for real."

"He's not here."

"I know."

"How do you know—"

"When I called, you wouldn't have worried for his safety if he was home."

"Oh. Right."

"When will he be home?"

"I'm not sure."

The baby in the background cried louder. Evidently, mom's attention was diverted elsewhere.

"What's this about?" she asked.

"Is this June Sumner?"

"Yes, your son's wife. Been married five years." She moved somewhere else in the house because the baby got quieter. "Too bad we had to meet on the phone."

"Do you need to attend to the baby?" Lee asked.

"I was feeding her. She's in the high chair. No food equals a mini tantrum. She's fine for a minute more. You want to tell me what this is about?"

"I want to see Nick; talk to him."

"That sounds nice and all, but Nick will want to know why. He's got a life now. He's moved on from what happened in the past."

"What happened in the past?" Lee asked, slightly surprised he was talking to June—a stranger to him—about a family issue.

"Nick told me his side of the story several times. Just know he's happy now. If whatever you want to talk about brings him down, he won't want any part in it."

"I have nothing negative to talk to him about. I miss him. That's all." He said it but wasn't sure he meant it. The call was set in motion because of an investigation. He didn't initiate the call on his own. Sarah told him to call. Reconnect. So he did. Did he miss his son? Of course, he did. "I miss him," he repeated. "I want to see him."

"Okay. I'll tell him you called. I gotta go."

"No, wait. When's he due home?"

"After dinner tonight."

"You said you saw my number on call display. Will you have him call that number?"

"I'll tell him you called. I'll give him the number. He'll decide what to do."

"That's fair. Thank you."

"Nice meeting you," June said, then hung up.

He held the phone to his ear a moment longer, blew pent-up air out of his mouth, then set the receiver down slowly.

It rang in his hand.

He jumped and jerked the phone back to his ear.

"Yeah?" he said, hoping it was Nick.

"It's Hallagan. There's been an incident in Vernon."

"Vernon?"

"When local officers responded to the site, they called us."

"Why?"

"They want to talk to Sarah Roberts."

"She's leaving as we speak. What would Vernon RCMP want with Sarah?"

"Two murders this morning in a coffee shop. There was a note on the front door. It said the murders were because of Sarah Roberts and what she did in Kelowna yesterday. The unsub wants to talk to Sarah, or the body count will rise."

"Holy shit. I have to get Sarah off that plane."

Lee slammed the phone down, flipped through a couple of scattered documents on his desk, found the one he was looking for, and scanned it with his finger for a name.

Officer Tom Mason and a select team of three other officers were tasked with ensuring Sarah and Parkman got on that plane this morning. Mason's contact phone number was printed below his name.

Lee dialed the number.

Chapter 12

THIRIO SET THE GUN on the table beside him to keep his hands free.

"Get up off the floor," he ordered.

The customer squirmed at Thirio's feet, sobbing and mumbling that he didn't want to die. A small dark puddle had formed on the floor near the man's abdomen.

"You fucking pissed yourself?" Thirio pulled his right foot back, then followed through with a kick to the customer's side. The man grunted on impact. "I oughta kill you for that. Now get up."

The man didn't move. His mumbling was too loud to hear Thirio's instructions well enough. Thirio leaned down, grabbed the customer's shirt collar, and pulled upward. The man spun around with something clutched in his hand. The light above bounced off the body of a canister of some kind.

Pepper spray!

Thirio released the customer and jerked his head away. A torrent of spray shot toward him, connecting with the side of his face. Thirio's eyes were clamped shut with no air moving in his nostrils as the liquid landed on his skin.

He dove several steps away, wiping the spray toward the back of his head with his hands in a frantic gesture to keep it out of his eyes.

A table moved behind him. What sounded like a chair tumbled to the floor.

My gun!

He'd left it on the table with the safety off. Without thought, without fear that the customer now had the weapon in his possession, Thirio spun around and lunged for the table, his one good eye wide open.

The customer got there first.

Thirio used his forward momentum to shove his right shoulder into the man's stomach and continued running until the wall stopped them abruptly. An exhalation of air shot from the man's mouth. His hands landed on Thirio. One in his hair and one on his shirt.

A sharp, intense pain shot through Thirio's head as the man tried to remove a large clump of Thirio's mane all at once.

His right eye had watered over with the scent of pepper spray so close to it, but now both eyes watered and gushed with the pain. He shouted a furious-sounding battle cry. In moments like this, Thirio always prided himself on how clear his thoughts were. He realized as his shoulder held the man against the wall and the man's hands pulled his hair and tried to rip the shirt off his back that those same two hands did not have a gun in them.

Thirio shoved his weight into the customer again, then dropped to the floor and felt around for the weapon, trying desperately to see through drowning eyes.

At the second his fingers bumped the barrel of the weapon, it was kicked away from him.

A fury he hadn't felt since his fiancée was murdered months ago rose, making him forget the gun.

He swiveled his upper body as he rose to his feet until he was face to face with the man. The customer backed away and headed for the opening to the coffee shop's back room.

Thirio lurched forward. He grabbed the man's neck and closed his hands even as the customer rained down fist after fist on Thirio's arms and upper chest. In this state, Thirio remained unfazed. After he'd killed himself for the world to see—his family and his enemies—he renamed himself Thirio, which meant beast in Greek, for he was the beast now, spawned by the devil himself. As Lucifer's pet, the anger and rage bestowed upon Thirio were magnificent and glorious. The inability to feel an ounce of pain while enthralled with a furious rage enabled him to hold onto the customer's neck until he watched the life dim from the man's eyes.

The man dropped to his knees. Thirio's arms followed, his grip tightening still. The customer's eyes fluttered as they bulged, his face a deep red, turning purple. A moan emitted from the man's throat. It signaled his fight was diminished until it was nothing but one of will—a will to live in a moment when he knew he would die.

The customer's arms weakened, then ceased their assault. When the body before Thirio slumped downward, and he was simply holding dead weight, he released the man's throat, took a deep breath, and stood to his full height.

"That'll fucking teach you," he mumbled, his voice deep with exertion.

His vision better by degrees, Thirio scanned the front window. It was void of onlookers. Not a single person in evidence. No one had happened by to try the door. As far as he could tell, no one had responded to the sound of the gunshots.

He jumped over the body and stopped at a sink behind the counter with a tall faucet. After a two-minute rinse of his face, he hit buttons on the till until the money tray opened. Upon quick examination, he counted a little over two hundred dollars in cash. This didn't have to look like a robbery. He just needed the money to forward his plan. They had killed his Julia. They had darkened his heart for years, then blackened it with her death. The demands of a blackened heart were insurmountable. The urge, the calling to right wrongs, started with the death of his oppressors and death of his enemies. Upon completion of that task, he would go on to serve his one true angel. It didn't matter to him whether he lived or died. He would serve his angel—the prettiest of them all—the fallen angel in life and death.

After wiping his face with water from the sink until most of the burn from the spray had dissipated, Thirio found a pad of paper and a marker on a desk in the back room. He wrote a note to Sarah Roberts. Then he signed it, Thirio.

When they found the bodies and realized it was Sarah's fault, she would come after him. Her calm, her ability to reason, would be contaminated by her desire to catch him. She would make mistakes, and he would be waiting for her.

He lifted his head in thought, staring off into space

momentarily. This made perfect sense. Sarah Roberts was something of a good person. Whatever psychic ability she possessed came from the other side. There was Lucifer and his angels, then the other side, where Sarah dwelled. Thirio's angelic father had offered him the chance of a lifetime by bringing her here and allowing her to get involved. How could he not have seen this before? Sarah Roberts was God's weapon, and Thirio was the devil's weapon. A few random souls were saved yesterday. So what? Thirio could right that wrong within hours, and no one could stop him.

Sarah Roberts was here because it was his job—his right —to remove her from existence for his father. He had to stop her from meddling in his affairs any further. It made complete sense. This was Thirio's test. Was he the avenger that his angel wanted? Was he dark enough to manage such a task as removing one of God's instruments?

He considered his ultimate purpose, what he meant to achieve. Upon that, it was easy to see how Sarah could be his first test, his first initiation into the Kingdom of Hell, where he hoped to rule alongside his master one day. The more souls he sent to his king, the larger the kingdom to be placed at his feet. And who better to send to the lake of fire than Sarah Roberts, one of God's puppets?

A plan formed. The idea solidified in his mind as he hunted for a piece of tape. He knew exactly what to do with Sarah Roberts. His enemies would play a large role in trapping her, providing she really was psychic and was here to save lives.

Thirio didn't often smile, especially not since Julia's death. But after what had happened yesterday, coupled with the idea of how to execute the meddling psychic, he smiled and thanked Lucifer. Thirio would have never been able to develop the idea on his own. Never. This was all his father's doing.

He placed the handwritten note on the inside of the coffee shop door, looked both ways, unlocked the door, then stepped outside. He strode to his nondescript work truck, eyes down, heading to work like anyone else. Once inside the truck, he punched the roof twice and let out a piercing scream. That woman couldn't be allowed to thwart him again. The bitch had to die, and she had to die in the worst way possible. His plan involved dismemberment, just as his father would want.

He started the truck and headed to the first house on his list. He had seven estimates set up for today. He would get to each one. Then maybe cancel tomorrow's estimates. By the end of the day, he would probably have enough money to finish what he had started. He would be scrupulous, watch his back, and look for suspicious cars following him.

Bottled in average-looking spray containers, he had the poison behind his seat, already made and ready for public consumption. If anyone got close, he would use the poison on them.

There could be no more risk. No potential for that woman to find him. He wouldn't stop. He would stick to his original mandate. He had come too far to stop now. The only alteration to the plan would be to lure Sarah Roberts into the trap set by the devil himself. Then he would take his time killing her. No one would be able to stop him.

No one at all.

He checked the side of his face in the mirror where the pepper spray had reddened his skin. It wasn't too bad. Just a little coloring on his right temple. Nothing he couldn't explain away to a potential client as a carpet burn.

Four blocks from the coffee shop, while sitting at a red light, a police car, lights flashing, raced by his work truck heading back the way he had just come.

Thirio smiled again.

He was getting used to things going his way.

Chapter 13

AT THE SOUND OF an airline attendant's announcement to commence boarding, Sarah and Parkman rose from their seats and lined up along with the other passengers.

The time was fast approaching when Lee's men would return for them. Sarah knew it as Vivian wasn't blocked at the moment. Several bits of information came through, preparing Sarah for what she had to do when the time came.

"They're still not here," Parkman said.

"They're coming." Sarah opened her passport to the picture page, then slipped her boarding pass in like a bookmark. "Just do what we're supposed to do until they arrive."

Parkman nodded. He wasn't one to question her.

Passports checked, Sarah led the way down the tunnel access to the plane. They got seated quickly in the twelfth row and waited. Parkman had the aisle seat. He fidgeted with his seatbelt, secured it, and rested his head back, eyes closed.

Vivian's presence was close. Like she was in the seat behind Sarah, whispering to her. Ever since Sarah had died in Denmark, they had maintained a very close relationship. This thing, whatever blocked Vivian, was new. What stumped Sarah was how Vivian didn't know what was blocking her. How could she not know? What could block Vivian's connection without Vivian knowing what it was? Could it be evasive on purpose? If so, to what end?

As a multitude of questions raced through Sarah's mind, she glanced out the plane's oval-shaped window to watch the ground crew finish with the last of the luggage. Men wearing fluorescent green vests worked on the plane parked to her right. She counted seven men with green vests and one man standing by himself in a suit jacket.

A suit jacket?

Sarah twisted in her seat to get a better look at the man in the suit standing on the tarmac roughly twenty yards from the plane. He wasn't wearing protective gear or headphones like the rest of the ground crew. The man simply stood behind the plane to her right, eyes focused on something on the ground. One glance at him, and she could tell he was depressed. An image of a depressed stock broker on a street corner came to mind. Or an embezzling businessman who had just discovered an audit was in his future.

He had to be with the airlines in some capacity. Otherwise, he wouldn't have clearance to stand out on the tarmac.

The captain announced the doors would soon close as they prepared for takeoff.

Parkman seemed restless.

"What's caught your attention?" he asked.

"That man." Sarah leaned back and pointed.

Parkman bent forward to look out the small window. He settled back in his seat, undid his seatbelt, then sat forward again and leaned across Sarah for a better view.

"I see a bunch of guys working with the luggage and one guy waiting with orange sticks. Which man are you referring to?"

Sarah kept her eyes on the man in the suit. He hadn't moved. The breeze didn't rustle his hair.

"That guy. In the dark suit." She pointed directly at him. "He's standing slightly behind that plane."

Parkman leaned out farther. "I don't see anyone in a suit."

"What? Really?" She looked at Parkman's face, then the direction of his gaze. He had a full view of the rear of the other plane. The only way he couldn't see the besuited man was if he was invisible.

"Can you see that cargo vehicle coming our way?" she asked.

"Yes."

"It will pass on the other side of the guy in the suit in three seconds. Two. One. Passing now, not two feet from the guy."

"I'm watching the vehicle, Sarah, but there's no one standing out there."

It dawned on her like a tormented epiphany. Her body shuddered at the prospect, at the reality. Goosebumps rose on her arms and legs.

"Sarah?" Parkman said beside her. "Your body just shook. Did you have a spasm?"

She ignored the question as she stared at the man, her eyes boring a hole in him.

Vivian? You there?

No response. Vivian's presence was no longer detected.

Her sister was gone. Blocked.

Understanding what was happening and why Vivian couldn't see it came to Sarah in a flash. If her suspicions were true, then a lot more happened to Sarah when she died in Denmark than Vivian was letting on.

The man on the tarmac raised his head in a blur of movement. He stared directly at her. There was no question in her mind.

He raised his right hand and motioned like he was trying to tell her something. This was the third time she had seen him, although she couldn't hear any gibberish this time. He was the man in the B.C. Medical Services building window. He was on the sidewalk outside Officer Lee's office window, and now he stood on the tarmac where no one but Sarah could see him. He had come with a message. Whatever he was trying to tell her seemed to be depressing him. Maybe the realization that Sarah wasn't getting his message meant he had failed her.

"Sarah?" Parkman said, his voice empathetic. "What's going on?"

She studied the man's roving hand. She tried to make sense of what he was saying. Slowly, a pattern began to emerge. His hand went up, down, left, and right like he was spelling something out. She detected a pause where his message ended; then, he started again. No matter how hard she tried, not a single letter formed in her mind.

"Excuse me, miss?"

Someone touched her arm.

Sarah turned a hint of anger on her face for being pulled away from the man in the suit.

The flight attendant jerked back, then gestured downward. "Your seatbelt."

Sarah nodded but didn't respond verbally, afraid anything she would say would come out unnecessarily mean. She quickly clasped her seatbelt and turned to watch the man in the suit.

The man had disappeared.

"Shit," she mumbled to herself.

"Sarah," Parkman whispered. "I don't scare easily, but this is scaring me. What's going on?"

The plane bumped as it started backward, away from the gate. Sarah faced forward in her seat, her mind filled with questions and a lack of answers.

"It's okay, Parkman," she said. "I will explain everything very soon."

"I trust that. You always do."

"I have some things to figure out first."

"Like what?"

"Things, Parkman."

"Right." He waited a moment, then added, "Things."

"When the men come, go back to Lee. Get him to work on his son. Look for pictures of his son's landscaping job." Sarah closed her eyes. "Find the before-and-after shots. Then encourage a healthy relationship between father and son. Nick's family needs Stephen."

"Landscaping job? Does the family need Stephen? What are you talking about?"

She blinked but didn't respond to Parkman's question.

"In those pictures, you will see the face of the man we're hunting. That'll be a step in identifying our perp."

Parkman shifted in his seat beside her. "The unsub's face would go a long way to solving this mess."

The plane stopped with a subtle shake. The engines revved up, and then it started forward as they taxied away from the gate.

"You're still sure they're coming for us?" Parkman asked.

"Yes. We don't fly today."

"They're almost out of time, then."

"I'm aware of that." She kept her eyes closed, listening for Vivian to return. "They'll be here."

"What are you going to do?" he asked. "I mean, while I'm with Lee pressuring him to talk to his son."

"I have to go underground to find our perp."

"Underground? I don't like the sound of that."

"I don't have a choice. Too many Kelowna police officers don't want me to succeed. And I don't respond well to bullies."

"Bullies? Who's a bully?"

"Officer Tom Mason."

Sarah opened her eyes as she felt Vivian close again. She exchanged a glance with Parkman and instantly saw torment in his eyes. He hated when they worked apart.

"It won't be long," she reassured him. "Vivian says it's the only way. You heard what Lee said about his superiors. They blame me for the death of their bomb-squad member. They hate me here. I don't care about their hate. What I do care about is when that hate hinders my progress."

Parkman nodded his understanding. She knew, as much

as he despised leaving her alone, he would do it because it was Vivian who had gotten them through the worst situations in the past, and if this were what Vivian wanted, he would go forward without doubt.

"Flight attendants, prepare for takeoff," the captain said over the speakers.

The engines revved, and the plane shot forward. If anyone questioned Vivian's ability to foretell the future, it would be at that moment that they would feel vindicated. But that moment would be short-lived.

By the time the plane got to take-off speed, the sound of the engines had changed, and the wing flaps adjusted. The plane decelerated rapidly. People whispered to one another throughout the plane. A feeling of unease filtered to everyone. Heads turned, and questions were raised.

"I apologize," the captain said over the speakers as the plane slowed enough to turn off the main runway. "It seems we're being called back to the gate. We will find out what they want and get you in the air as soon as possible. We're sorry for the delay."

Minutes later, the plane was met with four police cruisers on the tarmac. Sarah watched the cruisers approach, lights flashing.

Mason and his crew were back. They had been told to take Sarah and Parkman into custody. It had to be official at some high level to stop their plane from taking off.

Once the door was opened, five heavily armed officers entered the front of the plane, Officer Tom Mason leading the boarding party.

"Nothing to worry about," Sarah whispered. "Lee needs us. There have been two new murders this morning. Vivian's with me now." She patted Parkman's leg. "They need us back on the case."

"If I didn't have you, I'd think the worst, as this could be quite intimidating."

She offered Parkman a smirk. "Mason loves this sort of thing. Manhandling us off the plane in front of so many people raises his self-esteem. Makes him feel manly. His time will come."

The men came down the aisle as a unit.

"Sarah Roberts," Mason barked. "Parkman. Get out of your seats. You're leaving the plane with us."

"No, please?" Sarah asked. "No sugar on top?" She tilted her head sideways and fiddled with her hair.

"We will drag you out if we have to, but you're coming with us whether you want to or not."

"I think we'll be okay to walk," Sarah said. She nudged Parkman's arm. "You good with walking?"

He nodded. "Sure. Walking's good."

"Get out of your seats," Mason barked louder. "We haven't got time for this."

Sarah glared at him. "Watch yourself, Mason. Your clock is ticking."

He leaned in over Parkman, his upper body pushing Parkman back into the seat.

"You threatening me again, Miss Roberts?" His eyes bulged slightly. "Please tell me you're threatening me."

"Mason, I will throat punch you, take your gun, and kneecap you so you're in a fucking wheelchair the rest of your life if you get in my face one more time. You're a man. Nothing more. Don't be such a child to think I'm *threatening* you. Aren't we all big kids now?"

His face reddened with fury.

Parkman shoved forward, knocking Mason into the seat in front.

"Oops," Parkman said. "Didn't see you there."

Mason stood. "Get them out of here," he shouted to the men behind him.

Parkman unclipped his seatbelt and got to his feet. He shot a questioning glance back at Sarah. She shrugged to let him know it was no big deal.

"This one goes with me," Mason said, grabbing Sarah's arm.

She undid her belt and rose from her seat. Mason shoved her after Parkman.

"Make sure she's placed in my car."

Sarah followed Parkman up the aisle, avoiding the stares of the passengers whose flight was delayed. At the door, the late-morning sun warmed her. She paused on the top step.

"It's going to be a lovely day," Sarah said.

Mason pushed her from behind. "Get moving," he grunted.

She started down the steps toward the cruisers parked in a semi-circle at the bottom, already looking forward to the injuries Officer Mason would receive on the drive back to the police station.

"Hey, Parkman," she called.

He looked over at her from the side of another police car.

"Do what the note says," she called out to him.

"The note?"

"Yeah. The note. Just do what it says."

An officer placed a hand on Parkman's head and pushed him into the cruiser's back seat.

Mason opened the backdoor of his cruiser.

"Get in," he said.

"What? No handcuffs?" she asked, hands raised innocently.

"Shut up and get in."

She eased into the back of Mason's cruiser, knowing why he hadn't cuffed her. She had read his mind through Vivian and knew exactly what he had planned.

"Ohh," Sarah said loud enough for Mason to hear. "This is going to be fun. You should've brought along popcorn for the party you and I will have."

Chapter 14

THIRIO WORKED HIS MAGIC at the first estimate he performed in the city of Vernon. The incident in the coffee shop earlier that morning had brightened his spirits. Buoyed by what had happened, he wondered what Sarah would think when she read his note. How happy would the authorities be with their choice of hero?

He drove through town on his way to his next appointment, the trunk's stereo blasting The Dayglo Abortions's song, "Religious Bumfucks." It hadn't reached lunchtime yet, and he was already two thousand dollars richer for having done nothing but offer people hope. He was a king. He was on top. No one could stop him because he worked for the devil, and the devil made his mayhem possible. That had become his truth, his reality.

His idea to pose as a contractor to extract money from potential clients was brilliant. He prepared a website in under a day at a coffee shop using their WiFi. Something nice, but not too flashy, with fake testimonials. Once the email was set up and a prepaid phone card for the business number was placed in his unlocked iPhone, he was set. The UPS store gave him a business address for the city he would work in for only a few bucks. Then he entered that city's buy and sell pages on Facebook, dropped the name, number, and email, and talked about his contracting rates. His staff of six men could do the job quicker and more efficiently than any other contractor.

There was no company, no six men, and no job he would ever complete. There was only Thirio stealing unsuspecting potential clients' deposit money.

Within a week of his first ad on Facebook, appointments for free estimates were set up, and he was in business. In Kamloops, he visited over twenty homes, offered free estimates, and had eight people call back to want the landscaping work done. Two homes were prepared to have short retaining walls put in. Thirio had no intention of fulfilling any of these orders, but he collected the fifty-percent deposit for the work upfront. Since his company was popular and booking into next month (the lie he told all his potential clients), he would set dates six to eight weeks away for his crew to return and start the work. Within two weeks, Thirio had eight advances on work he would never do. He shut down the website, deactivated the email, pulled the sim card from his cell phone, and headed to Penticton to repeat the process. The two hundred dollar investment brought him thousands in return.

With enough money to settle in and build small explosive devices in Penticton, he rented an apartment downtown.

While there, he set up another company and began the estimate gig all over.

The delivery of the bombs became costly. He had bought small GPS trackers and had to find used furniture to sell. Once the prospective buyers contacted him about the reclining chairs he had for sale, he would qualify them. The buyers had to be from Kelowna, an hour away. All bombs had to be delivered to Kelowna, where his main goal of spreading terror was to be initiated. The bombs were connected to his cell phone for easy detonation. The buyers of the recliners would be the first to die, and with them went their knowledge of Thirio's location and description. The plan was genius.

Three bombs later, the cost of doing business had become too expensive to continue. He needed more money to get to his denouement.

Now in Vernon, seven estimates were set for the next two days, and he was feeling good about the results. Estimate number one had gotten him a cheque. He was en route to the next estimate with no care in the world about the people he met or the money he stole from them.

The only person on his mind was Sarah Roberts. How would she respond to the hand-written note stuck to the window of the coffee shop in Vernon? He'd told her for every life she saved, he would take ten until he caught up with her. Then he would send her to Hell, where she belonged.

Would the police waste time dusting for prints on the paper? Would they check for cameras in the area? Maybe try to match the bullet to a weapon?

Nothing they would do could bring them closer to him.

Absolutely nothing.

Because Thirio had thought of everything, he was the perfect kind of killer. Elusive, brilliant, and savvy. His fingerprints had been burned off the day he killed himself. The gun was unregistered, and the serial number was filed off long ago. If anyone ever gave the authorities his description, they'd be describing a dead man. Even a hair fiber DNA check couldn't lead to Thirio. It would lead to a man buried days after Julia was killed. They had nothing and would get nothing.

Except for Sarah. They had Sarah. And if she really were a psychic, then maybe she'd become a problem.

Or maybe not.

Something bothered him about his thought process. Something he had just deduced floated around in his mind, feeling like it was unfinished.

He turned off the main road by a casino and headed deeper into the city, his next appointment eagerly awaiting an estimate.

What bothered him so? It felt like he'd missed something important. But what did he miss? What could he have missed that would be so important as to bother him?

His fingerprints were gone. DNA was linked to a dead man. The witness statements would lead nowhere. Ballistic tests would end up—

Ballistics.

"Damn it." He smacked the steering wheel.

He'd left the gun on the floor of the coffee shop wherever that customer had kicked it. Fingerprints weren't an issue. The loss of the weapon was. He didn't have another gun.

"I need a gun," he said to himself in the rearview mirror

as the Dayglo Abortions ranted in their song "I Killed Mommy."

With the denouement fast approaching, he would do the landscaping estimates as planned while sizing up his potential clients on home security. Of the people he would meet that day, one of them would have a gun somewhere in their home. As soon as he found a protective, security-conscious customer, he would find himself a gun.

And that would be his final estimate of the day.

He sped up his work truck in the moment of excitement, clicking over to the next song. "I'm my own God" blasted through his cheap speakers.

"Apotheosis," he said to himself. "The elevation of a person to the rank of a god." That was who he was now. A ruler for Lucifer, a Lord. He was Thanatos, the ancient Greek personification of death. For Satan, he would be the death instinct, the deliverer of death.

"Thanatos." He looked at his own eyes in the mirror. "Man, does that ever sound good. That's so me."

More souls were heading south of the soil. More souls for his Father meant a higher rank on the Father's side. Maybe Thirio would be awarded a kingdom when he headed south of the soil. He'd presented himself as a god on Earth. Why couldn't he be one in Hell?

Who knew what the dark lord would offer him as a reward for his work? What Thirio did know was this work was exciting, and he never wanted to stop.

At least not until he dismembered Sarah Roberts. Then, and only then, would he be ready to meet his father to begin his reign over the legions of tortured dead.

"Thank you," he shouted in the cab of his work truck.

"Thank you so much for this opportunity to show you evil on such a grand scale. My Father, the bringer of darkness, the strongest of angels, I thank you for this chance to prove my worth."

Thirio punched the dash twice.

The pain in his knuckles made him smile. He would have to get used to the pain where he was going.

"No problem, there. No problem."

Chapter 15

SARAH SAT IN THE rear of Mason's cruiser, her knees uncomfortably jammed against the Plexiglas wall separating her from the front seat.

Officer Mason glanced at her intermittently in his mirror. Neither spoke after leaving the airport parking lot. Within a kilometer or two, the cruiser with Parkman pulled away and was lost to sight.

Mason signaled left, then turned onto Rutland Street. Sarah watched the street signs, committing most of them to memory. This wasn't the direction to the police station, and Mason wasn't driving her to Vernon, where Vivian had said two people were murdered that morning. Mason had other plans for her.

She stared at the top of his head, the hair thinning where a bald spot was forming. She thought about Mason's life, at least what she had the privilege of knowing. He'd done a lot of terrible things since becoming a man. What troubled Mason about Sarah was the death of his friend, Barry Ashford, the RCMP officer Sarah had antagonized over a year ago. Ashford had once been Mason's business partner, as close to him as a brother. Ashford had been involved with a massage parlor in Kelowna and prostitution. The mafia would have called Officer Barry Ashford a made man.

But Ashford was dead, and many people blamed Sarah for that. Sarah had kidnapped Ashford and tied him up in the house she'd rented in Kelowna to extract a confession from him. During that time, Ashford was murdered and dismembered. Since witnesses had seen Sarah nab Ashford, she became the prime suspect in the case until it came to light, mostly due to Parkman's help, that Debbie Ashford, Barry's wife, was the murdering sort. The story was twisted —reserved for the pages of fiction or movie screens—often never happening in real life. But this incident did happen, and Sarah was at the center of it.

Mason thought Ashford had been a good man and a solid cop. Mason believed Debbie was given an opportunity to end her marriage, so she took it. Debbie's plan to have Sarah blamed for the murder almost worked.

Mason blamed everything on Sarah. He'd been willing to let it go because Sarah was on the next flight out of Kelowna. But when Lee called Mason's team and ordered them to get Sarah and Parkman back downtown, Mason had made another decision. He would see to it Sarah would never set foot in Kelowna again.

All this knowledge was imparted to Sarah in seconds as Vivian relayed what Mason was dealing with internally. His rage worsened with each passing second. Sarah, complicit in

Ashford's death—according to Mason—was in his car. Vivian warned her this was coming.

This was a ghost of a different kind. Earthbound spirits were tethered by strong emotions of love or hate. Barry's ghost lived on in Mason's mind, bound there by some twisted brotherly love, a link Sarah would have to break to stay alive.

In her reverie, lost in the information from Vivian, Sarah had forgotten to pay attention to the street signs. The cruiser had gone up a back road that led past apple orchards. At a four-way stop, Sarah caught the street sign: McCulloch Road.

Mason continued along McCulloch, winding up its meandering length through rural residential, passing Gallagher's Canyon Golf Course until he came to a narrow road that crossed a one-lane bridge. After another minute, Mason turned up a road where a sign said something about Myra Canyon trestles.

"Taking me on a scenic tour of backwoods Kelowna?" Sarah asked, not an ounce of nervousness in her voice. She'd dealt with these kinds of confrontations before. She still felt nervous, though. Things could go wrong. Vivian couldn't show Sarah her own future—whether she had one or not. But revealing her state of mind to Mason, letting him see a glimpse of weakness, did Sarah no favors.

After a minute of navigating the dirt road, bouncing over large holes in the rough surface while making his way up the incline, Mason still hadn't responded to her.

"You do know your boss will wonder what happened to me?" Mason slowed as the road steepened and became bumpier. "I'm assuming you've got a plan to explain your detour, the loss of time?"

When Mason still hadn't responded, Sarah slapped the

Plexiglas. He jerked at the smack but remained silent.

The back seat was a mini jail cell. There was no way out short of breaking a window. Doing that would offer Mason a reason to hurt her—bad. Or kill her. She had no choice but to wait it out. See where he was taking her and deal with it then.

More than five minutes later, Mason pulled into a flattened clearing beside the road. He angled the car parallel with the road, the passenger side facing out.

When he turned off the car, he sat still as if waiting for something or someone. Or maybe he was having second thoughts. The car's engine ticked in the all-encompassing silence.

"Hey, Mason." Sarah interrupted the quiet. "You think the airline pulled our carry-ons off the plane? I'd hate to find out that my bag of undies is halfway to Toronto right now."

He fidgeted with something upfront. Sarah leaned forward. Mason's gun was in his hand. He was checking the weapon for ammunition. He clamped it shut, then holstered it at his waist.

"How about we play a game?" Sarah asked. Now that the cruiser had been turned off, the summer sun beat through the windows. She felt like an ant burning under a magnifying glass. A film of sweat broke out on her brow. "You like games, right Mason?"

He checked his mirrors, then his watch, still not saying a word. It occurred to her that even his police radio was silent. She hadn't heard the dispatcher since she entered the car.

Mason has a plan. God laughs.

"Do you believe in God?" she asked.

No answer.

"I hope you do. It would be odd to meet someone you

don't believe in."

Mason glanced out his window, a thousand-yard stare.

"How about this? Would you like to know when you're going to die?" Sarah asked. "Doesn't everyone want to know that sort of thing?"

He moved slowly. His eyes met hers through the rearview mirror.

"What?" Sarah shrugged. "You know I'm psychic. How about I tell you a bit about yourself? I can tell you how you die and when. Wouldn't that be fun knowing such things?" She smiled, dropped her head to the side, and bit her lower lip. "You know, Mason, I once heard someone say that the future has a way of showing up unannounced. It kind of just happens. Interesting, right? Well, not anymore." She raised her voice to imitate a game show host. "I can tell you your future right now. Everything that will happen to you right up until the day you die." She leaned forward, her nose an inch from the Plexiglas. "How about it, eh? You wanna know? Do ya?"

He slammed his right elbow into the Plexiglas. She flinched and drew her hands up in defense.

"Shut the fuck up!" he shouted. "Just shut up."

She relaxed her hands at her sides, staring at the back of his head, heart beating faster. The heat in the car had increased. For whatever reason, Mason wasn't turning the car on.

"Mason?" she said, her voice serious now, monotone. He didn't respond. "Mason, you need to know something." He looked at her in the rearview mirror. She lowered her head slightly but kept her eyes on him. "I never lose. I either win, or I learn. But I never lose. That's what your problem is. You rarely win, and you never learn." She licked her lips. "Get it, Mason? Because if you don't, you will die while I'm in Kelowna. And I won't be here too long."

His eyes remained riveted on her.

"I leave Kelowna very soon, and I will never come back. In the meantime, I will offer you one free lesson from which to learn. If you fail, you die. If you learn, you live, and you'll become a better person—"

"Oh, my shit," Mason shouted. "Will you just shut up with your psychobabble? Just shut up. It's not me who will be dead soon. It's you."

His cell phone beeped. He grabbed it, read the screen, then set it back down. After typing something on the keyboard just below the lip of the dash, a small screen lit up, providing a view of the front of the car. The dashcam.

Mason exited the car, leaving the driver's door open. Sarah saw the dashcam recording, then suddenly understood Mason's entire plan.

The door to her left clicked and swung open.

"Out," he ordered.

She edged sideways, pulled her knees away from the back of the front seat, and stuck her head out.

Mason stepped in. With a blur of movement, he slammed his fist into Sarah's jaw. Her vision flashed white, then came back. She hadn't seen it coming. The sucker punch knocked her downward. She would've hit the gravel face-first if her hands hadn't been free of the vehicle to stop her descent.

"Get out, witch," Mason shouted. "You think you know me? You think you know how I treat women? You don't know shit, whore bitch."

He grabbed the back of her shirt and hefted her up and

out of the car even as blood slipped from her mouth. She landed on her feet, bent over at the waist. He released her and walked to the front of the car, where he stopped and gestured with his hands for her to follow.

Her teeth had cut her cheek inside her mouth, which slowly filled with blood. She felt around the minor wound with her tongue. None of her teeth were broken, just a slight sting where the flesh was torn. She rolled her shoulders twice while rotating her head and offered Mason a wide smile, revealing teeth tinged in blood.

Never show fear.

An adage she'd learned years ago. Take the pain. Ignore it. Move on. Let things go. It was the only way to stay alive in a man's world. Guys like Mason were thrilled when they could intimidate. A person's behavior always came with a payoff, and Mason's payoff was the enjoyment of someone weaker asking for forgiveness. He was the boss. He was in charge. It had to be on his terms.

"Is that why you became a cop?" Sarah wiped the side of her mouth and glanced down at her hand. Blood smeared from wrist to knuckle.

Mason placed a hand on the butt of his holstered weapon.

"I'm warning you, Sarah," he said. "Drop the weapon."

She held out her hands. Both were empty. Mason stood in front of his cruiser, on the dashcam, recording himself for later defense.

"Bold," she said. "I'll give you that."

He drew his weapon. The tip aimed at her face. Behind the extended hands, Mason's eyes were cold, decisive. He was ready to pull the trigger, to execute her, surrounded by nothing but trees and shrubs. He had even taken care of the witness factor. Of the three cruisers at the airport, one drove Parkman into town, and the other two had broken away. One cop now sat at the top of the Myra Canyon Road, the other at the bottom, both blocking access to the road. That was what Mason had been waiting on. When his cell phone dinged, his men were in position. Parkman was entering the police station at that moment, minutes away from a rendezvous with Lee, oblivious that Sarah wasn't right behind him.

What Vivian failed to mention was how Sarah could get out of this. Sometimes leaving her alone to fend for herself was welcomed. Other times, not so much.

Sarah stepped forward.

"One more step, Sarah," Mason said. "I'm warning you. Put the gun on the ground, or I will have to shoot."

"Would it help to say I don't have a gun?" She shivered as the sweat beaded all over her body, and it cooled fast. "Does your dashcam record audio as well? Or will they read your lips later when they investigate my death?"

Mason eased into a shooter's stance. His index finger slipped inside the trigger guard. She had seconds left. Maybe less.

She stepped closer.

"How will you explain the location? The middle of nowhere? Huh?" She moved closer still, her heart skipping in her chest, blood dripping from her chin. She didn't want to swipe the blood away, fearing Mason would just shoot at the sudden movement.

"You told me there was a dead body up here," Mason said, his mouth enunciating each word, making it easy to read his lips. "I believed you. And now you aim to kill me. I've got backup coming. When they arrive, I will take you into custody." He eased back. "Sarah, drop the weapon. We can work this out. I will be forced to shoot if you don't drop the weapon."

"Mason, before you kill me out here, give me one thing."

"What?" he asked, his lips barely parting this time. It looked as if he'd taken a breath. He appeared to be building the nerve to take the shot.

"Make it count," she said.

"What?"

"Forehead. Center of the eyes. Don't fuck this up like you fucked up your life. I don't want to *almost* die and end up in a hospital for six months only to come out with half a face, eating from a fucking straw until I'm sixty-something when I eat my own bullet properly." She moved closer again. He was within reach now. "Just promise me you'll do it right, and on your count, I'll lunge at you. It'll be justified then."

"What?" He frowned. "You have a death wish?"

"There's no end game here for me, is there? You've set this up, and now you win. I'm okay with that." She adjusted her feet. Inches closer. "You think I like walking around with all these voices in my head telling me shit about rapists, serial killers, and asshole cops like your friend Ashford?"

At the mention of Barry Ashford's name, Mason's body tightened. Sarah didn't give him a chance to shoot.

Lightning quick, her right hand grabbed the gun barrel, adjusted its angle away, and pulled him toward her in the same movement. Her left wrapped around his elbow.

The gun fired beside her head as she cranked down on his wrist and shoved upward at his elbow—the way it wasn't meant to go. Her hearing, momentarily lost after the report of the weapon so close to her ear, meant she didn't hear his bone break. Mason's right arm dangled at an impossible angle, the flesh of his exposed forearm protruding upward as the inner bone—now broken—fought to escape.

Sarah spun on her heels in a circle while swinging her right hand around. Before impact, she formed a fist. With the momentum of the spin and Mason's weakened bravado, she brutally connected with the side of his head and knocked him off his feet. He sprawled onto the hood of his cruiser, where Sarah delivered a kick to the back of his knee. The gun was forgotten, his broken arm twisted backward, and Mason dropped like a lump to the dirt. Sarah kicked the gun out of reach and dropped down on top of him. She grabbed his collar—her senses on full alert after thinking she'd be shot—and lifted him up to meet her face. He blanched at the sight of his arm.

She spit on him. "There," she said. "That brought a little color back to your face."

He moaned. Soon, those moans would amount to screams as he registered the broken bone. The splatter pattern of blood and saliva on his face and the arm twisted backward would make for a grotesque zombie costume for Halloween.

"See what I mean?" Sarah asked. He shook his head and looked up at her, blinking rapidly. He moaned deeper in his throat. "You never learn."

Sarah dropped her forehead hard and fast. The contact with Mason's nose broke it instantly. His body jerked under her. She released him and got to her feet. He dropped to the dirt and curled into a ball, his good hand holding his face.

The road was empty each way. His buddies were still doing a fine job of blocking it off.

The doors on the driver's side of the cruiser were wide

open. Sarah grabbed Mason's feet and started dragging him toward the car. He had to weigh at least a hundred and seventy-five pounds, but she was able to move him to the back door within a minute.

Sweat blinded her. She swiped at it, took a couple of deep breaths, and got her hands under his shoulders. Mason moaned much louder as she lifted. The movement caused gravity to swing his broken arm downward. When it bumped the ground, his body jerked and spasmed while he shouted in pain.

"What the fuck, Mason," Sarah whispered while lifting him. "You gonna die on me here? It's just a broken arm. How much of a pussy are you? Fuckin' baby."

Blood spilled from Mason's nose, covering his mouth, chin, and neck. His eyes fluttered almost shut.

"Maybe it's better you just go to sleep for a while," Sarah said as she dropped his upper body onto the back seat. It took more time than she wanted, but she finally got Mason stretched out in the back of the cruiser, his legs folded up so she could close the door.

Something heavy dropped in the footwell below Mason's waist. Sarah paused before shutting the door, then leaned back inside the hot car. A shiny black pistol lay on the cruiser's carpet. It had fallen from Mason's front pocket. No doubt the gun that would be planted on Sarah's dead body. The one she was supposed to have been holding on him.

"You never learn," she said, shaking her head.

Sarah grabbed the pistol and checked for a serial number. Of course, it was gone. Filed off.

She slammed the door, locking Mason in the back of his own cruiser. After moving a few steps away from the car, she tossed the pistol as far as she could into the woods. It came down deep inside the tree line to the sound of leaves pushed out of its way. A dull thud followed. Hopefully, that pistol would never be found or used again.

She slapped her hands together to rid them of dust and dirt and walked over to Mason's police-issue gun, where it lay on the ground. After retrieving it, she slipped the Smith & Wesson into her waistband. It was flat enough to rest at the back of her pants easily.

Inside the front seat, she retrieved Mason's cell phone, left the door open, then walked around and opened the other front door. She couldn't have Mason dying from the intense heat on this hot summer day in the back of his own cruiser. Murder charges being what they were, that sort of thing would slow her progress in finding the unsub she was called to Kelowna to deal with.

The phone showed no texts since he released her from the back of the cruiser. The battery was over ninety percent. She would deal with the cruiser blocking the road to the south of her. She would let Lee deal with the one to the north. As long as one of them was out of the way, a *real* police officer could get her out of there. Or maybe she would just borrow a car.

She laughed to herself. She used to hate cops. Trusting them was not an option. And now she was going to call the cops—Officer Stephen Lee—to pick her up and get her away from the cops who had tried to kill her.

"What the hell is going on in this crazy fucking world?" she muttered out loud.

Sarah started down the road at a decent pace, her cheek numb, only aching slightly now. Myra Canyon Road was mostly downhill from Mason's cruiser, meandering left and right with nary a shoulder. At each corner, she eased around it slowly. The element of surprise couldn't be lost. The road veered to the left, then right again. She followed it quietly, watching for the RCMP cruiser blocking the south at every turn.

She checked Mason's phone frequently.

Why hadn't his partners texted him to see what was taking so long? After a brief communication with Vivian, she understood. They were waiting for word from him. A call for backup. A plea for help. Then they would come running.

In a few turns, she would come upon the cruiser of Officer Brent Waters, the man who helped Mason cover for the beating he gave his ex-girlfriend Vicky.

Sarah grinned, flaring up the pain in her cheek.

It was Brent's turn to learn an important lesson about being a responsible adult. By blocking the road so Mason and Sarah would be alone, Brent was complicit in Mason's actions. Brent was, in fact, an accessory to her attempted murder.

Sarah quickened her pace. Maybe he'd have a water bottle in his car, too. Forget calling Lee to get her out of there. She would take Waters's cruiser. By the time she took the car from him, she would definitely want a drink.

According to Vivian, waiting for Lee to get her out of there wasn't the answer. He wouldn't get her to Vernon fast enough, and that was where Sarah needed to be within an hour or so.

At a grocery store.

A grocery store?

Vivian's nod seemed urgent. At least, that's how it was

conveyed in her consciousness.

Sarah started running.

Chapter 16

MASON STRUGGLED TO ATTAIN consciousness as the pain swallowed him whole. The heat had become unbearable. Breathing through his nose; impossible. Mouth open, inhaling searing breaths of hot air, he rolled onto his side. His broken arm bumped the Plexiglas. White hot pain flared through his body. The kind of pain he associated with severing a limb. His eyes fluttered, then shut. Drowning in the misery of his agony, consciousness waning, he allowed himself to let go for a moment.

Thoughts of Vicky dashed into his mind. Where was she now? What man had she run to after they broke up? How could Vicky leave him? They had a good thing. Nothing would've happened if she'd just done what she'd been told to do. She wouldn't need dental work to fix the teeth he broke.

Women always complain about men losing it and attacking them. Or the husband kills his wife and ends up in jail. Follow the trends. If you're a woman, buck up and listen to your man or pay a price. Each man had a different idea of what that price was, but Mason knew his exactly. He had enjoyed causing Vicky pain. It was for the better. It taught her a better way. Why wouldn't they get that and just thank him for his efforts?

He pushed thoughts of violence out of his mind as an image of Sarah came to him—what she had done to him. The pain he would cause her when he caught up with her spurred him on.

Suddenly, he was walking in a field. At the edge of the field, a line of something light brown had been set down, covering the foliage in all directions. He headed toward it. Moments later, he got to the brown section and discovered it was sand. As he crossed into the sandy area, the temperature changed to desert-like conditions. He broke out into a sweat. It was hard to breathe. The air was thick, humid, choking.

Something bumped into him. He spun around to see what it was, and the light brown sand all around him disappeared to form a white light.

Mason screamed.

He opened his eyes, batted them, then squinted. The sun beat through the back window of his cruiser onto his face. Inside his mouth, his tongue felt fat as it tried to move to the side to allow air in.

He must've drifted off. He needed to get up. Stay awake. What he needed to do was call for help. With his good arm, he grabbed for the burn phone he had in his pocket.

It was gone.

Sarah must've taken it.

He felt around to his front left pocket and pulled out his

own cell phone.

"Missed this one, bitch." His voice surprised him. A deep nasal quality that made him think of the stuffed nose of a nasty cold.

He held up the phone to his eyes, flipped it around to the front, and almost dropped it. His body jerked as he caught it, sending more waves of pain through him.

"Sarah Roberts," he moaned, teeth tight, jaw firm. "Your death will be my pleasure. Your pain, my ecstasy."

Was it Calder parked at the top of Myra Canyon Road or Waters? Which one blocked the north? Calder or Waters? He couldn't remember for sure but decided on Calder. He scrolled through the menu on the phone and dialed Calder's number.

"Yeah?" Calder answered on the first ring. "We good? You need *backup*?" he said the last word sarcastically.

"Yeah," Mason mumbled. "And an ambulance."

"Mason?" Calder stammered. "That you?"

"Yeah."

"What happened to your voice?"

"Bitch broke my arm, then my nose. Call an ambulance. Get me out of here."

"Holy shit. On my way."

"Wait."

"What?"

"Call Waters, too. Warn him. Sarah's probably headed his way. She's on foot and armed."

"Holy shit. On it."

The line died.

Mason wondered how far Sarah would get before she was murdered by one of his team. He laid his head back on the seat. He set the phone on his chest. The second Calder got there, they would send out a BOLO for Sarah. Hopefully, she stayed alive long enough to get put in jail. In jail, she would be abused. Then she might end up hanging herself. He'd see to it.

Either way, it didn't matter to Mason how she did it—or how *he* did it. What was important to him was that Sarah Roberts would be leaving Kelowna in a body bag.

His eyes fluttered closed. He focused on his breathing. He lost consciousness again.

Chapter 17

After the second estimate didn't pan out and the third was a lost cause, Thirio was convinced he wouldn't be able to steal a weapon. Canadians, as a rule, did not have guns in their homes. Sure, there were knives, baseball bats, and several other implements that could become a weapon, but he could go to the local Home Depot and purchase those items himself.

He walked around the backyard of an old Victorian-style home in rural Vernon, assessing the viability of digging up the overgrown grass and planting a vegetable garden. The owner, Mr. Ray Durowitz, wanted the garden to combat all the chemicals in the food that killed his wife. Durowitz was in his eighties, lived alone, and seemed fit enough to manage his own garden.

None of that mattered to Thirio. What mattered to Thirio was if he could convince Durowitz that he was the man for the job and entice a fifty-percent deposit up front on the work.

Thirio talked. He engaged Durowitz and made suggestions. He wasn't just a salesman; he was a master closer. Everything he did or said was to close the deal, and Durowitz was falling into his trap.

The summer heat warmed Thirio's back and matted his shirt up against his skin. He welcomed the heat. One day soon, he would reign in the heat of Hell, unbearable to human flesh.

At the edge of the proposed garden, Thirio surveyed the assembled tools Durowitz had placed out in anticipation of digging a garden. Old folks had no idea how contracting worked. The estimate came first. The deal was arranged next. A deposit was paid. Then a date was set for the work. Today was—arrange for the deal and retain deposit day, just like dealing with a lawyer. People had to pay something to retain services. Only with Thirio, he would never return to do the work.

He retrieved a shovel from the ground, hefted it to check its weight, then set it up against the fence.

"Nice shovel, Mr. Durowitz. It'll work for you, but my team will bring our own tools."

"Ray."

Thirio turned to glance over at Durowitz. He set a palm over his eyes to block the sun.

"Excuse me?"

"Ray. Just call me Ray."

Thirio nodded. "Okay, Ray. I was saying that my team —"

"I heard that," Ray cut in. "What's important to me is the

initial placement of the garden. The seeding, too. Once that's done, I'll tend it." Ray looked away from the overgrown grass and weeds, his eyes watering as if he was about to cry. "How long before your team could have this job done?"

"That's a two-part question, Mr. Durowitz—Ray. The job itself would take one afternoon. We tear up what's here and lay rich topsoil. Then, on day two, we seed and water it. When can we do it is another question."

"Any day is fine with me," Ray said.

"My team is pretty busy, Ray. It'll be at least a month before we can get here."

"Too long," Ray said. He turned away and started for the house.

"Wait up, Ray," Thirio said, stumbling after him. "I could look at my schedule and see if we could make it earlier."

"It's already midsummer," Ray said as he slowed and turned back to face Thirio. "I need that garden in, so it produces something for September and October. I want vegetables stored for the winter. You can't come in September to do the work. It'll be too late."

"Okay, I understand." Thirio pulled out his cell phone. "Let me call the office. I'll have my secretary look at the schedule and see if there isn't room to fit this job in this week."

Ray faced Thirio and crossed his arms. "I would like that very much."

Thirio dialed his own cell number and turned away from the customer. Back at the proposed garden area, he pretended to be talking to Maria at the office. He begged her to find room. He explained to the dead phone line that Mr. Durowitz had lost his wife—he lowered his voice but made sure it was loud enough for Ray to still hear—and that the garden was a necessity. After a moment, he glanced over his shoulder.

"On hold," he said. Then pointed at his phone. "She's checking with one of the crew."

Ray nodded his understanding, then shuffled inside the house and shut the door.

Alone in Ray's backyard, Thirio held the phone to his ear and stared at Ray's garden tools. Handheld digging implements included a small shovel and a pitchfork with three tines, about the same size as the shovel. He grabbed the pitchfork. The handle was new, the grip tight. The tines hadn't seen much use, if any. Steel tines painted red. An image of Lucifer holding a pitchfork filtered into his consciousness. When the epiphany hit, he couldn't believe his luck. Here he stood in the backyard of Ray Durowitz's house, holding the weapon he was looking for. Instead of a gun, he would kill Sarah with a pitchfork. The estimates he regularly did never had anything to do with gardens. But today, when he needed a new weapon, he had a garden estimate. A garden that had a pitchfork. It was like Satan was talking directly to him.

The door banged behind him. Ray was back outside.

"Yes, I understand, Maria," Thirio said into the phone without turning around. "That's right. I'll tell him. Thanks."

Thirio hit a button on his cell and slipped it into his pocket. When he turned to face Ray, he offered him a smile so wide he showed all his teeth.

"Ray, you're in luck. Doing anything this weekend?"

Ray shook his head.

"My team can come Saturday. They'll plant and water Sunday morning. That work for you?"

Ray wiped his eyes. It must have something to do with getting old because the man wasn't crying, but his eyes leaked.

He nodded. "That works fine for me," Ray said. "The sooner, the better."

"Let's head on into the house and write this up so I know exactly what you're looking for. I'll need the paperwork for the team. Once we get the deposit, I can commit them to Saturday and Sunday."

Ray started for the house with Thirio on his heels. He'd never killed anyone as old as Ray Durowitz before. It would probably be quite easy on account of the man's age. Thirio would watch those watering eyes to see if he saw relief as he strangled the life from the old man. He hoped he didn't see relief. Thirio wasn't doing it for Ray. He was doing it for his own pleasure. Maybe he'd burn the house down once Ray was dead.

Just before entering Ray's house, he took one last look around. The neighborhood was small. Only two houses had a view into Ray's backyard, and both had curtains drawn, empty driveways. He was sure no one had observed them talking by the proposed garden.

Thirio was in the clear to send Ray to another world far from this one. He only hoped he wasn't reuniting Ray with his long-lost love. That would upset Thirio. He didn't let the door bang shut after him. In fact, he didn't let it make a sound as he locked it behind him.

He headed into the kitchen to obtain a deposit cheque. Then he would steal a soul. An old man's wretched soul.

One more soul headed south of the soil.

Chapter 18

Parkman entered Lee's office, pushed past Officer Amparo, and stormed to Lee's desk.

"Where's Sarah?" he demanded.

Lee looked up from a stack of papers, a bewildered expression on his face. "I have no idea," he said, then glanced past Parkman at Amparo. "Isn't she with you?"

Amparo shook his head.

"They went another way," Parkman said. "At first, Mason took Sarah and disappeared within two or three street lights. Then the other two cruisers broke off a few lights after that. Amparo here," Parkman gestured at the officer to his left, "drove me here." Parkman ran a hand through his hair and then crossed his arms. "You want to fill me in on what's happening here?"

Lee looked from Amparo to Parkman, then back to Amparo. "Where's the rest of the team?" he asked Amparo.

The officer shrugged. "No idea, sir. They didn't fill me in."

Lee placed his hands on the desk, eased his chair back, and stood up.

"Why do you have no idea, Officer Amparo? Mason volunteered for this delivery job. It was simple. Take Sarah and Parkman to the airport. When I called to have them brought back here, you were supposed to come as a unit."

Amparo stepped closer to Lee's desk. "I understand, sir. Mason's a senior officer. When they told me to bring Parkman here …" He shrugged again. "I'm sorry, sir. I have no idea what's happened. I'm sure they'll be on their way soon."

"They'd better be," Lee said, his voice harder, an octave lower. "Or it's all of your jobs." He pointed at Amparo. "And if anything's happened to Sarah, I'm holding all of you responsible."

Lee hit a button on his desk. "Julie Deighton. Get me Officer Tom Mason on the phone."

"Yes, sir," a female voice responded.

Parkman detected a slight British accent. Lee had a secretary? He hadn't seen one when he walked into Lee's office.

"Amparo," Lee said. "Take a seat. I want you close when I reach Mason and get to the bottom of this."

"Yes, sir." Amparo walked over to the far wall and sat on a small couch.

Parkman studied Lee's face. Was the man truly on their side? Could he trust his old colleague?

"I'm sorry, Parkman." Lee sat back down in his office chair. "I'm sure nothing's going on. Mason wouldn't risk his career."

"Who is this Mason fellow?" Parkman asked as he took a seat opposite Lee's desk. From his back pocket, he pulled a toothpick and popped it into the side of his mouth. An idea struck him. "Did Mason know Barry Ashford?"

Lee snapped his head to face Parkman. After a moment's hesitation, he rolled his chair closer to the keyboard, where he typed furiously for a moment.

"Oh shit," Lee mumbled.

"What? I don't like the sound of that."

"Mason and Ashford go way back. They were partners once."

"Not good," was all Parkman could think to say. The toothpick dropped from his mouth. "Lee, you have to find these guys." He raised his voice. "Right now."

Lee slapped the button on his desk. "Julie, anything on Mason?" He released the button. "I'm sorry, Parkman. I don't know how I missed it."

Julie's voice came over the speaker. "Mason isn't picking up."

"Try Calder's phone. Or Waters. Do it and get back to me."

"Yes, sir."

Lee leaned back in his chair and stared out his office window. A palpable silence fell over the room. Parkman reached for another toothpick, disregarding the one on the floor. He shuffled his foot over it until it rolled under Lee's desk.

"What about our luggage?" Parkman asked. "Did someone think to grab that?"

Lee swung his chair toward Amparo and raised his

eyebrows. Amparo rubbed his palms along his thighs.

"We were told to bring them here," Amparo said, his voice sounding nervous now. "I can't account for the others, but I did what I was told."

"You're telling me everything?" Lee asked.

Amparo nodded. "Absolutely, sir."

Parkman felt Amparo was probably in the dark as to what the other members of the volunteer foursome were up to. The young officer's forehead glistened with worry. He may not know what his fellow officers were up to, but he knew he'd be held accountable for it.

After a few more moments of calm, Parkman had a chance to put his thoughts in order. Sarah could take care of herself. Her connection to Vivian was stronger than ever after what happened in Denmark. He wasn't psychic, but something told him she'd be fine.

"Why were we pulled off the plane?" Parkman asked.

"A double murder occurred at a coffee shop in Vernon this morning."

"Same MO?"

"It's our guy."

"You're sure?"

Lee nodded. "He left a note on the store window for Sarah."

Parkman sat forward and flipped the toothpick to the other side of his mouth. "He knows about Sarah?"

"After yesterday, of course. Everyone knows. The papers went crazy with Sarah coverage. I said this would happen. Our unsub put it all together. He'll know who Sarah is and what she's done to sabotage his progress."

"What did the note say?" Parkman asked, flipping the

toothpick to the other side again and biting down on it.

"It basically said that Sarah was to blame for the deaths of those two people. Because of her interference, Thirio would go on a killing spree, and no one could catch him."

"Thirio?" Parkman said the word out loud. "You know the guy's name?"

"Whoever wrote the note signed it, Thirio."

"Did it come up in any databases?"

Lee shook his head. "Nothing. We're assuming it's not his real name."

"Fingerprints?"

Lee shook his head again. "No, but the perp left his gun behind. No prints on it, either."

"Can he be that good to leave no trace?" Parkman crossed his arms. "Why leave the gun behind?"

"We suspect he wipes everything down or wears gloves. The gun was loaded. It might have been an oversight."

The intercom buzzed on his desk.

"No answer on Waters's phone," Julie said. "Nor Calder's."

"Fuck," Lee shouted. He pressed the button. "Okay, I need you to send someone out to the airport for Parkman's and Sarah's luggage. Please confirm when you have it."

"Will do."

Parkman glanced at Amparo, then back to Lee.

"GPS Mason's phone," he said. "Send out a BOLO. Do something, Lee, before I lose my fucking mind."

"I'm on it, Parkman."

Lee picked up his phone.

Chapter 19

Shirt pasted to her back, Sarah continued along the dirt road; the only relief from the heat was the high trees keeping the direct sun off her. The arid conditions in her mouth made her imagine chewing sand. Mild swelling had blossomed on her inner cheek.

How far up Myra Canyon Road Mason had gone before turning off to park was unknown. She hadn't memorized that part of the ride. It couldn't be too much longer. At every corner, she anticipated seeing Waters's cruiser parked sideways across the road. Or maybe he would get tired of waiting and drive toward her.

She retrieved Mason's gun from her waistband, wiped her hand on her shirt, then gripped it tight, her palm moistening again almost immediately.

The next corner had to be it. The clock was ticking, and she needed to be in Vernon in just over a half hour.

Lee was going to be pissed. But not as pissed as when he learned that his cops had planned to murder her. Unless he had something to do with it. He was the man who sent Mason's team, after all. How could he not know of Mason's loyalty to the dead Barry Ashford?

A voice broke through her thoughts. Someone was talking up ahead. She trotted to the side of the road and hid at the corner.

"What are you talking about?" Waters said. "Slow down." There was a pause. "She did what?" Another pause. The sound of gravel being disturbed probably meant Waters spun to look up Myra Canyon Road—toward her. "How long ago?" Waters asked. "Okay. Got it. I'll find her." Silence. She waited. Was the call done? Then Waters said, "Okay, Calder. There's no way I'm bringing her in. With what she knows now? Forget it. I'll shoot on sight." Sarah lowered her head, stared at the small pebbles by her feet, and shook her head. *No one ever learns.* "Okay. I'm on it."

Waters had to be twenty feet away. She heard his footsteps and tried to calculate the distance. Was he walking toward her or his car?

A lock clicked. *The trunk.* He's retrieving something out of the trunk of the cruiser.

Cops have bigger guns in their trunks?

The trunk lid slammed down.

Calder knew what was going on now, too. To call Waters and warn him meant Calder had made it to Mason.

Or Mason had another cell phone. The one in her hand was a burn phone. *Shit!*

Waters's footsteps drew closer. Sarah dropped lower and assumed a shooter's stance, the weapon aiming for Waters's legs.

In the distance, a car engine revved. Something deep, like the growl of a large truck. Waters's footsteps ground to a halt. Sarah leaped up and quietly stepped out into the open, Mason's gun aimed at Officer Waters. The cop was six feet away, his back to her. She had been right about the weapon in the trunk of the cruiser. He held a large police-issue shotgun.

Remington Model 870, Vivian whispered to her softly. *A 12-gauge, pump-action shotgun. Police and military issue.*

Fuckin' great, Sarah said back.

A monster truck at the bottom of the road saw the cruiser, slowed, and stopped. As Waters watched, with Sarah behind him, the truck backed up and began a three-point turn.

Waters pivoted on his heels. He started when he saw her. Their eyes met. The shotgun jerked in his hands.

Sarah fired Mason's weapon with no time to wait and see Waters's intentions. Then fired again even as the first bullet punched into Waters's left thigh.

Waters did a spasm of a dance as he got hit—twice—then dropped his weapon and wrapped both hands around the wound. He hopped on his right foot, trying to stay upright.

She was lucky enough to nail him with both bullets, one in the thigh, the other entered at the top of his left foot. He'd stumbled with the thigh shot, but it was the foot impact that made him dance on his good leg.

Sarah lurched forward, grabbed him around the lapels before he could fall, and half lifted, half propelled him back toward his cruiser. Within three steps, Waters's legs came out from under him. He fell with a grunt and a whiny moan.

"I hate shooting cops," she shouted at him.

"Then why did you?" he grunted. Curled in a ball, hands

on the wound, blood seeped past his fingers at a surprising rate.

"Because you're not doing your job." She pushed his arm out of the way, latched onto his belt, undid it, then ripped it from his belt loops in one strong tug.

"What?" he said, teeth tight together, face already blanched.

"You're supposed to be out finding the guy blowing shit up. Instead," she leaned in closer and smacked his face, "instead, you're out here trying to hurt little old me."

Waters groaned. Sarah smacked him in the face again, this time the other cheek, then wrapped the belt around his upper thigh and cinched it tight.

"Why … you hitting me?" Waters asked, his jaw tight.

"I'm pissed off. And I'm trying to get blood into your cheeks. You seem to have gone pale."

"I've been shot, for fuck's sake!"

Sarah backhanded him. Blood formed on the edge of his mouth.

"Oh yeah," she said, making an exaggerated attempt to look up and to the left as if she had just remembered something. "You're a bully." She met his eyes. "You beat women. You helped Mason beat a woman. I know, it's mostly your girlfriends and women you hire." He spit at her. The effort was pathetic, the phlegm a paltry display of bravado. "That's why you're pissed off. Because I'm a woman, and I'm," she tightened her hand into a fist and drove it down onto his cheek, "hitting you."

Waters's head bounced off the stones below his face. His eyes closed, and his head rested downward at an odd angle.

She checked for a pulse. It was firm, strong. Happy she

hadn't killed him, she rummaged through Waters's pockets until she found his phone. After a moment, she had Calder's name from the contacts. She quickly typed a text that told him to get to Waters before he died. Two bullet wounds and a tourniquet—will need hospital attention. She sent the text, relieved Waters of his wallet and weapons, grabbed the pepper spray from his belt and the car keys, then whistled to herself on the way down to his unmarked cruiser.

She turned it on, aimed it south, and started back toward Kelowna. In the cup holder, she found two water bottles unopened.

"Awww, Waters, it's like you were expecting me."

She opened the first one and drank half in one go, then after a few breaths, drank the other half. She tossed the empty onto the passenger side floor as the golf course passed by, the same one she remembered from earlier.

Two ambulances passed her going the other way moments later.

Then Waters's phone lit up. Call display said it was RCMP HQ. Sarah ignored the call. She opened the maps app and typed Vernon. Once her route was set, she hit start and listened to GPS as it guided her toward Vernon.

She only hoped she wouldn't be too late. When she was done in Vernon, would this mess be over? Somehow, she didn't think so. The shit with Mason would need to be dealt with.

The dashcam.

She dialed Lee's cell nummber from memory. He answered on the first ring.

"Waters?" he snapped into the phone. "What the fuck is going on?"

"Don't speak," Sarah said.

He gasped. Then said, "Go ahead." There was a click. Like he'd turned it onto the speaker function.

"It was a trap. To murder me." Someone else gasped in the background. "To settle a score for Barry Ashford. Three officers involved. Mason, Waters, and Calder. As far as I can tell, Amparo was not aware."

"Sarah—"

"Shut up," she shouted. "How complicit are you, Lee? Look, don't answer that. I'm on my way to take out the unsub. Then I'm done here." She cleared her throat. "You want proof? Mason's dashcam. He recorded the whole thing. When watching it back, remember one thing. My hands were empty."

She ended the call. It didn't ring again.

"Now, Vivian, since we have some time to ourselves, you want to tell me where I'm going?"

Nothing.

"Vivian? I need to know which grocery store and why?"

It was as if Vivian wasn't there. Sarah couldn't feel even a spark of Vivian's presence.

Sarah drove on in silence. Up ahead, a man stood on the side of the road behind a car. His arms were moving. She was driving too fast. One second, the man was there, then she was passing him—he watched her, gestured at her—then he was in the rearview mirror.

It was the same man she'd seen outside Lee's office window. The same man on the tarmac at the airport and in the office window of the B.C. Medical Services building. He had a message for her, and she wasn't getting it.

But most importantly, his presence blocked Vivian's.

How? And why didn't Vivian know about him?

Ten minutes later, as Sarah pushed the cruiser hard along the highway toward Vernon, her sister showed up.

"Where have you been?" Sarah asked.

I couldn't find you. It became a futile exercise in patience. Where were you?

"Someone's playing games with us, and they're on your side of the field."

That's impossible.

"Afraid not."

Chapter 20

Parkman lunged across Lee's desk and snatched the cell phone, but Sarah was gone. He rolled off the desk and confronted Lee in his chair.

"What the fuck was that?" Parkman snapped. "Your officers tried to kill her? Tell me how that is even possible."

Lee got up from his chair but found it difficult as Parkman continued to crowd him.

"Look, Parkman, you know me. I called you and Sarah here because I have a problem. I thought she could help—"

"You have a problem, all right. A pissed-off Sarah is a huge problem."

Lee pushed his chair out of the way with the backs of his knees.

"I know how upset you are," Lee said.

"You don't know the half of it."

"But Parkman, you have to let me get to the bottom of

this. I will figure out what went down, and those officers will pay for what they did."

"Knowing Sarah, they're already paying."

Lee's phone rang in Parkman's hand. He checked the screen.

Officer Calder.

"Here," Parkman handed over Lee's phone. "Play it cool. As far as you know, we're patiently waiting for Sarah down here at the office."

Lee nodded. Parkman was grateful for the nod. It meant they were still on the same page.

"Lee here," Lee said as he placed the call on speakerphone.

A good play by him.

Calder's voice came through raspy, like he was out of breath. "We need a BOLO out on Sarah."

"A BOLO?" Lee asked, feigning surprise. "Isn't she with you guys? Where are you, by the way? You're supposed to be here by now."

"She got the drop on us."

"The drop? What are you talking about?"

"She told Mason something about a dead body up off Myra Canyon Road. He took her up there, and she pulled a gun on him. Broke Mason's arm, then busted his nose to shit." Calder talked so fast that Parkman leaned in closer to catch it all. "Then she shot Waters in the leg and the foot and stole his cruiser."

"Sarah shot a cop and stole his cruiser?" Lee asked. He mouthed the words, *holy shit.*

"She's insane, sir. Put out a BOLO for Waters's cruiser. We have to get her off the street. I've called for a pair of ambulances. They're on their way."

"Okay, Calder. Stay with your men. We'll deal with this."

Lee hung up and glanced at Parkman. "She really messed those guys up. This is going to have a ripple effect that'll ruin careers."

Parkman allowed a grin to crease his lips. "This situation is fucked, but I have to admit, I do feel a little better."

"She doesn't get off scot-free, Parkman. We have to watch Mason's dashcam. There'll be an investigation."

"I'm well aware of that. But for now, Sarah's doing what she came here to do. She's going after the unsub. If you could just keep your guys out of her way for a while, maybe she could stop this terrorist asshole."

Lee started for the door.

"Where are you going?" Parkman asked.

"Myra Canyon Road. I want to see what's on Mason's dashcam for myself. Then we need to go to Vernon. I want a firsthand look at what happened at that coffee shop this morning." He stopped at the door. "I was waiting for you and Sarah before I went to Vernon, but we won't get Sarah now, so we go. Just the three of us."

"Three?"

Lee turned to Amparo, who was still sitting on the side couch. "Get up. You're coming with us."

Amparo shuffled over to Lee, who put his hand out.

"Cell phone?"

Amparo frowned but reached into his pocket and produced an iPhone. Lee dropped it in his pocket.

"I'm not taking any chances, Amparo. Sarah said you're clean here, but until I know what went down, you were with those other three."

"I understand, sir."

"Now, come on. It'll take us fifteen minutes to get out to Myra Canyon."

"What about Sarah?" Parkman asked. "You gonna put out a BOLO? GPS the location of the cruiser she's driving?"

Lee seemed to think about that for a split second. He blinked, then looked at Parkman. "Nothing of the sort. Sarah knows what she's doing. Bringing her in only risks her life further. As far as I know, she's gone to do her thing somewhere, and that's how it'll stay until Sarah decides to come in on her own."

"And if she needs help?"

Lee stepped past him. "Then we'll be there for her when she calls. You and me."

Parkman followed him out of the office. "Let's just hope no one has erased any part of that dashcam." Parkman stayed close to Lee. "For your cops' sake."

"I agree," Lee said as he looked back at Parkman. "For Sarah's sake, too."

Chapter 21

Ray Durowitz turned out to be the easiest person to kill. Thirio had struggled with several people in the past, but Ray succumbed without much fight. Halfway through the act, it seemed as though the man welcomed the end of his life. Could someone love a deceased spouse that much to want to die to be with them? Was that love or insanity?

Thirio almost stopped killing the man at one point because he wasn't doing it for Ray.

"Why does everything always have to be about you?" Thirio shouted at the old man's corpse. "That's the problem with our narcissistic society today. Everyone thinks the world revolves around them. The stars, the universe, billions of people on this planet, and yet somehow," he leaned in over the corpse, "you thought it was all about you. Fucking pathetic."

He stood up and headed for the back door, Ray's deposit

cheque secured in his wallet.

"And don't think I don't see the irony in that statement, Ray. I'm not saying the world revolves around me, either. It isn't about me. Or you. It's about the bigger picture. The process. It's why we're all here. To check and see who you will follow. God or Satan. That's the big test of humanity." He reached the door, took one last scan around the kitchen in case he left something behind, then opened the back door cautiously. "It's like an election, Ray." He said, his voice lowered in case someone was in Ray's backyard. "You vote for the winning team by your actions. Everyone knows what side I'm on. That's what this is all about. Not individuals. It's about teams. Good and evil. Sarah's good. I'm evil. And what does evil do?" Thirio watched the backyard as he talked. No one was in evidence. He closed the back door, walked over to the garden tools, grabbed the pitchfork, and started for his truck.

"What does evil do?" he whispered to himself. "Glad you asked. Evil destroys good."

He laughed maniacally, tossed the pitchfork into the back of his pickup truck, and drove away from Ray Durowitz's house.

That was his last estimate of the day. There would be no more in the future. He had the money he needed to finish what he had started. The pitchfork would be the perfect weapon for Sarah. A man like Thirio didn't need a gun anyway. Too clean. Too easy.

A pitchfork to pierce her legs, her groin, her face. The anticipation of placing one of the tines over Sarah's eye, then watching as it squished the small orb aside, moving deeper to impale the soft tissue of her brain, was too much to bear. The mental image of Sarah squirming under that assault gave him an erection.

Thirio drove to the bank Ray's cheque was drawn on. Once cashed, he left without regard for the cameras that might snap his face. A conventional investigation couldn't stop him.

Twenty minutes later, Thirio pulled into the parking lot of The Fast Way, one of the largest grocery store chains in British Columbia. He retrieved a bottle of homemade poison from behind his seat, slipped it inside his jean jacket, and got out of the truck.

How many people would get sick because of what he was about to do? How many would die? The bottle contained a mixture of water, hand cleaner, and mice poison. The mice poison was in high concentration but still low enough that no one would really notice it over the taste of the fruit or vegetable they were eating. Even a rudimentary wash of the vegetables he was about to spray wouldn't remove all of the poison, as certain vegetables would absorb an amount that could cause problems for several people. Especially geriatrics and the very young. It was amazing what information the internet offered the casual terrorist in the way of information to terrorize.

He strode toward the front of the grocery store, head held high, purpose written all over his face.

While they chased him in Vernon for the three people he'd murdered so far today, then dealt with a large number of people entering the local hospital with symptoms of poisoning, they would have their eye off his denouement, his final act. No one would see it coming.

The destruction of an entire family. That's where this all

started, and that was where it would all end.

The Campbell family was the root of his pain, his suffering. If it weren't for them, Julia would be alive. If they hadn't pushed so hard, the feud wouldn't have started all those years ago. And now, in their honor, he had stricken fear in the public's heart as the Campbells struck fear in his.

They had relatives in Penticton, Kamloops, and Vernon. They were the owners of the grocery store he stood in. Over time, the Campbells hadn't backed down from the feud between their families. Escalation of incitements continued until recently, and Julia had been killed.

When Thirio was done, every Campbell family business and relative would suffer. He would leave no stone unturned, no member unscathed. With the final act coming, his own family would learn of the sacrifice he had made to set things right. They would understand. He'd let his plans stray to some degree with the innocents that had died along the way, but who was really innocent? And when the Campbells attacked, hadn't Julia died? Wasn't she an innocent?

Everyone's a sinner. We're born into it.

Nothing justified what they did to Thirio's family. By that same token, nothing justified what he had undertaken as a course of retribution. Two wrongs didn't make a right. But who wanted what was right, what was just? This was about good and evil, plain and simple. They thought they were good and Thirio was evil.

His final act now involved Sarah Roberts, providing he could lure her to the Campbell guesthouse. Or maybe he wouldn't need to. Maybe the psychic bitch would know where to be and when to be there.

That remained to be seen. But for now, he would leave

messages for her. She would follow his trail of breadcrumbs. She would get closer, and Sarah would lose her life. Thirio would win. His time on Earth would end, and his time in Hell on his new throne would begin.

In the produce section of The Fast Way grocery store, Thirio waited until he was unobserved. Then he eased the bottle out far enough to spray and started with the green apples. He covered them until they glistened. Then the grapes were showered in poison. It would appear to a casual observer that the store's staff had watered the fruit.

A minute later, he sprayed the potatoes, then moved on to the lettuce and onions. He sprayed and sprayed until the bottle emptied. Then he left the store unobserved and unaccosted and headed to the other Fast Way on the opposite side of Vernon.

What a lovely day it had turned out to be. There were three Fast Ways in Vernon and three in Kelowna. He had five more bottles of watered mice poison in the truck.

He clapped his hands together, then flapped them at his side as if he had wings. Wings of an angel. A pretty angel like Lucifer.

It was such a lovely day.

Chapter 22

LEE GOT OUT OF the car and slammed his door before Parkman got out. Something Sarah had said yesterday came back to Parkman. She'd talked about poisons of some kind. But she'd also said sharpshooter.

He joined Lee by Mason's unmarked cruiser. Amparo stayed in the back seat of Lee's car, not saying a word. Two uniforms stood on either side of Mason's vehicle. Parkman assumed Mason, Calder, and Waters had vacated the area in ambulances.

Lee barely nodded at the two officers as he dropped into the front seat of Mason's car and began to fiddle with the dashcam.

"Lee?" Parkman said.

Lee grunted as he worked.

"Are any of these guys snipers? Or have any experience in that field?"

Lee turned to gawk at Parkman. "Not that I'm aware of." He swiveled back to return to what he was doing.

"Sarah said something about a sharpshooter yesterday."

"And?"

"Poison."

Lee stopped what he was doing and stared out the windshield. "You don't think she meant poison as inside the department, do you?" Slowly, Lee turned to face Parkman.

Parkman shook his head. "She's never cryptic or spinning riddles. When she says poison, she means the kind that makes people sick and kills them."

Lee looked away. A moment later, the dashcam started up, playing out the scene in front of the car. Parkman leaned down to get a better look.

Mason moved onto the camera, a hand on the butt of his weapon. They watched as everything unfolded on the recording. Sarah attacked Mason after he'd pulled his weapon. Then the video went back to recording the road and the trees a few feet ahead of the car.

"What do you make of that?" Parkman asked.

"It could be argued Sarah did have a weapon trained on him. Mason would just say she tossed it before attacking him."

"This isn't a courtroom. We're not lawyers. Now, I'll ask you again. What do you make of that?"

Lee set his feet outside the car, took a deep breath, and stood up. He moved close to Parkman, a hand on his side, a grimace on his face. Then, in a low voice, he said, "I think Sarah was brought up here to be killed. Calder and Waters blocked access to the road, north and south. Once Sarah escaped Mason, she walked south and had to shoot Waters—

and take his car—to get out of here and feel safe."

Parkman put his hands on Lee's shoulders. "For a man who's not psychic, I feel that's a very good depiction of what probably happened. Sarah said they were gunning for her."

"She did?"

Parkman nodded. "At the airport. She said Mason had hurt an ex-girlfriend of his. A girl named Vicky, I think. Apparently, Waters had helped him cover it up. She taunted the men because she saw what they were going to do. Her last words suggested they think about their actions because they would come with consequences."

"Wow," Lee said, shaking his head. "I'm sorry for bringing you both here. I had no idea Sarah's life would be in danger." Lee moved away from Parkman. He stopped by the car's trunk and stared at the ground. "That's some girl you've got, Parkman. When three cops plan something like this, that person's usually dead."

"This is Sarah we're talking about. She's never a victim."

"I can see that." Lee started back toward his car, where Amparo waited patiently in the back seat.

After a moment, Parkman followed. "Where to next?" he asked.

"Vernon. I want to visit the crime scene at the coffee shop."

Lee's phone rang. He snapped it up and hit speaker. Parkman hustled over and bent down to listen better.

"Officer Lee here."

"Lee, it's Sarah."

"Sarah," he nearly gasped her name, fumbling over his tongue. "I'm sorry, you know, what happened out here—"

"No time for that. Come to Vernon. Bring trusted cops."

"Can do. Where are you?"

"Go to the hospital. Start interviewing people as they show up. Bring a police sketch artist. Then call your son back. It's the only way we get a composite of the unsub."

"Where will you be? Can we meet up? I want to talk to you about what happened out here on Myra Canyon Road." He waited a moment, then said, "Sarah?"

But she'd already hung up.

"Let's go, Lee," Parkman said. "No time to waste. Make calls on the way."

Lee stopped at his car door, holding the handle. "What are we looking for? The hospital will be full of sick people. Who are we to interview?"

Parkman stared at him across the roof. "We'll interview the people coming to emergency who are suspected of being poisoned recently. I'd say that's a good start."

They both dropped into the car at the same time.

Lee swore as he shoved the accelerator to the floor, leaving a dust cloud behind as they headed back toward Kelowna and, ultimately, Vernon.

Five minutes later, Lee made a phone call. A team of officers was to head to the Kelowna hospital, locate Calder, Waters, and Mason, and detain them until Lee could get back.

They were to be held on suspicion of attempted murder.

Chapter 23

SARAH WAS TOO LATE. Vivian had directed her to the first Fast Way grocery store as she entered Vernon's city limits. While parking the unmarked cruiser, Vivian shouted for a location change. Sarah sat behind the wheel, wondering how Vivian could be wrong. She'd held back information in the past. She'd even been silent for periods of time. But everything Vivian did held a purpose. A greater purpose that Sarah always stumbled upon. But misinformation? That was certainly a first.

Sarah drove out onto the road heading deeper into town, and started off toward another Fast Way on the other side of Vernon.

Could it be the mysterious man with the flapping arms that Sarah kept seeing? As much as she suspected that man was blocking her sister, could he have the kind of power to steer Vivian wrong? If so, they would need to fix that.

Have you seen the man I've been seeing? Sarah asked her sister as she waited at a red light.

What man?

The one on the tarmac. In the building. Outside Lee's office window. Always staring at me, motioning something with his arms. Some kind of signal or a word.

A few moments passed without anything from Vivian.

Then, *There's no man, Sarah. I would know.*

There's a man, she said matter-of-factly.

Sarah, you're scaring me.

Sarah focused on the road. Vivian had no idea what was happening, which confused Sarah. How did Vivian account for the times they had been blocked?

Sarah spied the sign for The Fast Way grocery chain coming up ahead.

Vivian, what am I looking for here?

There was no answer.

Vivian?

Nothing.

"Shit," Sarah said as she slammed the steering wheel. "How am I supposed to stop this asshole if you're not talking to me?"

She pulled into the parking lot, slowed to let two women walk by, then parked a few spots from the front of the store. Once out of the cruiser, she stood by the car door and scanned the parking lot for anything that stood out. Why was she here? What would the perp be doing traveling from grocery store to grocery store? None of this made sense, and the one person who could clear matters up had gone AWOL.

Why tell Lee to go to Vernon Hospital? Shouldn't she be heading there as well?

"What the fuck?" she whispered to herself.

A light summer breeze stirred up her hair. The sun beat relentlessly on her swollen cheek. She thought about applying some ice to it.

A landscaping pickup truck had parked at a weird angle beside her parking spot. In the rear of the pickup was a pitchfork with three blood-red tines. Who ran a landscaping company with only one tool? Something about the truck bothered her. She asked Vivian if it meant anything but got no answer.

"How good am I without you?" she asked under her breath. "I'm as good as Jack and shit."

She headed inside The Fast Way without knowing what she was looking for. Just inside the doors, she watched people come and go. Shoppers carried bags out. Tills rang in purchases. A young man in a green apron restocked oranges from boxes suspended on a small, gray dolly. Everything seemed normal, nothing out of place. No bad guys with guns. No balaclava-clad assholes trying to shoot the place up.

Hopefully no bombs either.

With her sister quiet, she had no idea what she was walking into. She reached around to the back of her shirt to ensure it covered Mason's Smith & Wesson. If this was about the unsub, she needed to have it handy but concealed.

She continued into the store to avoid unwanted attention and aimlessly walked the aisles. Cereal boxes galore, then coffee and teas. Jams and peanut butter. But no terrorists.

The utter feeling of uselessness came over her. She asked herself over and over what she was doing there. And if she was, in fact, being blocked from communicating with her sister, who was blocking them and why?

Who has that kind of power?

As she turned up the baking supply aisle, she almost bumped into an old man in a suit.

"Excuse me," she said as she shuffled sideways around the man.

He turned toward her. Their eyes met. His hands were already up and motioning in the air like he was conducting an orchestra only he heard.

Something hard in Sarah's stomach dropped. This was new to her. Sure, she'd seen the man several times in the past twenty-four hours, but never up this close.

"What are you trying to tell me?" she asked.

His right hand fluttered, shot back and forth several times, then started again.

A woman with a small child edged by her. Sarah moved sideways to offer the woman room. When she did, Sarah caught the look on the woman's face. A skeptical frown, accompanied by a quick sideways glance. The woman only saw Sarah in the aisle, talking to herself. Just as Parkman hadn't seen the man standing on the tarmac, neither did this woman see the man in the aisle, waving his arms in frantic gestures.

What gives? she asked with her mind. *Is this how we communicate?*

The man nodded, the edge of a smile pulling at the corner of his mouth.

Sarah stumbled backward, reaching out to the shelf to steady herself by a box of chocolate cake mix.

There's more, she stammered. *There's more than Vivian? Like, I can see—*

He waved his right hand again. Then made that same

motion with it. Sarah studied the motion. It was always the same thing. Up down, a looping arc, then a sideways motion, starting back near the bottom and working his way upward. He lost her for a moment, scratched in the air, and started up again.

A couple in their forties walked by pushing a cart. Neither one glanced at the man or Sarah.

She was more stunned than she would have expected. After years of talking to the other side, she would have thought she could handle this scene with more confidence.

He scratched the air again, then motioned the message. A series of letters? Or numbers?

He nodded slightly, his hand never wavering from its path, its mission.

It looked like a nine, followed by a two or a five. Another number followed, then he scratched the air and started again.

"Excuse me," someone said from behind her.

She started at the proximity of the sound. A man maneuvered his cart past her, reached close to her shoulder, and grabbed a vanilla cake mix. He offered her a smile, then continued by her.

Before he got two feet, the cart touched the man gesturing at Sarah. But it didn't touch him. It *entered* him. The shopper paused to look at something on the shelf, the side of the shopping cart an inch inside the man's—the ghost's—suit jacket. He scanned the cake mixes, frowned, then turned away and walked directly through the old man in the suit.

A moment later, the man in the suit was whole again, and the cake-mix shopper had turned the corner and was gone.

A cool wave of sweat broke out on her forehead. She was

staggered. Disbelief, wonder, amazement, joy. If she could *see* the other side now, the possibilities were limitless. But why did it have to block Vivian? Was this spirit malevolent? What was his goal?

Not one to be intimidated easily, she lurched out and tried to grab his suit jacket. Her hand drifted through the man's presence.

A wave of understanding coursed through her. There had to be a reason he was here. Something important. Something so important that he overrode Vivian's powerful connection, which had been forged almost a decade ago.

Once more, she focused on the man's message. The first gesture had to be a nine, then a five. After that, a two and an eight.

The man shook his head.

"Nine, five, two … six?" she asked out loud, then remembered herself and repeated it internally.

He nodded.

Then scratched the air, back and forth.

"Ma'am, can I help you find anything?"

The manager, a man in his fifties, stood a few feet behind her. Beyond the manager, the woman who had passed her with the child earlier watched from the beginning of the aisle.

"I'm fine." She pointed. "I'm talking to—" she stopped. That was a rare mistake. She would need to pay more attention in the future. "I'm talking to myself, trying to decide what cake to bake tonight. Is there a problem?"

"No problem, ma'am. Just wondering if we could help you along."

She knew how it looked. No shopping cart. No bags. Nothing in her hands. Just a random girl, swollen cheek—no doubt bruising, too—standing by herself, talking to herself. Mothers with children would wonder. The manager was called to get her out of the store. It all made complete sense.

She gave him a warm smile. "Maybe I'll bake a cake another day."

"That sounds fine," the manager said with a smile.

When she turned around, the man in the suit was gone.

As she left the store, a thousand questions filled her mind. What had happened when she died in Denmark? Did the door Vivian used to access Sarah on this plane open to allow others in somehow? Were the days of just Vivian and Sarah over? Or was this a bad turn of events?

When she reached the cruiser, the work truck with the pitchfork was gone.

She dropped into the front seat of the cruiser no further ahead for having come to the grocery store. Maybe Vivian sent her here to talk to that old man in the suit.

"Nine, five, two, six? What's that for?"

The early afternoon breeze raised the corner of a piece of paper stuck under the windshield wiper. She snatched the paper off the window. After dropping back in the car, she unfolded it. A message was scrawled in blue ink. At the bottom, the name *Thirio* was scrawled in cursive.

Many more people will die today in your name. You can't stop what I have done. Come see me. Try to stop me. We will end this together.

Thirio

Sarah crumpled up the note and shouted her sister's name. She didn't expect a response and didn't get one.

A minute later, after using GPS for directions, she pushed the cruiser hard toward the Vernon hospital.

Chapter 24

THIRIO HAD PARKED IN a way that offered him an easy exit from the grocery store parking lot. He had entered the grocery store, emptied his bottle of poison on the produce unnoticed by the minimum wage staff, tossed the bottle in the garbage, then started for the exit when he saw what looked like an unmarked police cruiser pull in beside his work truck. His stomach had dropped. Could they have found him so easily? He still had so much left to do. He had walked over to the magazine rack by the front windows, grabbed an Entertainment Weekly, and idly watched to see what the cop would do.

A woman got out of the car. A tall, pretty blonde woman, her back to the store. She scanned the parking lot, her attention drawn to his truck. Thirio would swear she stared in at the pitchfork. It was like she knew everything. Who he was, where the garden tool came from, who he'd killed to get it. Moments passed—he held his breath—then the woman faced the grocery store and started for the door.

Sarah Roberts.

"Not possible," he muttered, letting the magazine fall from his hands.

He realized how possible it actually was—she was brought in on the investigation because she was psychic.

Thirio snatched the magazine off the floor, opened it to a random page, and turned away from the front door as Sarah entered the store. He weighed the odds of attacking her right then and there and quickly deduced he wasn't ready. He didn't have his gun—accidentally left behind at that coffee shop—or he would have emptied it in her face. He didn't have a knife or any other implement that could be used as a weapon. The pitchfork was in the bed of his truck.

The last time he'd seen Sarah, she had a gun. And the woman was driving an unmarked cruiser. How the hell could the authorities offer her a car? If they gave her a car, then they gave her a weapon.

Of course, the witch is packing.

She strolled by him, only three feet between them. Thirio pivoted slowly, watching her head toward the far aisle. He set the magazine back on the rack, grabbed a shopping cart, and headed for the aisle parallel to the one Sarah had disappeared down.

He turned to the right at the end of the aisle and meandered along the chips and soda pop row.

Minutes later, having walked three aisles without locating her, he turned a corner and saw her staring off into space at the front end of the baking aisle.

He edged closer, pretending to be studying products on

the shelf. Halfway up the aisle, he noticed how strange she was acting. Like she was talking to someone. Maybe she was on a cell phone with earbuds hidden under her hair.

He moved closer.

This was his chance. She faced the front of the store, her back to him. Nothing was heavier or larger than a bag of Robin Hood flour on the shelves, so he would have to use his hands. As long as he attacked swiftly and decisively, he could possibly knock her out or at least shove her to the floor, where he could stomp on her head until he crushed her skull. Then there would be no Sarah Roberts on his ass every step of the way.

He moved closer until he stood within one foot of her. A punch to the back of the neck. Or maybe kick the backs of the knees out. Anything to drop her fast. Then jump up and down on her chest, throat, and face.

No more pretty girl.

He collected his breath for the attack. Clenched his fists and raised his right hand.

A cart's wheels squeaked behind him. People were in the aisle. There would be screams, havoc. How much time would it take to stomp her to death before people interfered?

His right hand opened, the fist gone. He touched a box of cake mix on the shelf.

"Excuse me," he said from behind her.

Sarah started. Thirio pushed his cart around her, reached up to the shelf by her shoulder, and grabbed a small box of vanilla cake mix. He offered a friendly grin, then continued past her.

Something was wrong with the way she stared at nothing. There was a look of consternation, her eyebrows squished together, yet bewilderment in her eyes.

Thirio paused to stare at the cake mixes. If she knew it was him she was looking for, she'd do something about it. He could tell that about her with one look. They'd fight. She'd die.

He waited a moment more, inviting the attack that didn't come. He offered her a frown if she was watching, then turned away and headed toward the end of the aisle.

She didn't recognize him. She may have psychic leads as to where he had been and what he was doing, but she had no idea what he looked like. That confirmed it for him. No one knew what he looked like yet. Even though they had witnesses at the coffee shop and even though the woman who bought the chairs in Penticton didn't die in the explosion, his description was still unknown.

He replaced the cart at the front of the store, strode to his truck, hastily wrote Sarah a note, and then placed it on the cruiser's windshield.

Won't she be angry when she comes out of the grocery store to find a note from the man she's hunting? Questions of how he knew what car she was driving and where she was at any given time would drive her nuts. It was good to turn the tables on her for a change—like he was the psychic one.

Back in the truck, he stared at the front door of the grocery store for a few heartbeats, then pulled out of the parking space.

They would meet up again very soon. And the next time would mark the end of Sarah Roberts. There was no doubt in his mind that he was her exterminator.

No doubt whatsoever.

Chapter 25

Sarah parked near the hospital exit, pocketed the cruiser's keys, left the doors unlocked, and entered the building through the main admittance doors. She noticed four marked and two unmarked cruisers when she pulled into the hospital parking lot. Lee had followed her instructions.

Sarah wasn't at the hospital to meet them, though. She was there to meet two people connected to the unsub. They had a picture of the unsub. Officer Lee's son, Nick, also had a picture. But since Lee's issue of reconnecting with his son had not been resolved, and Sarah and Lee weren't investigating this case together anymore, Vivian had sent Sarah to the Vernon hospital to meet two people in Room 404 so she could obtain a picture of the culprit and locate the bastard herself.

She headed straight for the elevators, hit the button, and stepped inside when the doors opened. On the fourth floor,

Sarah walked directly to room 404. At the door, she rapped softly, then opened it.

A man lay on the bed inside the private room while a woman stood by the window. The woman looked over her shoulder. When it was clear she didn't recognize Sarah as a doctor or nurse, she turned around all the way.

"Can we help you?" the woman asked. "I think you have the wrong room."

The man watched Sarah from the bed, a white sheet drawn up to his neck.

Sarah entered slowly, a kind, soft smile pasted to her lips.

"Do you two have a minute?" she asked.

They exchanged a glance. The woman rubbed the back of her neck, then let her hand fall to the side as she stepped closer to the bed.

"Not really."

Sarah stopped walking. She put her hands up in a non-threatening way. "I'm here to talk. Just for a few minutes. Then I'll leave."

"Talk?" the man said. "About what?"

"Your condition and my condition."

The woman touched her husband's hand. Their fingers laced together. She blinked, cleared her throat, then raised her head and stared at Sarah.

"Your condition?" she asked.

"How about this?" Sarah said. She advanced closer. "I'll say my piece. When I'm done, we can talk more, or I'll leave."

They looked at each other again. He nodded, and she nodded back.

"Go ahead," he said.

"You are Lori and John DeBeau. You've been together for many years, and despite ups and downs, challenges, and obstacles, you always got through everything together. It's your selfless ways, your kindness that pulls you two through." Sarah paused to let her words sink in. She eased closer to the bed.

"Lori, you're forty-eight, and John," she turned to him, "you're fifty-four. You've had memory loss issues and were recently diagnosed with Lewy Body Dementia, for which I am so sorry." Sarah turned back to Lori. "You are a pediatric nurse. I see you take care of special needs children. Together, you and John have ten kids. I'm amazed at the kind of people you two are and the things you've done. I mean, I can see you read to him as he has difficulty reading now."

"How do you ..." Lori swallowed an emotional gasp. "How do you know all that?" Her eyes watered over.

"I'm Sarah Roberts, and sometimes I talk to the other side about people like you. Good, kind people. The true warriors out there, helping with children, giving your life to bettering others." She turned her attention to John. "Then to have something like his diagnosis rip it all out from under you. It's cheap. It's mean. But I'd like to tell you, there's hope."

"Hope?" John asked.

"Hope, because this isn't our real home." She pointed at the ceiling. "That's our real home. Make do down here, then go home. They're waiting. Many speculate, and many have faith. I, for one, know the truth because my sister has laid it out for me." She moved closer. "We're here, on this plane, to do what we're supposed to, then move on. It's like, maybe you hate to fly. Begrudgingly, you get on that plane, land safely, and say it wasn't all that bad after all. In fact, you're happy you did it. That's probably not a good analogy, but when you leave here, you'll look back from the other side and be happy you did it—you lived that life—but wow, it'll be so good to be home."

"Why are you telling us all this?" Lori asked.

She looked at John, then Lori. "I need your help with something."

"Our help?" John sounded skeptical. "How can we help?"

"One of those obstacles, those challenges we spoke of earlier, took place at your home in Kamloops about a month ago. A contractor gave you an estimate on yard work. Something you wanted to be done with stones around the kidney-shaped pool in the back." Lori was nodding. "This contractor asked for a sizable deposit. You gave it to him. The cheque cleared, but the man never showed up for the work. When you checked on his company, it was gone. Kamloops police have nothing for you. As far as they're concerned, the investigation's closed."

Lori nodded vigorously. "John has been having trouble with his disease for some time. I don't want him working around the yard anymore. Since we'd been so busy this summer, I called for a maintenance crew to do the work. I found that guy on a Facebook page. It looked good. His estimate was twenty percent less than the other two I had come by."

"And he took the deposit?" Sarah asked.

John was nodding now.

"Yes," Lori said. "And screwed off with it. We don't need that sort of thing in our lives right now. I needed that work done."

"Here's how I can help," Sarah said. "I think I know who that man is. All I need is a picture of his face—"

"A picture?" Lori cut in. "We don't have a picture."

"I'm afraid you do," Sarah said. "On John's phone."

Lori turned to her husband. "John? You took his picture?"

"I'm not sure. My phone's over there in the pocket of my jeans. Grab it, and let's see." Lori started for the small pile of clothes by the side table that was littered with flowers and gifts. As evidenced by the gifts, John had a lot of people that cared. "I was taking pics the day that guy was doing the estimate because I wanted before and after photos for our album later."

Lori touched his phone screen as she walked back over to stand beside Sarah. On the screen, Sarah watched as Lori scrolled through family pictures of Niagara Falls, then slowed as she hit pictures of their backyard.

"There," Sarah said. "That man."

Lori touched the picture, enlarging it. The pool area was gorgeous. The concrete around the edges had overgrown grass and misshapen stones. Lori stood beside a man of medium build, medium height, clutching a clipboard in his left hand. The man faced the other way.

"That him?" Lori asked.

"Can't tell from behind. Are there any others?" Sarah asked, knowing there was one of his faces coming up. Vivian wouldn't have sent her for any other reason.

Lori thumbed to the next photo. Then the next. Backyard fence. Large stones. The man's shoes are in one photo. She moved to the next one.

Sarah gasped.

"You okay?" Lori asked.

Sarah wrapped her fingers around Lori's hand and angled the phone to see better.

"That's him," Sarah said.

The man in the grocery store. The empty cart. Vanilla cake mix. The shopping cart penetrating the image of the old man with flapping arms as he walked away. That was how the note was left on her windshield. Thirio had watched her pull in and got close to her on purpose.

Why didn't he try anything? He had no issue with killing random people. His bombs didn't discriminate. Her body shook for a moment at how vulnerable she had been, entranced by the old man and his message.

"I need that photo," Sarah blurted.

She yanked Mason's phone from her pocket and got Lori to text the photo to the phone.

"I'm so glad we had this on John's phone," Lori said. "Does this mean he'll be caught for what he did?"

"Absolutely. Because of you, we will catch him."

Lori tilted her head to the side, staring at Sarah. "Hey, aren't you that girl the police in Kelowna brought in to help with their bomber?"

"I am."

"I saw what happened in the news. Crazy stuff."

"They say you're psychic—" Lori stopped as she understood how Sarah knew everything she'd told them about their situation. "Oh, I get it. That's how you knew everything."

"And how I knew you had this photo on John's phone."

Lori stuck out her arms and looked down at them.

"Ohhh, I've got goosebumps." She glanced at her husband. "John, look at this."

"It's been so nice to meet you both, but I must leave now." Sarah moved backward toward the door.

"Wait," John said. "Can you tell us a little more about my condition?"

Lori moved around the bed and grabbed her husband's hand.

Sarah stopped by the door.

"I'm sorry." She lowered her head. "Sometimes this job can suck." She looked back at them. "I can see what has happened. I see your names, information, and when you were born. The future? That's a whole other ball game. I rarely get to see the future. But that's a good thing. Usually, when I do see the future, it's bad. Take comfort in that."

Sarah opened the door.

"Will we see you again?" Lori asked. "How will we know you caught the guy who took our money?"

Sarah paused in the open doorway. "Unfortunately, I won't be around long enough to see you again. When this business is over, I'm flying back to Toronto." She held the door open with an elbow. "But you'll know I caught the guy because it'll be front-page news. His picture will be everywhere."

She let the door close slowly.

"Thanks, Sarah," Lori called after her, but the door closed, cutting off Lori's voice.

Hospital security walked toward her. Two men in uniform. Sure they weren't there for her, she turned and headed for the stairwell anyway. Once on the stairs, she quickly dropped to the first floor and exited the building through a side door. The second the door clicked closed, a car raced by, going too fast for the parking area.

An unmarked cruiser.

She wasn't close enough to get a good look at who was inside but suspected it was Lee and Parkman.

She started across the parking lot toward Waters's vehicle, wondering when Vivian would be back in touch. Wasn't the man in the suit long gone? At the car, she stopped and scanned the parking area, the road ahead, and the sidewalk. Was the old man in the suit the only one? Or was she now able to see more people from the other side?

Two women were on the sidewalk. A man smoked outside the emergency doors. A red Kia navigated the parking lot, looking for a spot. An ambulance bounded into the area by emerg, preparing to unload its human cargo. No one stared at her. No one tried to signal her.

She faced the hospital. Squinting to look into individual windows, images rose from the tinted glass. As if forming from the air, dozens of faces stared out at her from those windows.

Sarah stepped back, bumped the car, and held onto it for a moment.

"What the fuck?" she whispered.

Another ambulance, sirens blaring, turned into the hospital, snapping her from the trance the people in the windows had over her.

She blinked, shook her head, and without looking back at the hospital windows, dropped into the driver's seat and slammed the door.

It was her turn to have goosebumps. She had talked to and listened to Vivian for so long that she almost forgot her sister was on the other side. Seeing those faces in the windows was something else altogether.

She left the Vernon Hospital and headed back to Kelowna, her hands shaking.

Would Vivian be blocked when others reached out to Sarah? As souls by the dozen left hospitals all the time, would hospitals be off limits to Vivian's connection going forward? She hoped Vivian would come back soon and explain some of this shit. It was starting to get old. And fast.

She grabbed Mason's phone and called Lee. They needed to coordinate the investigation.

Chapter 26

Parkman snatched up Lee's cell phone while Lee drove. Call display told him it was Sarah. Lee gave him a dirty look, but Parkman ignored him. "It's Parkman," he said. "You good?"

"Yeah," Sarah said. Wind distorted her voice. She was driving. "Tell me something."

"Go."

"Why hasn't Lee tried to apprehend me? Or come for the car I have? He was livid when I snatched the cruiser to go to the mall's coffee shop. What changed?"

"Trust." Parkman stole a look at Lee. "He trusts you. And wants you to trust him. Those officers today—Mason, Calder, Waters—went rogue. Right off the fuckin' map. There was no way anyone could've predicted that." He paused, then added, "Well, other than you."

Sarah didn't respond for several moments. Parkman

waited.

"It's good to hear your voice, Parkman. I don't like working like this. We should be together."

"Agreed."

"Did you get your luggage yet?"

"No."

"There's a note in your bag. Do what it says. Your life could depend on it. Promise me you'll get the note."

"I will." He didn't bother asking what was written on it. If she were going to tell him, she would've.

"Parkman?"

"Yeah."

"I'm scared."

He wasn't sure he heard her right.

"Say again."

"I'm seeing things."

"Things?" He watched the white lines of the road zip by, waiting.

"People. That have passed on."

He sat up straighter. "Passed on. As in dead?"

"As in dead."

"But how?"

"Not sure. Maybe something opened when Vivian got close to me in Denmark after I died. Like some sort of metaphysical portal."

"Could be. Are you okay, though?"

"They appear to me like flesh and blood. When I see them, I can't tell the difference. I mean, it's hard."

"Wow. That's just wow. I'm speechless."

"There's something else."

His stomach dropped. "What?"

"When they come around, staring at me, paying attention to me, they block Vivian. At the hospital in Vernon, Vivian was completely silenced."

"You saw de—" he stopped, turned toward the window, then rephrased his question. "You saw that kind of thing there?"

"Yes."

"Are they talking to you?"

"No. Not talking. But they're communicating."

"How?"

"Gestures. Messages. Like sign language."

"You can read sign language?" Parkman asked, his tone one of surprise. What other revelations was she going to offer up?

"No. I said it was like sign language."

"Oh. Right." He cleared his throat. "What would someone like that want to say to you?"

"I'm as lost with this as you are, Parkman. I hope Vivian returns and lets me in on what's happening. Then we'll all know. Has Lee talked to his son yet?"

"He tried but didn't get through."

"Tell him to try again. His son has a picture of the unsub. Did you talk to the people at the hospital?" Sarah asked.

"Yes. When we left, more people were filing in. Most had been poisoned by something. Through preliminary interviews, a pattern formed. They were all coming from one grocery store. But then others who had been at another store showed up with similar symptoms."

"The unsub, his name is Thirio, sprayed some kind of poison on fruits and vegetables at The Fast Way grocery stores in town."

"How did you get his name?"

"He left me a note on my car window when I went to The Fast Way to stop him. I was too late and got tied up with a dead man in a nice suit. Anyway, Thirio and I were in the cake mix aisle together. We met there. I saw him today."

"You what?" he gasped into the phone. "This conversation has gone from weird to off the rails."

"In a grocery store, Parkman. I met Thirio at The Fast Way."

"That's why you were there? To meet him?"

"You're listening, right?"

"Yeah, yeah." He nodded even though she couldn't see him.

"I was there to stop the poisonings but couldn't. I was too late. He walked by me when I was busy with a dead man."

"Okay, I heard you, but," Parkman shook his head, "did I hear you right?"

"You did." Sarah waited a heartbeat, then said, "Are you still in Vernon?"

"Yes. The Vernon RCMP detachment got a call that a man in a rural area was found murdered about half an hour ago. We're heading to that location to see if there's a connection. Vernon saw two people dead this morning. A third would be a huge coincidence if it isn't our unsub—sorry, Thirio. Where are you?" Parkman detected Lee looking at him at the mention of the unsub's name.

"Heading to the next location Vivian has instructed me to go. A house on the outskirts of Kelowna. I don't have an exact address, but I have the street name. I basically know where it is and what I'm looking for. But I've got another stop to make on the way."

"We're headed back to Kelowna after this. You want to meet up? Talk things out? Lee's on our side. I'll vouch for him."

There was another pause. He would have been convinced she'd hung up if it weren't for the sound of the wind in the background.

"Not yet."

He knew not to ask her reasons. If she were going to offer them, she would have. Lee slowed the cruiser as they neared the house, where several emergency vehicles parked every which way, covering the lawn, the driveway, and the street.

"We're here, Sarah. When you need us."

"Be careful, Parkman."

The phone clicked in his ear. He set it down, already missing her. This wasn't supposed to be the way things were done. They worked together. Even though he was with Lee, surrounded by other members of law enforcement, Parkman felt so alone.

It was good to talk to Sarah. He needed that. But what did she need? And what was that about a note in his luggage?

"Hey, Lee. I need my luggage from the airport."

Lee frowned. "You gonna tell me about that call? Or do I have to assume most of it from what I heard you saying?"

"I'll tell you what I can after we're done here and heading back to Kelowna."

"Okay."

They opened their doors at the same time and exited the cruiser.

"Thirio," Lee said as if tasting the name, rolling it off his tongue to see how it felt. "What kind of name is that?"

Parkman popped a toothpick in his mouth, then offered a don't-really-care shrug.

"No idea."

He started for the house with the large garden fenced off at the back, thinking about Sarah's newfound ability to see people that had passed on. Would Esmerelda Hall or Dolan Ryan drop in to say hello to Sarah? He disabused himself of such a notion. Sarah had a unique purpose. The other side got involved only when serving that purpose. People who have passed on wouldn't drop by to say hello unless they were forwarding Sarah's aims.

At least, he thought so.

Chapter 27

MASON STARED DOWN AT the white cast covering his broken arm. Bandages covered his face, surrounding the broken nose. The drab hospital room drove him insane with the smell. Instruments hung from the walls and were attached to the cabinet. Tools were in cupboards on the side above a sink and counter. Everything reminded him of a dentist's office, and he hated dentists.

This was the second time he'd broken a bone. The first was a broken rib in his back over two decades ago. Without a cast on that one, the doctor said the bone would fuse in four to six weeks and firm up in eight weeks. He always remembered that injury because of the month-long nights in a recliner. Sleeping in a bed had been agony.

That bone broke because he was stupid enough to try to impress a girl. Tom had accepted that price as a lesson learned, paid in full. There was nothing authentic about impressing a woman in his life after that day. Sure, he still went on to charm the ladies, but it was only to sleep with them. He even kept one around—otherwise known as a girlfriend—for a while, so he didn't have to go through the routine of courting each time he needed his urges satisfied.

That was why Barry Ashford, the good cop that he was, had been such a dear friend. Barry ran a clean establishment for years. The hottest babes were always willing to satisfy Tom for such little pay. That was all gone now because of Sarah Roberts. Even Barry was gone, killed, and dismembered. For such a man, even if he had done a few things that were suspect under the eyes of the law, that was no way to die.

Tom rose from the hospital bed and made his way over to the window to look out on Kelowna. Sarah Roberts had some nerve coming back to his city. She had Barry killed the last time she was here and then just up and left the city with impunity. As far as Tom Mason was concerned, that wasn't an expiable crime. She was culpable, and since no official, no authority or court of law was willing to make her pay, it was Tom's job to exercise judgment.

His arm throbbed under the cast. He closed his eyes and lowered his head, feeling his body, listening to his heart. He had to keep his blood pressure down. He couldn't let Sarah Roberts bother him. He was a cop. He would locate her, execute her, then burn her body and destroy any and all evidence. They wouldn't find her dismembered body like they found Barry's. No one would ever find Sarah again. He had lived in Kelowna long enough to know where to hide bodies. He knew where to go, how to do it, and how to ensure he would never get caught. He was a cop, after all.

And a good one at that.

He opened his eyes as they watered in anger, his heart beating a solid rhythm in his ears. Adrenaline flowed through his body as his pulse increased. His muscles oozed a sense of increased strength, even with one arm broken. The throbbing in his nose didn't cause him alarm. Pain reminded him he was alive, awake, and ready to hunt Sarah.

"A woman," he muttered to the empty room. "A fucking woman."

He placed his fist against the window and slowly crumpled his hand inward until all his knuckles cracked.

"I'm ready for you, Sarah. You will rue the day."

He thought back to what she had said about never losing and how she always won. Or something like that. Then the pretentious bitch went on to threaten his life. Mumbled something about how he would die before she left Kelowna and that she wouldn't be there long.

"How dare she?" He spat out the words. "We'll see who loses, you fucking whore."

Someone knocked on the door.

"Come in," he shouted. His free hand dropped to his side, leaving a tiny smudge where his moistened flesh had marred the pane. The door opened behind him. He didn't turn around, only stared at the moisture until it disappeared.

"Mason?" Officer Jeff Calder.

"What?" Mason kept his voice low.

"We're all checked out of this place." Calder had moved closer. "Want me to take you home?"

Mason turned slowly from the window. "The security posted to my door will allow this? Or are we under arrest?"

"I talked to them. They understood the order was to

guard your room. Someone said something about attempted murder charges, but that was laughed off. You survived a direct attack on your life. The attempted murder charge is real, but it's Sarah who will be arraigned, not us. I'm sure something got mixed up somewhere because Lee can't be reached. He's somewhere in Vernon."

Mason smiled. Vernon. That's nice. Almost an hour's drive away in another jurisdiction. Out of the way, which would allow Mason to track down Sarah without interruption.

He started across the hospital room floor, grabbed his jacket, and stood beside Calder.

"Are you with me?" Mason asked under his breath.

"Of course, I'm with you," Calder said.

Mason detected a slight hesitation in his response but didn't ask about it. When Calder said he was committed, Mason would hold him to it until the end.

"Good," he said. "Then get me out of here and call that friend of yours that tracks phone apps."

"Tracks phone apps? You mean Marcus?"

"Yeah, that's him."

"Why do you want Marcus? You lost your phone?"

"No, fucktit. I want him to track Waters's cruiser. Sarah stole it, didn't she? And since it hasn't been located, we can assume Sarah is still in it."

"Wouldn't Lee have done that already?"

"No. I doubt it. He brought her here. He's working with her and not us. And if he did, it doesn't hurt for us to find out, now does it?" He edged past his friend. "We might get lucky and locate that bitch before anyone else does."

"Mason," Calder said from behind him. "What happens

when we find her?"

Mason stopped at the door, his hand on the knob. He squeezed it tight, the skin over his knuckles stretching. After two breaths, he turned back to lock eyes with Calder.

"You leave that up to me. Just contact Marcus. Find that car, and we find Sarah. Then your part is done. Understood?"

Calder nodded. He rummaged in his pocket and retrieved his cell phone. "Yeah, no problem. I can find the car. That's easy."

Mason opened the door and stepped out into the hallway. The guards assigned to his room were gone.

"Where did they go?" he asked as Calder came out behind him.

"I relieved them for lunch."

"No complications?"

Calder shook his head. "None." He clucked his tongue. "Nothing will stick with what your dashcam has on it. Anyway, I got our boys to go for lunch. It's handled." He motioned at the phone as if someone had answered. They started for the elevators as Calder spoke into his phone. "Hey, Marcus. Calder here. I need you to track a car for me."

By the time they exited the building and Calder got Mason situated in the front seat of his cruiser, his phone rang.

"Calder." He paused. Then said, "You're sure about this?" He met Mason's eyes, then nodded. "Thanks, Marcus. You're a pal. I owe you one." He snapped his phone shut and smiled wide.

"Out with it," Mason ordered. In his anger at Sarah, he wasn't interested in prolonged games.

"Waters's cruiser is in Kelowna. In fact, it's about a ten-minute drive from us right now."

"Then get in. Take me there."
"Done and done."

Chapter 28

S ARAH PULLED INTO THE parking lot of the security store she had visited when she was last in Kelowna. Once parked, she exited Waters's cruiser and started for the store. Two vehicles up, a bearded man left his car at the same time and started for the store. He walked with purpose, plodding toward the entrance. He beat her there by several steps, then held the door as he'd noticed her coming in behind him.

"Thanks," she said as she took the door.

A large man with black wavy hair, easily six feet and a half tall, eased his bulk out from behind the counter and greeted the bearded guy before Sarah. While they talked, she browsed the latest gear and surveillance items they had in stock. She loved the cans of Coke that were storage areas for cash. Just plop the cash inside the can, screw on the top, and leave it in the fridge. A burglar would never know about the few thousand in cold hard cash in the ice box unless, of course, that particular burglar got thirsty during the heist. The store offered high-end tracking devices and gigantic home security kits with quad cameras and remote access.

When she moved to the GPS tracking devices, the bearded customer said something that piqued her interest. He identified himself as a real estate agent. He was looking for information about securing a home for an elderly client.

This guy is good. What realtor today went to these lengths to aid in a home purchase?

She moved closer to the men to eavesdrop. Kelowna's break-and-enter rate seemed out of control in the downtown area. With the recent terrorist acts, one of his elderly clients wanted advice on securing the perimeter of her home.

The men edged past Sarah.

"Be with you in a moment," the large clerk offered in a soft voice that didn't match his bulk.

Sarah smiled, nodded, then continued her browsing. After a minute, the clerk left his bearded customer and shuffled over to Sarah, his long thick shoes clomping her way.

"How's your day?" he asked.

"I need something unique." She lowered her voice. "Where would I be able to purchase a Kevlar vest?"

The clerk rested a hand on the shelf to his left. "Can't say I would know something like that." He watched her with a wary eye, his body angling even farther away. "Why would a pretty young thing like you want a bullet-proof vest?"

"To avoid being killed," she stated matter-of-factly. "Look, I don't see that kind of hardware here. I was hoping you'd direct me to where I can find it."

"Excuse me," the real estate agent called from the other

side of the small store. "I need you again when you have a second."

"Sure thing," the clerk hollered over his shoulder. He stepped back twice, then wrung his hands in front of him. "Sorry, can't help you. We offer what you see here."

"Your boss. Can he help me? I just need directions to someone in Kelowna that sells that sort of thing."

"I am the boss. No one here can help you. Sorry." He said the last few words with disdain.

This had been a waste of time. But with a sharpshooter in her future, she had no choice but to pursue this avenue. She needed something for protection.

"Damn it," she muttered on her way out the door.

Back in the unmarked cruiser, she hesitated, the car key in her hand. Maybe the realtor could help. He would know the city. He might even be able to tell her about the address she was headed to later that evening.

She slipped the key back into her pocket and exited the car. Leaning on the passenger side to be closer to the agent's car, Sarah waited for him to exit the store. She didn't have to wait long. One minute later, he strolled across the parking lot. When he glanced her way, she waved.

"Hi there," she said. "I couldn't help overhearing you're a real estate agent." He slowed, probably curious about who he was talking to. "Would you have a few moments to offer me some advice?"

"Of course." He stopped at his car door, opened it, crossed his arms, and leaned them on top of it. "Ask away."

"I'm in need of a particular piece of self-defense."

"Driving that unmarked cruiser?" the man asked. "What kind of protection would you need?"

Sarah wiped her mouth and rubbed her hand on her pants. "Let's start again. I'm Sarah." She extended a hand. He came off the door, shook it, and went back to his leaning.

"I'm Trever Florko, at your service."

Words flitted into her head. "Century 21, right?"

"Yes." He sounded surprised. "How'd you know?"

"You're something of a talented agent. Not sure what they call it in your business, but the people of Kelowna know your name."

"I try." His smile was genuine.

This guy was the real deal. His neatly trimmed beard gave him a GQ look, and his neatly pressed collar shirt wasn't too business-like that he wasn't approachable.

"As I was saying," Sarah leaned in closer, "I need a Kevlar vest." It was out. She waited for his response. He blinked, looked left, then turned back to her.

"There's an army surplus store a block over on Dayton Street. You might want to try there."

"That's great. Thanks." She paused momentarily, then pulled a piece of paper from her back pocket. "You wouldn't be able to tell me a little about this street, would you?" She handed him the paper. "Seeing as you're a realtor."

Trever scanned the street Vivian had given her. He seemed to read it twice, furrowed his eyebrows, then looked up and handed the paper back.

"As far as I know, the Campbell Winery residence is on that street. Without looking it up online, that would be my guess."

"Campbell Winery?" Sarah repeated. The name meant nothing to her.

"Yeah, it's a large winery in these parts. Kelowna is

home to dozens of wineries. The Campbell's place is smack up beside the Martin's winery. They're the only two addresses on that road. I should know because I love Campbell's wine. They do a great ice wine as well."

"A winery?" Sarah said, almost to herself. What the hell did Vivian give her the address to a winery for? What could possibly be up there?

"Anything else I could help you with?" Trever asked.

"Not at the moment—"

Get out of sight, echoed through her head.

Sarah ducked below the edge of the realtor's car. She had to assume the worst without knowing why she had to drop out of sight.

"You should get down," she advised.

To Trever's credit, he got down below the door. "Why are we ducking?" he asked.

"We'll know in a second."

She waited, balancing herself with a hand on the hood of Trever's car. On the street, a vehicle eased by. Sarah swiveled to watch the vehicle. It was an unmarked cruiser, just like Waters's car, and Calder was driving. Before it drove by, she was sure she saw Mason in the passenger seat because the bandages on his face were visible through the side window briefly.

"Actually," she said, her eyes tracking the back end of their car as it slowed and prepared to pull into the parking lot. "You could give me a lift to that army surplus store."

"That's not your car over there?" Trever asked.

Calder had stopped behind Waters's cruiser. Sarah crawled around the front of Florko's car until she reached the passenger door. She opened it and slipped into the seat, keeping her head down.

"Come on," she beckoned. "It's only one block. Take me to Dayton."

Trever hesitated, then sat beside her in the driver's seat. "One block," he said. His demeanor had changed.

There was no time to explain her actions. She would be out of his life in one city block, and there was no danger to him—providing he left immediately. Calder was now peeking inside the front door of Waters's cruiser.

Trever backed out of the parking space, then headed for the exit. As they came into view of Calder's vehicle, Sarah dropped below the window line.

"Is everything okay?" Trever asked, his tone flat. "I'm not aiding and abetting here, am I?"

"Not at all." Sarah eased the gun from her waistband. If Mr. Florko needed any persuasion, she couldn't afford a travel delay. "Just drive." She leaned up far enough to glance out the side mirror and watch Calder look around the parking lot. He scratched his head and started for the security store.

"Not a problem," Trever said, snapping a glance down at the gun in Sarah's hand. "I'll just drive."

Chapter 29

"WE JUST MISSED HER," Calder said as he tried to catch his breath. He had been in the store all of a minute. "She was here," he panted. "Left with a real estate broker, according to the guy behind the counter."

Mason punched the dash above the glove box. "What did she buy?" he asked.

"Nothing. She was looking for a Kevlar vest."

They exchanged a knowing glance. Mason knew what Sarah was doing. She was gearing up for a fight, preparing herself for when he came calling. A vest wouldn't help her, though. He would be shooting for the head.

"Did he sell her one?" Mason asked.

Calder shook his head. "No, they don't stock that sort of thing. All he could tell me was the girl left, talked to the real estate agent by his car, and then they pulled out as we got here."

"Did he get the agent's name?" Why was it like pulling teeth with Calder?

His partner offered him one of those ear-to-ear smiles. "The agent's name is Trever Florko."

"I know him. Get in here. Call Century 21. Get them to connect you to Trever's phone." Calder dropped into the car and yanked his phone out. "He can't have gone too far."

Calder got on the phone and waited for an automated answering machine to put him through to the operator, then he asked for Florko.

Mason watched the road while listening to his partner. They were minutes away from arresting Sarah Roberts and then making her disappear forever. She would have no idea what hit her. It was late afternoon. The sun was still high. He took a deep breath, then exhaled. Today was a good day to execute a meddling bitch. Barry would be proud.

"I understand," Calder was saying. "Fair enough. Thank you." He paused, rubbed his chin, then tapped his hands on the steering wheel. "Mr. Florko. This is Officer Jeff Calder with the Kelowna RCMP. Could you return my call at once? It is an emergency." Calder recited his cell number twice, then hung up.

"They wouldn't put you directly through to him?" Mason asked.

Calder shook his head. "Wouldn't give his cell number out over the phone."

"You're a cop," Mason nearly shouted.

"I know, but this is unofficial. I can't play that card all the time."

Mason slammed the dash again. "Okay, think. Where would Florko take Sarah?"

"Or better yet, where would Sarah force Florko to take her?"

"I hadn't thought of that." Mason tapped his leg twice, then turned to Calder. "Where can the public access something like Kevlar?"

Calder shrugged noncommittally. "No idea. Never had cause to buy one."

Mason thought about his city, his contacts. Was there any kind of arms dealers in Kelowna? The Hell's Angels' clubhouse on Ellis Street was tied up in a court case as the government was trying to take their house. Would they have Kevlar that Sarah could access? If so, could Florko have those kinds of contacts? Mason didn't think so. He didn't know Florko all that well, but what he did know of him, the man was clean.

"This is maddening," Mason said. "While we sit here sucking our thumbs, Sarah's getting away. Did that clerk tell you anything else? Like how Florko and Sarah got together? I mean, did he see them meeting for the first time? Did he overhear anything they said? Like where he was taking her?"

Calder opened his door. "I'll go check." Then he was gone.

Mason closed his eyes and steadied his breathing. The wounded bone in his arm throbbed, and his nose ached something fierce. The broken nose affected his voice, but Calder hadn't said anything about it—which was a safe move on his part.

He ground his teeth as heat flushed through his body. Making him chase her would only make it worse for her. When he finally caught up with Sarah, he would be unable to contain his fury. He had never hated someone as much as he hated Sarah Roberts.

Why? Because she had murdered his best friend and cop, Barry Ashford. She had attacked Mason, broke his arm and nose, and guards had been placed at *his* hospital room door.

"Who the fuck is this girl, anyway?" he asked out loud. "Why is she so important? Who made her King Shit?"

Soon, very soon, she would learn that she was not King Shit or Queen Shit. She was a piece of shit, and when he was done with her, he would wipe the shit from his shoe.

The door opened, and Calder dropped back in the car. "The clerk knew nothing." He cranked the ignition. "So I called Marcus and had him get me Florko's cell number. Took him seconds."

"And? Did you call him?"

Calder shot a glance at Mason. "No. I did something better."

"What?" Mason shouted, his nose aching because of it.

"Marcus did some magic like that find my phone app. He'll be able to tell us where Florko is in seconds, and then we'll go grab him." Calder's phone dinged. "There it is." Calder grabbed his phone and stared at it. "Looks like Florko is minutes away on Ambrosia Road." He put the car in gear and skidded out of the parking lot. "Let's go grab that bitch."

Chapter 30

Sarah waited inside the army surplus store until the clerk was freed from talking to another customer. The store was mostly hunting gear and clothing. She had spied pepper spray canisters and various hunting knives near the counter, but nothing like what she was looking for.

After several minutes, the clerk plodded toward her. "Can I help you find something?" His age hadn't crept into his voice yet. The man had to be in his sixties, but he had the voice of a thirty-year-old.

"I'm in need of a Kevlar vest," Sarah said, wanting to get right to the point. She studied the man's blue eyes. He stared back at her, unwavering.

"I might be able to help with that. How much you looking to spend?"

"Whatever it costs."

His eyebrows rose, but his eyes remained fixed on her.

After a moment, the man's lips parted. He tapped them with his finger. "You a cop?" he asked.

"Do I look like one?" He didn't respond. "The answer is no, I am not a cop."

"Give me a minute. Let me deal with this customer, and I'll lock up for the day. Stick around. I might have what you're looking for."

Sarah stayed by the side window of the store. She thought about what might be waiting for her at the Campbell Winery. Was Thirio directly connected to them? Or maybe it was the Martin Winery farther up the road, as Florko had mentioned.

She wondered if Florko would go to the police after seeing her gun. If so, she needed to leave this army surplus store very soon.

Her cell rang. She yanked it out to see Lee's number.

"Yeah," she answered.

"It's Parkman. We're leaving the location of the murder in Vernon."

"And?"

"Looks like it's our guy, Thirio. A witness placed a guest in the house about the time of the murder. The owner of the house and the guest walked around the garden. The neighbor said it looked like Ray Durowitz, the deceased, was getting an estimate for something."

"Makes sense. Thirio is driving a lawn maintenance pickup truck. Before going into the grocery store in Vernon, I noticed a red pitchfork in the back."

"That's him. The neighbor said he saw the guest take a pitchfork from the garden and place it in the back of his truck before driving off. Lee requested Vernon police check

Durowitz's bank accounts. As a courtesy, that information was provided by the bank. It appears Mr. Durowitz's account had a cheque written on it and was withdrawn today. The bank is pulling surveillance cameras as we speak. We'll get a photo of this guy within hours."

"Good work. Listen, Parkman. You still need to get Lee to call his son."

"For an ID? We're going to get that."

"No. Not just an ID."

"Then why? Give me something."

She hesitated a moment, watching the clerk cash out the other customer. "This is his last chance. Nick is terminal, and he doesn't know it. He does have a picture of Thirio. I thought that would bring these two men together. But since it might not, tell Lee he needs to fix this thing with his son anyway."

"I will. And Sarah?"

The army surplus store clerk used a thumb lock to secure the door. He flipped the open sign to closed.

"Parkman. I've got to go."

"Wait. Sarah—"

She hung up, slipped the phone away, and meandered through the overburdened clothing racks to where the clerk waited by a side door. The opening led down into a basement.

"What's down there?" Sarah asked, her hand twitching, ready to reach for the gun if needed.

The old man held up his hands. "I don't have a Kevlar vest, per se." He coughed into his elbow, then started down the stairs. "Come on down and see what I do have. It's something far better than Kevlar. It's British-made."

Chapter 31

THIRIO MADE IT BACK to Kelowna in good time. He drove the busy streets, whistling to himself while driving. The sun's warmth soothed him as it slowly dropped from the sky toward dusk. He'd listened to Blue October, then the Dayglo Abortions again, but ended up playing Sevendust, keeping the bass high, the treble low.

Once he'd made it through the most congested areas of Kelowna, he took Chute Lake Road to Upper Mission Drive and finally turned off onto Gillard Forest Service Road. This road allowed him access to the rear of the winery where he'd been staying recently. The Campbell Winery had a long history of being a detested rival in the wine business. His previous family, before he killed himself and, by doing that, excommunicated himself—the Martins—had their winery abutting the Campbell's property. Like the Hatfields and McCoys, a long-standing feud between the families had originated before Thirio was born. Stories his grandfather had once relayed to him led Thirio to believe the conflict was sparked by land disputes—disputes that were never settled or had been dealt with unfairly. No arbitrator or mediator, whether private or from the city, could ever appease either side equally. In the decades-long fight, there had been property damage, random fires, and even gags that went wrong. Thirio knew, without a doubt, that the gags weren't actually meant as jokes. The Campbell family had always intended to do harm, and the harm they did.

His fiancée Julia had died at their hands; her death ruled an accident. The Campbell family got away with it—no criminal charges. The legal system let them off the hook. Thirio wouldn't make that mistake. He meant to make the Campbell family pay.

Thirio parked in a cutaway area just off the road, then locked his truck and started up the embankment with the last of the tools he would need. If he survived the night, he would take the rest of the poison-filled bottles and use them tomorrow. With the extra money he obtained today, he would create more havoc and not stop until he was killed and brought before the ruler of Hell, his new father.

The forest road behind him was rarely used. With the work truck parked there, no one would pay special attention to it.

He used the valley behind the Campbell Winery property to access their land and moved from tree to tree undetected until he reached the empty guesthouse. He always tried to come when the shadows were long and the sky darkening. In these particular trees, the light had to fight to reach the ground, and it was a losing battle at this hour of the day. At the back of the winery property, the Campbells had left an abandoned guesthouse to rot. It hadn't seen visitors since the 1960s. The building had no running water and no electricity, but Thirio had used it just fine in the first month of hiding. The irony was that it was in their own abandoned guesthouse that he'd cooked up his plan of revenge to murder their family or as many as he could kill before someone stopped him. But first, he would cripple them with his bombs and destroy their financial interests with the poison.

His denouement, his final act, was the sharpshooters. Once the winery got a taste of the glassy-winged sharpshooter, there would be no coming back. Thirio had released them on Campbell's Winery over a month ago, and even though the sharpshooters weren't indigenous to the Kelowna area, they had a strong will to survive. Kelowna was known for its intense summer heat. These grapevine enemies usually survived in warmer climes like Florida, Texas, and southern California, where they wreaked havoc by releasing Pierce's Disease. The sharpshooter decimated the Los Angeles basin in the 1880s and again in the decade between 1930 and 1940.

Importing a batch of them had been easy. After driving to southern California, he met with an entomologist, bought a group of them, and drove back across the border with the insects stuffed in a suitcase in the trunk of his family car. All this was done before Julia was murdered. The irony wasn't lost on him. The timing, simply perfect. The Campbells had brought their own destruction upon themselves by going after Thirio.

He made it to the guesthouse undetected, as usual. Their main house was a couple of hundred yards away and separated by a fifteen-foot row of hedges. Someone would have to be standing in a specific spot on their winding driveway to catch a glimpse of a dark shadow crossing the front stoop of the guesthouse in order to see him. All his work and preparation were done in the basement of the guesthouse, where using small lights never posed a problem. And now all that work was coming to an end. Soon the Campbells would discover the aggressive leaf-hoppers and the Pierce's Disease bacterium in their vines that the glassy-winged critters spread. Since there's no known cure for Pierce's Disease, the Campbell Winery would succumb to ruin.

The poison Thirio had sprayed in their grocery stores would make headline news, and their stores would suffer financially. The random bombings throughout the city would lead back to the Campbells after Thirio's last explosion—on their property—and all would be right with the world.

Thirio used his iPhone flashlight to lead him down the stairs to the basement, watching for the second last stair as it had lost its integrity years ago. Once in the basement, he swung the light over onto the table and bench where all his bomb-making tools waited discovery by the authorities. He'd had his twin brother help him bring everything down there, then when his twin brother got cold feet—which Thirio suspected would happen and prepared for it anyway—Thirio came up with his most brilliant plan. With his brother dead and disposed of—his body dumped in Okanagan Lake— Thirio could continue his work without anyone knowing he was alive. His identical twin would take his place in death. There were two sides to the family dispute, and his brother never saw Thirio's side. There were always two sides. Good and evil. You were either with the Martins, or you sided with the Campbells, and Thirio was a Martin through and through.

When Julia died, family and friends from all over the globe began arriving for her funeral. It was all very pompous because no one knew her like Thirio had. No one really cared about Julia. It was an excuse to come to sunny Kelowna for a vacation at the Martin Family Winery.

When his long-lost twin brother called from Rome, Italy, it just so happened that Thirio had answered the phone. His brother had been away an entire decade since he'd talked to their mother. No one had gotten a hold of him in over five years. Then he called to come to the funeral after reading about it in an online Kelowna newspaper.

Thirio impressed upon his brother to keep his arrival a secret. Thirio would fetch him at the airport and set him up in a hotel. On the day of the viewing, it would be Thirio who would bring his brother to the funeral home.

His brother agreed to everything, and Thirio got to work. When he picked him up at the airport, he had him spend the next sixteen hours—with minor rest times—setting up the basement of the Campbell's abandoned guesthouse. It had been a decade, Thirio had argued. To make things right for the family, especially Julia, his brother needed to atone to his identical twin, and atone he did. His brother needed to show him due respect.

When his brother had cast doubt on Thirio's plans and attempted to talk him out of it, he'd sided with the Campbells. At that moment, his brother became the enemy, the very enemy that had murdered Julia.

Even before his brother flew in from Rome, Thirio had lost any feelings for him. The brother who had abandoned the family. The brother who had walked away callously left an abundance of pain for their mother. Furious, Thirio had argued that his twin had no right to return as the prodigal son. Thirio would show him who was the real son, what a real family looked like, and that he did.

When the body was found in the lake, everyone would think it was Thirio. The family would perform a positive ID at the city morgue. It would make sense, too. With Julia gone, how could Thirio go on? But who killed him? The police would never know. More importantly, they wouldn't perform a DNA test on a body that looked like him, especially after his own family identified him, but if they did, it wouldn't have mattered.

His was a perfect crime, the perfect murder. His asshole brother was gone—no one was looking for him—and Thirio was free to do what he wanted with wanton abandon. The triumph of evil over good.

As he prepared the last bomb in his possession under the dim gleam of a tiny penlight, thoughts of Lucifer drifted into his mind. He wondered what the angel would look like. Would he still have his wings? If so, would they be black or white? Thirio guessed they'd be black. Would the devil's laugh cause chills? He was so excited with the opportunity of heading south of the soil that he almost hit the wrong key on his cell phone and detonated the bomb.

"Damn it," he murmured.

He set a six-digit deactivation code on his phone in case, for some unknown reason, he sat in the chair it was attached to or was pushed into it. Whoever sat in the plush furniture would disintegrate with the blast. Actually, anyone inside the basement would most surely die. There was no hope unless they had Thirio's cell phone and its deactivation code.

As he prepared the rest of the damning evidence against the Campbells, he only hoped that Sarah Roberts would sit in that chair. Seeing her blown to tiny bits of flesh and bone would be a delightful sight.

Chapter 32

On Ambrosia Road, Calder parked half a block from the address Marcus had texted.

"Did he give you a unit number?" Mason asked.

Calder glanced at his phone, slid his thumb along the screen, looked out through the windshield, and pointed. "It's that one."

Mason opened his door with his good hand. "Then let's go get her."

They approached the buildings, a more modern version of townhouses. These units were wider and higher, with some offering an outside patio on the roof. Mason couldn't recall how old they were, but he knew a couple of people who lived on this street. One was a friend, and the other was a guy he'd arrested for possession last year.

At the door, he stayed back a few feet, ready to pull his weapon if needed. Sarah was unpredictable. He'd never admit it, but she was also very good in close quarters.

Calder hammered on the door. "Open up," he shouted. "Police." He waited the requisite five seconds, pounded on the door again, shouted, "Police," once more, then checked their flank.

Footsteps approached from the other side of the door. The peephole darkened. For some reason, that always pissed Mason off. They'd shouted "Police" twice, but everyone always checked. He had yet to meet a group of home invaders running around the city banging on doors and yelling "Police."

"Open up," Mason shouted.

The snick of a lock was the first sound of compliance. Then the door eased open enough for a bearded man to peek out.

"Can I help you?" the man asked.

"I'm Officer Calder." He flipped open his ID wallet, then snapped it shut. "This is Officer Mason. And you are?"

"Trever Florko. Is there a problem, Officer?"

"Can we come in?"

Florko opened the door farther and stepped aside, his left hand holding a full glass of red wine.

Before Calder moved, he said, "Are there others in the house?"

"Just me and my wife."

Mason fixed him with a cold stare, his hand still at the ready. "You wouldn't be lying to us now, would you, Mr. Florko?"

Florko shook his head, mouth open, the wine sloshing in the goblet. "No, sir. Why would I lie?" He looked like he'd been caught cheating on his taxes, and the auditor just asked damning questions.

"Because if you're harboring a fugitive—"

"Harboring a what?" Florko said, composing himself. "You mean that girl from the security store?" He looked from Calder to Mason, then back to Calder, no doubt wanting to only deal with him. With the bandages and the cast, coupled with Mason's glaring, Florko probably felt the intimidation Mason was pouring on.

Calder slipped past Florko and entered the man's foyer. Mason moved inside the townhouse beside Calder, pushing the door closed behind him. Florko moved back several feet to a comfortable distance.

"What can you tell us about that girl today?" Calder asked.

"Uhm, she ahhh, she acted weird. A subtle hostility about her. She reminded me of a caged animal. The wrong move, and you're liable to lose your head." Florko slurped his wine. Probably needed a drink after meeting Sarah.

"That's her," Mason said. "What did you talk about? Where did you take her?"

A woman emerged from a room up the hallway. Mason and Calder tensed at the same time.

Florko turned, "It's okay, honey. It's the RCMP. They just have a few questions."

"What was that about a girl?" she asked.

"I'll explain in a moment—actually, just listen so I only have to say it once." Florko looked back at them and nodded toward her. "My wife."

"You were telling us about Sarah Roberts."

"Sarah?" Florko frowned. His eyes lowered to the wine in his hand as if he was thinking. "Sarah Roberts?" he muttered. He looked back up, sipped the wine, then blinked a couple of times. "She only told me her first name." Then his eyes widened as he thought of something and lightly slapped his forehead open-palmed. "I knew I recognized her."

Calder exchanged a glance with Mason, then turned back to Florko. "Yes, Sarah Roberts. Look, Mr. Florko, we don't have a lot of time. What did she say to you? Where did you take her?"

Florko had a stunned look in his eyes. He stammered a moment, then caught his breath. "She asked about a bulletproof vest. She wanted to know where she could buy one. I told her to go to the army surplus store on Dayton. Then she jumped in my car and asked me to drive her the one block over. So I did. Although, she was quite persuasive."

"How persuasive?" Mason asked, easing closer.

"Once in the car, she produced a gun. She didn't point it at me or anything. Just set it on her lap. How could I refuse? It wasn't like she was kidnapping me. The gun just showed up. I drove to the army store. She jumped out and disappeared inside. Then I came right here and poured this tall baby." He held up the wine and drank from it again.

"Is there anything else you can remember? Did she say anything else?" Calder asked.

"She asked about a street."

"A street?" Calder and Mason exchanged a glance. "What street? And why ask you something like that? Did she think you were directory assistance or something?"

"No, nothing like that." His wife had moved up to stand beside her husband at the mention of the gun. She rested a hand on his shoulder, but he didn't seem to notice. "She knew I was a realtor and that I knew the area."

Calder waved his hand, exasperated. "What street did she ask you about?"

"She had it on a piece of paper. It was the Campbell Winery street on the other side of Mission. Trumpeter Road."

Calder turned back to Mason again. "Campbell Winery?"

Mason gave Calder a who-fuckin-knows shrug.

"Anything else?" Calder asked when he turned back.

"No. Nothing."

"Are you aware that you aided and abetted a known criminal today, Mr. Florko?" Mason stated in his best authoritative voice. Although listening to himself speak sounded like he was talking through a pipe because of the broken nose.

"It wasn't like I had a choice," he pleaded. "She showed me a gun."

"Did you report the incident to the police after dropping Miss Roberts off?" Mason asked.

"Well, no, but—"

"Then it's bullshit. If you were actually threatened with a weapon, kidnapped—even if it was for only one minute— and made to drive someone somewhere, you should have reported it to the police. Instead, you came home for a glass of wine. Or are you commonly kidnapped at gunpoint? Does it happen so often that reporting it was a practice in futility?" Mason stepped closer. "Or have you lost faith in the RCMP?"

"Well, no, but—"

"Stop saying *well, no, but*!" Mason yelled.

Calder pulled out a business card and proffered it to Florko, who had stepped back when Mason shouted. "Take this. Call us if you remember anything else." Florko's wife snatched the card from Calder's hand.

Mason ripped open the door and almost fell as he stumbled down the steps. Calder caught up to him.

"Bit hard on the realtor, dontcha think?" Calder said.

"Fuck you."

"Just saying."

"Yeah, and look at my nose. Look at my fuckin' arm." Mason held up the cast. "Fuck you and fuck Sarah. But most of all, fuck people like Florko, who are just *helping out*. He didn't help a young girl out. He helped her escape from us. He should pay for that." Mason looked back at the townhouse. "I'll remember his name."

"Good," Calder said as he dropped into the car. "Buy a house from the guy one day, so he doesn't file a complaint with your name stenciled all over it. Now, get in the fucking car, and let's go get that bitch."

Mason bumped his cast on the center console, grimaced as the pain shot up his arm, and then cursed under his breath for an entire minute.

"*Well, no, but*," Calder said in a mockery of Florko's voice. "Can you believe that guy?"

As Calder drove toward the army surplus store, Mason finally got his breathing back under control.

"One day, you're going to drive me to a rubber room where I might have to kill you."

"Fuck you, Mason. I'll kill you first."

They drove the rest of the way in silence. Mason didn't want to tell Calder how much he hated him at that moment. None of this would be happening if Calder had backed him up better out on Myra Canyon Road earlier. If Calder were a better cop, Sarah would be dead, and they would be back at the station doing paperwork for days—but the bitch would be dead.

Fuck you, Calder. Just fuck you.

Chapter 33

Sarah gazed in awe at what the old man offered. The technology had advanced in ways she was unaware of. She'd worn Kevlar vests before, even ones with tiny bombs attached, but nothing like the one in front of her. The British had invented a revolutionary device made of some kind of liquid.

"It's a BAE Systems liquid body armor vest," the clerk said. Sarah kept poking it with her finger.

"It's very lightweight," she said.

"The projectile's impact is spread over a wider area with this unit—unlike Kevlar—because of the liquid. Kevlar vests sandwich about forty-five layers together to create a substance five times harder than steel." His rudimentary demonstration by bringing his hands together didn't offer much in the way of a visual. "Because of that, no bullet enters the body." He tapped his chest. "But the force of the bullet is localized and can cause severe bruising and even broken ribs. What the Brits have done is sandwich ten layers," he touched the outer rim of the BAE unit, "with their special gel between two layers of Kevlar to create an ultra-light vest that spreads the impact of the bullet over the entire surface." He looked up to meet her eyes. "This reduces the intensity of the injury standard Kevlar allows."

The basement of the army surplus store was a warehouse for the store's extra stock. Two single lightbulbs dangled from the ceiling. Behind the clerk, a wooden door was barred and bolted shut. A weapons cache was Sarah's guess. Upstairs, the door was locked. The old man had never met her before and couldn't possibly know her, yet they were alone.

"Why are you helping me?" Sarah asked.

"Because of what you're doing for the city."

She tilted her head sideways and eyed him suspiciously. "How do you know what I'm doing for the city?"

The old man coughed into his elbow, turned away, and found a chair in the corner.

"Don't mind me." He tried to clear his throat, then coughed once more. "Cancer in the lungs." When the fit was over, he placed a hand on each knee and righted himself. "Ever since those bombs went off in the city, everyone's been watching the news. Is it ISIS? A terror cell? Business picked up here." He inhaled, stopped to breathe, then let it out. Color returned to his face. "The news said you were here and that you'd stopped other bombs from going off." He shrugged. "I was hoping I'd get the chance to meet you." He waved toward the upstairs area. "Then you waltz on in here looking for a vest. So I will ensure you get the best one I have to offer because whatever you're doing, lady, make no mistake, you're volunteering to enter the ring." He raised an index finger. "No, you're willingly walking into a war zone, and you're doing it with your head held high. I respect that. I'd volunteer to go with you if I were younger or fitter."

"I appreciate your kind words, Mr. …"

"Mike. Just call me Mike."

"Okay, Mike. How much for the BAE vest?"

"Nothing. It's yours. Just go and stop whoever's tearing up my city."

"Oh, I can't do that. You have to take something—"

"Consider it my contribution to the effort." On the last word, he was lost to a bout of coughing. His elbow wasn't sufficient shelter this time. He grabbed a box of Kleenex, wadded up half a dozen, and gagged into them.

Sarah stepped back to give him privacy. After a moment, Mike collected himself, then got to his feet.

"It's the dank air down here. Always does this to me." He started for the stairs. "I locked the doors upstairs because I wanted privacy when showing you the vest but also because it's closing time." On the second step going up, he paused. "Grab that vest and come on up. This basement'll kill me if I stay down another minute."

Sarah did as she was told. She looped an arm through the center and carried it up after Mike. Upstairs, the lights were off except one by the exit door. The sun was almost down, the shadows long. She needed a taxi, and she needed to get to Campbell's Winery before the end of the day to see why Vivian had given her the address.

"Can you call me a taxi?" she asked.

Mike coughed into his Kleenex. He was right—the air

upstairs was much easier to breathe.

Movement caught her eye, and she ducked down in reflex. The man in the suit who had been haunting her for days stood three racks over. A chill raced down her back at the sight of him. The man lifted his left arm and pointed at the rear exit. Then he tapped at his wrist to signify time was running out.

Sarah frowned. Messages from the dead? What happened to Vivian? She tried to summon her sister, but as before, in the presence of this man, she felt nothing from the other side.

Out front, a car took the corner that led onto Dayton a little too fast, tires screeching in protest. Sarah bent at the waist and peeked through the windows. An RCMP unmarked cruiser continued turning and ended up in the army surplus store's parking lot. The besuited man gestured at the rear exit with more urgency, his arm jerking that way twice. Then he, too, looked out at the cruiser.

How could they find her so fast? She thought back to the Spy Vs. Spy store and tried to remember if she had mentioned where she was going next. The realtor had given her a ride to the store. Had Mason gotten to him? Or did the realtor call them to complain about the gun? However it had played out, they were here.

"You wanted a taxi?" Mike was asking.

"Not now. I think I'll just use your back door."

Mike had turned around at the front counter and watched the two men leave the cruiser and approach the store.

"Friends of yours?" he asked.

"You could say that. If friends are rogue cops who want to kill you."

"These guys?" he asked, glancing over his shoulder at

her. "They have a problem with you?"

She nodded. "Those guys. It's personal with them. They're trying to stop what I'm doing."

"Well, fuck them," Mike mumbled. "I fuckin' hate bad cops." He walked over to the glass door at the front of his store and crossed his arms. The cancer hadn't taken everything away from Mike. He appeared formidable in his stance as he eyed down the cops on the other side of the glass.

Mason and Calder hadn't listened to her warning to leave her alone at the airport. Like hounds with a scent, they wouldn't give up. She peeked out the rear door, saw the alley was clear, then leaned back in to listen to Mike's exchange with Mason and Calder.

"Got a warrant?" Mike yelled through the locked doors.

"Did you have a female customer looking for a Kevlar vest within the last hour?" Calder shouted back.

"I need to see your warrant." Mike stood his ground.

"I don't need a warrant to ask you a question," Calder shouted.

"And I don't have to answer any of your questions as a private citizen other than to identify myself."

Calder's mouth formed an O as he exhaled his tension. He turned to Mason to see what to do. Mason's face was bandaged, and his arm was in a cast. Looked good on him. Mason stepped closer to the door, his nose touching the glass. Mason and Mike would feel each other's breath on their cheeks if the glass weren't there.

"The woman we're looking for is a fugitive of the law," Mason said. "If she's in there, you're breaking the law, and if you are, then I will come through this glass to arrest you, old man."

Mike uncrossed his arms, lowered his hands, and gestured with his fingers to come forward. "Bring it on, fucking pigs. I got nothing to lose. And if I'm alive when this is over, those cameras over my shoulder will show how much of a bully the RCMP really are." He slammed the glass, and Mason jerked backward. "Fucking cocksuckers!" Mike yelled.

Sarah spied a pair of steel handcuffs sitting outside their clamshell case on a small bench by the door. Behind the open case sat another dozen handcuffs still wrapped and piled neatly in a box.

Sarah grabbed a pair, tossed the small keys in her pocket, and exited the back of the store. The British BAE vest slipped over her head easily and covered her comfortably under her bulky shirt. Close by, the busiest street would be Harvey Avenue, where she expected to find a taxi pretty fast. As she walked, the sun dipped behind a distant mountain on the West Kelowna side of Okanagan Lake, offering her better cover in the early evening dusk.

As vile as Mike had sounded, she was proud of him for standing up for what he believed in. Not all cops were bad. But for the few that were, they tarnished the image of the boys in blue. She had one regret, though, and aimed to fix that before she left Kelowna. She didn't get a chance to thank Mike for the vest. And she would have to return to pay for the cuffs.

Chapter 34

Parkman had to run to keep up as Lee body-checked his office door and barreled inside.

"Of all the fucking shit that goes on here," Lee shouted in his empty office. "I cannot believe this."

Parkman stopped to catch his breath. He leaned on the doorframe and waited for Lee to calm down. The officers he'd sent to the hospital had gone for lunch at the same time, and Mason and Calder had walked out. No one knew where they were, and neither answered their cell phones.

Lee stopped at his window and grumbled something under his breath as he stared outside. Parkman knew better than to ask what he said. Never interrupt a man when he was having a tantrum unless you want your head cut off in the resulting tirade. Adulting can be tough for some.

Lee turned and kicked the table beside his small couch, knocking it over and spilling the lamp. It crashed to the floor, shattering the base into dozens of sharp-edged pieces.

"Okay, Lee." Parkman stepped inside the office, hands up. "Take it easy."

Lee glared at him. He pointed at Parkman, jabbing his finger in the air with each word. "No, I will not take it easy," he growled. "Cops are expected to do their jobs. It's bad enough that the Abbotsford detachment is investigating my cops." Lee moved to his chair, where he dropped like a sack of meat.

"Abbotsford Police?" Parkman sat on the couch, avoiding the shards of glass on the floor. After replacing the toothpick in his mouth, he asked, "What are they looking into?"

"The Kelowna RCMP detachment is under investigation for a series of allegations is all I can say. The Abbotsford detachment is acting as an independent policing agency investigating my boys. They won't tell me anything because they're still investigating. They just keep interviewing cop after cop and several witnesses about things I'm oblivious to." Lee ran a hand through his hair and took a deep breath, exhaling slowly. "They're gathering information. You know how it's done. But it's raising my fucking blood pressure." He gawked at Parkman. "I'm 140 over 95. Can you believe that?"

"Lee, that's hypertension area. You gotta calm that shit down. Lose a few pounds. Reduce the salt intake."

"Blah, blah, blah. I've heard it all from the doctor. First, find Sarah. Then, arrest my own cops for attempted murder, neglecting duty, and other shit charges. Then locate this terrorist Thirio guy. Once that's all done, I'll not just consider losing weight, eating better, and bringing this blood pressure shit down, I'll consider retirement." He placed his hands on the large square calendar in the center of his desk and studied the room. His gaze moved from the pictures on the walls, the diplomas hung proudly, to the furniture, and finally stopped at Parkman. "I'm done, Parkman. I'm fucking done with all the bullshit."

"I was there once. In your chair. I left, too. Couldn't handle the bullshit." He tossed the toothpick back and forth with his tongue.

"I mean," Lee took a breath, "we had that Geoff Mantler thing years ago. Then the Barry Ashford shit. So many other incidents I can't even begin to explain. Now our superintendent has just retired. They're looking at choosing the next detachment commander for the Kelowna regional detachment. There's just so much going on inside the police force and not enough policing outside the force. It's ballooned to something unmanageable, and the people trying to manage it are being constantly sidelined and derailed. Our numbers are shooting through the roof. We're about to have the highest crime rate in years. It spiked in the last quarter by almost nine percent."

"Okay, listening to you is raising my blood pressure."

Lee swung his chair to face Parkman. "And what about the guy that died the other day? We're being investigated for that, too."

Lee needed to vent. He needed someone to listen to him. The man had to get it all out so he could release some of the weight on his shoulders.

"What guy?" Parkman asked, leaning forward, genuinely interested. A lot of people had died recently because of Thirio. Why was one particular case more special and in need of an investigation than another?

"My cops responded to a complaint of a male in need of medical assistance at the bus station. My guys, along with emergency health services, attended. The man died the next morning."

"What?"

"Yeah, and now we're being investigated to see if we're culpable in any way. We'd released the guy from custody just eight hours before he died."

"That's a full plate." Parkman relaxed back on the couch.

"A full plate? It doesn't stop there. Our city's on fire. Did you see in the papers what Kelowna Cabs did a few nights ago?"

Parkman shook his head and waited to be told.

"Driver picks up a fare—a man and a woman—after a night out. During the ride, the driver fidgets with his in-car computer and crosses the yellow line slightly. Later on, the driver allegedly does this again, but this time he drifts right over to the other side of the road before correcting it. Allegedly."

"Wow."

"Get this." Lee leaned forward. "The fare tells the driver he doesn't appreciate having his life risked while in his cab and could he just concentrate on the road. The cab driver gets upset. Fare orders the driver to call his boss. I'm not sure what happened after that except cuss words were exchanged —allegedly—and the fare tells the driver that he isn't going to pay for the ride because of the shit service."

"What did the cabbie do?" Parkman asked.

"He calls all his other drivers, and, I don't know, half a dozen yellow Kelowna cabs show up. The drivers all get out of their cars and stand there, arms crossed, staring the fare down. Intimidation or what? It's like two in the fucking morning. So the fare calls the police. My cop shows up, confirms multiple yellow Kelowna taxi vehicles at the incident, and quells things before they get out of hand."

"How was it resolved? Anyone arrested?"

"The fare was paid for the ride to avoid the escalation, and all the cab drivers left. I've got enough to worry about with cops like Mason and Calder and Barry Ashford without having to worry about the Kelowna taxi drivers intimidating their fares like a street gang or the fucking mafia." He raised his voice at the end of his speech.

"Okay, you're right. Maybe you need a drink. Something to calm down the blood—"

Lee's cell phone buzzed on his desk. He snatched it up. "What's up?" he barked. After a moment, Lee turned to Parkman. "Okay. Hold him. Don't let him go anywhere. That man leaves the building; you lose your job." He paused. "I don't fucking care," Lee shouted. "Cuff him if you have to."

Lee jabbed a finger at the phone as he jumped from his chair. "Let's go. Downstairs now."

"Why? Who's here?"

"A realtor." Lee half ran, half jogged for the door.

"Wait. What? A realtor?"

Lee stopped at the door as Parkman rose from the couch. "Apparently, he saw Sarah today. Then he was visited by two cops, Mason and Calder, who threatened him. He thought it best to report everything to the police so he was in the clear."

"And he's downstairs right now?" Parkman asked.

Lee started down the corridor. "In the flesh."

"Then what are we waiting for?" Parkman bolted past

Lee and hit the stairs running.

Chapter 35

SARAH HAD THE TAXI drop her off on a city street a mile from the Campbell Winery. She paid the driver and walked toward town. When the cab was out of sight, she turned around and headed back along Upper Mission Drive toward the Campbell Winery. Ten minutes later, she passed the Taste of Belgium Bed & Breakfast. Instead of continuing to Trumpeter Road, she stopped to consult a map on the cell phone. The forest service road leading to Kelowna Mountain was to her left, traversing behind the winery. There was a possibility she could access the winery from the back and have time to watch the place to see why it was so important.

She started up the sloped service road. The entire walk was uphill. After more than five minutes of puffing up the hill in the near dark with only the moon to guide her, she caught sight of a vehicle parked on the side of the road up ahead. Cautiously, she edged toward the black bulk in the dark until she could make out the size and make.

Thirio's truck. The one from the grocery store in Vernon.

She dropped down in case he'd been watching her approach. When she could tell no one was inside the vehicle, she moved closer until she leaned against the bumper. It struck her as ironic that she would use Thirio's truck to hide from him.

After several attempts to mentally summon Vivian proved fruitless, she waited a full five minutes without moving. She breathed in and out through an open mouth, barely maintaining a sound. Eyes closed, Sarah listened to the night. Crickets sounded close by. A frog croaked out a mating call. In the distance, a car backfired, followed by a screech of tires. Unless Thirio was also in hiding and waiting for her to lift her head, he wasn't close by, and she couldn't hide behind his truck all night.

She raised a hand above the truck's hood, then lowered it. When nothing happened, she raised her head higher, conscious of the notion that she might see that old man in the suit watching her. With Vivian gone, the other spirits had to be around, but when she stood up beside the truck, she was alone. The address to the Campbell Winery, supplied by her sister, directed her to where Thirio would be. Regardless of their communication issues recently, Vivian had been able to deliver her to the man behind all the turmoil in the city of Kelowna.

Sarah could end this tonight. Now she just had to find him.

As quietly as possible, she climbed a small rise on the other side of the ditch and started toward the rear of the winery. A building came into view up ahead. It was hard to see in the dark once she'd entered the trees, as the moon's limited light couldn't penetrate, but the house was easy enough to see because of its bulk. Sarah stopped behind the trunk of a blue spruce and watched the house. To her left, she could make out the lights of the main house in the distance. It was a large estate-like building with lights running along the roof's perimeter. Several windows were illuminated. A circular fountain with water rising from the outside and being cast toward the middle appeared to be in the front driveway.

Then what was the big building in front of her? It was too large to be a groundskeeper's house. Maybe it was a guesthouse, but that was a stretch because of its massive size. Maybe the Campbells were so rich they had built this place as a guesthouse, and since it was dark, no guests were visiting.

She moved from behind the blue spruce and started toward the dark house on her right. Something flickered by a basement window. She froze on the spot. The flicker came again. Someone was using a small light in the basement. Something told her it was Thirio. The BAE vest in place and her handcuffs open and dangling from a belt loop, Sarah pulled the gun from her waistband, kept her finger out of the trigger guard, and walked to the building.

She grew more certain that Thirio was in the basement with each step. When she was ten feet from the building, something moved on the house's front porch. Sarah dropped to her knees and raised the gun. When her eyes focused better, she saw the old man, her personal demon.

"What do you want?" she whispered.

He was doing that gesturing thing with his hands again. The one where she had to read the numbers. Nine, five, six, two, or something like that.

Back on her feet, her knees dampened by the moist ground, she continued forward, ignoring the old man as his image shimmered in the dark. It amazed her that she wasn't more frightened by him. If she hadn't seen him several times before in the daylight, if this was the first time they'd met, she probably would've shouted something or shot at him.

Taking easy steps to avoid creaks, she stepped onto the porch and put her back to the wall beside the front door.

After two calming breaths, Sarah pivoted, used the tip of the gun to push the front door open, and entered the Campbell Winery guesthouse foyer.

Chapter 36

Parkman bought a sandwich from a store across the street, then ran back inside the police station, where he snagged a coffee and observed his friend Lee in action. Lee got the man —Trever Florko—a coffee and offered one to Trever's wife, but she declined. Once everyone was seated inside one of the interview rooms, Lee eased into interrogation mode.

He took Trever's statement like the complaint it was, asked appropriate questions, then set his pen down. Parkman took the last bite of his sandwich, then popped a toothpick in his mouth.

"How threatened did you feel around Sarah, Mr. Florko?"

He looked at his wife, then down at his hands. "I didn't feel threatened." He met Lee's eyes. "I only felt threatened when those two cops came to my door."

"Those men will be dealt with," Lee said. "But first, I

have to ask, did you tell them about Trumpeter Road?"

"Yes. I told Sarah it was the road where the Campbell Winery was and told those cops that I'd sent Sarah there."

Lee tapped his pen as he glanced down at Trever's statement. "Okay, go home. Relax. I'll take care of this and ensure those cops don't bother you again. You've done nothing wrong. Although, the next time someone shows you a weapon, it would probably serve you well to tell us about it."

"I understand that now." Trever's wife wrapped an arm around his shoulder. "I just thought I'd recognized her, and when I learned it was Sarah Roberts, the same girl from the news, I was happy to've helped her."

"We know, Mr. Florko. It's okay." Lee got up from the table. "I've got your statement. I'll call those pesky cops back in here and give them a sensitivity training course myself."

"I sure appreciate that, Mr. Lee." Trever and his wife rose from their chairs. "We're free to go now?"

"Absolutely."

Lee opened the door and gestured for them to go ahead of him. Once outside, they shook hands, and the Florkos walked away.

"Parkman, be ready in five minutes."

He didn't have to ask but decided to anyway. "Be ready for what?"

"We're going to the Campbell's house."

"I hope you're bringing an army."

Lee turned back to Parkman. "Why's that?"

Parkman raised his hand and checked off finger after finger as he spoke. "You've got Sarah there. Thirio's probably there. Calder and Mason will be there, and who knows who else. The place will be crawling with trigger-happy idiots, and your biggest problem with whomever you take with you is that they may be firing on other cops."

"Got that covered. I'm bringing in an Emergency Task Force team. Men I know personally and have worked with for decades. This has escalated into a hostage situation, in my opinion. Get Sarah out alive and arrest anyone else on site." He started away. Over his shoulder, he said, "Or shoot to kill." At the elevator, he pushed the button, then looked back at Parkman. "I'm done with this shit." The door opened. "I'm fucking done." He disappeared inside the elevator.

Chapter 37

Sarah knelt in the corner of what was once the guesthouse's living room. She used the light from the screen of her cell phone to look around the room. It was mostly empty. A wooden chair sat tilted to the side in the far corner, one of its legs broken. Scraps of decaying paper and a discarded doll with one eye gouged out rested in the middle of the room. Wallpaper was in the act of removing itself from the walls, which only decades of disrepair could encourage. The building itself seemed intact as long as she stayed close to the walls. The wooden floor hadn't emitted more than one creak before she stopped to kneel and examine the room.

Something bumped below her. Whoever was downstairs —she was sure it was Thirio—was hard at work. Probably preparing another bomb or some toxic substance. Whatever he was working on didn't matter. He would never get to use it.

Sarah wore the BAE vest and was armed. The handcuffs were to tether him to her and take him to his truck before Mason and Calder showed up. Their investigation would lead them to the winery as she had told that realtor where she was headed.

She stared up at the dark ceiling, listening for her sister. The old man outside on the porch had blocked them again. Soon he would leave, and Vivian would return. With everything coming together so fast, she needed her sister close.

Sarah really needed to learn if Parkman ever got his suitcase back from the airport. If he did, everything would work out. The note she left him would save his life. She didn't want to think about the consequences if he didn't get his luggage.

After three slow, deep breaths, she rose from her crouch and advanced along the edge of the wall toward the main corridor. After several floor squeaks, she reached the door leading down to the basement.

Like a hunter in a blind, she stood soundlessly and waited. If the person downstairs had heard her advance, they would be waiting, too. The first person to make a noise would lose, and Sarah was prepared not to budge until morning.

A minute later, something thunked below her loud enough to be heard on the front porch. Thirio certainly wasn't concerned about noise.

She opened the basement door just far enough to squeeze through and gently stepped onto the first stair. Her heart was the loudest noise in the house now. It beat a rapid pulse throughout her body, drilling her ears with an incessant thrumming. She breathed quietly through her mouth and thought about her future. How long could someone handle this lifestyle, provided they lived long enough to examine the answer?

She touched the second stair with the softness of a feather, her weight easing onto the wooden step, pound by grueling pound. She held the gun in front of her, the handle covered in sweat. On the third stair, she changed hands, wiped her sweaty palm on her pants, then changed hands again. The fourth stair was low enough to bend over and glance into the basement, but there was no need at this point —the basement was pitch dark. She descended by feel alone. As much as the blackness was unnerving, it also settled her. If she couldn't see the perp in the basement, he couldn't see her.

She moved to the fifth step. What if Thirio had infrared goggles? Slightly bent at the waist, Sarah felt the wall beside her until her hand rounded the edge where the wall became the basement ceiling. She had descended the stairs far enough to be able to see the expanse of the basement with the benefit of light. Since the dark was impenetrable and the moonlight had no reign down here, she would have to continue down the stairs, move to a side wall, prepare her weapon, and turn on her cell's flashlight option.

It occurred to her she hadn't heard the person in the basement since that last sound several minutes ago. Waiting on the stairs to hear something from him would be ridiculous as she was too vulnerable. She needed to get to the bottom of the steps and move to relative safety until she could grasp what she was dealing with.

She eased down another step. Then another.

Someone moved close by. She froze, the grip on her weapon tightening, all her senses on alert. Was it a shuffle of clothing? Or maybe it was a footstep momentarily brushing the basement floor? How close was he to her?

Too vulnerable to remain where she was, Sarah moved to the next step, then the next. But there was nothing there. The stair wasn't where she expected it to be. Her balance lost, her ankle twisted under her weight, Sarah spun sideways as she pinwheeled her arms for balance. Emitting no noise while clenching her hands to avoid dropping the gun or the phone, she closed her eyes in the seconds it took to smash onto the basement floor.

Pain flared in her shoulder upon impact as the air was thrust from her lungs. If her approach to the basement could be considered mouse-like, then her fall was a lion's roar. Anyone would've easily heard the expelled air and the heavy thud on the concrete floor, even from upstairs. Some kind of film, probably dust, had billowed up and was descending back earthward to land on her face. She blinked her eyes in the dark, then closed them to keep the offending particles out. She rolled onto her back, slipped the gun away, and waited until her breathing got under control.

Something moved close by again. That same scuffling sound. Rodents? An animal?

She rolled to her good side, got a knee under her, and then got to her feet. She needed light. She needed to know what was down there with her. After one more deep breath to help manage the pain in her throbbing shoulder, Sarah flipped on her cell phone's flashlight.

When she glanced upward and raised the cell to illuminate her surroundings, Thirio stood beside her.

She let out a small yip.

"Good evening, Miss Roberts."

Thirio dove forward and, like a professional striker on any FIFA team, kicked Sarah in the side of the face. A flash of lightning entered her head, then all the light dimmed, and the basement's darkness enveloped her.

Chapter 38

Parkman waited in front of the police station, leaning against Lee's car. He'd had two coffees—wishing he'd had a small flask of whiskey to help with the stress of being away from Sarah for so long—while constantly checking his watch. Would Lee go to the Campbell Winery without him? Parkman was a civilian, and this was police work. Maybe Lee felt things had gone to where he couldn't keep Parkman on the case with him.

He pushed off Lee's car and started for the front door of the RCMP building just as the door opened and Lee ran outside holding a bulletproof vest.

"If you're coming with me, you're going to have to put this on," Lee said as he ran up to Parkman.

"What took you so long?" Parkman donned the vest over his collar shirt. The toothpick in his mouth nicked the edge of the vest and was ripped from his lips, falling end over end to the dirty, cracked sidewalk. "Shit," he muttered to himself.

Lee was already at his door. "Organizing this response team takes time. These guys are the best of the best."

"How many?" Parkman asked, already feeling naked without his pick. His last one lay on the sidewalk.

"Including you and me, six."

Parkman dropped into the passenger seat, waited for a heartbeat, then turned to Lee, who remained outside standing by his door. "You coming?"

Lee looked at Parkman through his open window. "Yeah. Just waiting on a guy."

"Where's the rest of the team?"

"Already en route. They'll meet us there."

Parkman waited—it seemed he was always waiting for Lee. They should have left an hour ago. The delay might put Sarah's life at risk.

"You coming?" Parkman shouted, agitation setting in. "We have to go. Don't wait for this guy any longer."

Lee leaned down again to look in at Parkman. "We have to. He was the one who retrieved your bag from the airport. Once he gets here, we go. When we have Sarah, I'm dropping both of you back at the airport and personally sending you both back home to Toronto. This ends tonight." He shook his head. "I can't have her death on my conscience."

"Your conscience? What about mine?"

Lee motioned with his finger. "Get in the back, Parkman. You're not here officially. We're calling this a ride-along, even though we stopped doing ride-alongs a while ago."

Parkman opened the door, left it open, and got in the back, leaving that door open as well.

Finally, after about a five-minute wait, a man in a jean jacket that barely fit him exited the building toting Parkman's and Sarah's bags as if they were small toys. The guy was a monster in denim. He was so large his pants probably had to be tailored because no men's store could clothe this guy off the rack.

"The brown one's mine," he shouted out the door.

"Put the red one in the trunk," Lee said. "Give Parkman the brown one."

Parkman grabbed his case from the monster of a man, placed it on the seat next to him, and closed the door. Once the cop was inside the car, Lee introduced him as Officer Mark Gossett. The guy's shoulders were so broad they were the width of the front seat he rested his back against. How long in the gym did it take to get that big?

Lee raced along Lakeshore Road, passing slow-moving vehicles when he could. A dash light strobed through the dark streets, but he kept the siren off.

Parkman opened his suitcase and rummaged around inside to locate the note Sarah told him to look for. He hoped the note wasn't time sensitive and it wasn't too late to do what she might have asked of him. The back seat was lit only by passing streetlights, but it was enough for him to find the small note.

"What's that?" Lee asked.

Parkman met Lee's eyes in the rearview mirror. "A note from Sarah."

"What'd she say? Anything about tonight?"

"It's all about tonight. Thirio has one more explosive device, and he's planning his final act tonight."

"Did she say where?"

The monster in the front passenger seat twisted around to look at Parkman, his face deadpan.

"Yeah. The Campbell Winery."

Lee smashed the steering wheel with his right hand. "Oh, my shit."

"What?" Officer Gossett said, his voice deeper than Parkman thought it would be. "We're heading to the bomb?"

"The Campbell family is rich," Lee said. "They've been in the Kelowna area since the 1800s." He met Parkman's eyes in the rearview again. "The Campbells own The Fast Way grocery store chain."

"So Thirio, whoever that is, has a thing for the Campbells."

"There's a group of people who hate the Campbells more than anyone else."

"Who?"

"The Martins. They own a winery next door to the Campbells. Those two families have been feuding for a century."

"If this is a family feud, why use bombs on strangers?" Parkman didn't buy it. "Why kill innocents?"

"As soon as we get there, we'll ask."

Lee got on the radio and ordered two available units to attend the Martin Winery and detain all persons at their home until he could arrive to question them.

"This ends tonight, Parkman," Lee shouted to be heard over the dispatcher's voice on the car's radio. "All of it."

Parkman looked down at the note. He reread the rest of what Sarah had written for him—the part that he didn't tell Lee. The part about locating the blue spruce tree and how vital that was. He also read the part about Officer Mason's and Officer Calder's death, just like Sarah predicted back at the airport, which seemed a lifetime ago.

Why didn't people ever listen to Sarah?

Chapter 39

Mason ordered Calder to stop a hundred yards from the front driveway of the Campbell Winery's main house. Calder pulled over and killed the lights and the engine.

"Why stop here?" Calder asked.

Mason stared out the windshield at the large family residence up ahead on the hill. The Campbells were one of the richest families in the city. They owned grocery store chains, two booths at the Kelowna farmer's market, and sold wines known around the world. That didn't include their philanthropy and the charity work they performed.

"We have to assume Sarah's already here. I'll work my way to the side of the house and cover you while you knock at the front door. We explain who Sarah is and that we have reason to believe this fugitive is coming to their home."

"This approach makes me think we're afraid."

"Fuck you," Mason said. "This approach is sane and

keeps us alive. Sarah's fuckin' nuts."

"Okay. We'll do it your way. But just look at all those windows."

Mason stared up past the large circular fountain in the middle of the driveway. The front of the house had at least twenty windows. At least half of them were lit up, with the large window in the middle illuminated by a huge chandelier.

"You think Sarah's in there with all those lights on?" Calder asked. "And what would she be doing here, anyway?"

"You're not paying attention, Calder." Mason tapped the side of his head with his knuckles. "Sarah's a fraud. She shows up in Kelowna and kills Barry Ashford way back when. She comes back to Kelowna and does this to me." He raised his cast, then set it back down gently. "She's after the Campbells for one reason, and that has got to be money. She's a crook, and she's here to steal from them. Somehow, she's here for the money. I just know it." He shrugged. "Maybe she's offering some sort of psychic bullshit reading or something, and because she can leverage the fact that she works with the police, she's making a killing. Who knows?" He wiped his nose gingerly, making sure not to bump it. "All I know is that the Campbells are a great target for someone like Sarah." He turned to Calder. "How do we know? She was probably behind this whole thing from the start. She could've set these plans in motion when she was here the last time. All she has to do is show up, and the bombings stop. Sarah looks like a hero." He snapped his fingers. "How else does she know where the bombs will go off if this isn't her doing?" He raised his voice. "She's the criminal here. This terror assault on our city is her doing. When we break this case, they'll give us fucking medals."

"Medals?" Calder asked, the skeptical look on his face told Mason everything he needed to know about how Calder understood how things worked.

"Fuck you. Twice." He cracked open his door, then shut it. "Kill the interior light, you ass."

Calder adjusted the dial on the dash.

Mason opened the door, twisted in his seat to place his legs on the ground, then pushed up and out of the car.

"Let's go," he said. "You knock on the door. I'll be watching your back."

Calder got out and started up the street toward the house without saying a word. In another world, at another time, Mason would have drawn his weapon and shot Calder. He couldn't believe the asshole had no imagination and couldn't figure these things out on his own. Questioning Mason's brilliant logic wasn't just disrespectful, it was revealing. It revealed who Calder really was, how much he trusted and believed in Mason, and to what length he was willing to go for Mason.

In other words, Calder was just here because he didn't want to deal with Mason if he chose the alternative. Calder wasn't here because he was after Sarah Roberts or trying to right a wrong. However tonight played out, Mason understood Calder's heart wasn't in it.

He was deadweight, and Mason wouldn't carry him after tonight. In fact, Mason had grown to hate Calder. If bullets started to fly and people started to die, Mason would ensure Calder went first and not the other way around. There was no way Mason was dying for that piece of shit. Not with that attitude.

As Mason traversed the lawn toward the side of the

house, he whispered under his breath, "This is the big time, baby. We stand side by side or not at all."

When he got in position, he signaled for Calder to knock on the front door. Calder raised his hand, but before he could knock, the door opened. Calder stepped back. "Mr. Campbell," he muttered in surprise.

"What are you two cops doing running around my property?" James, the Campbell Patriarch, asked Calder.

"Two cops?" Calder said. He sounded surprised.

James stepped out past Calder and pointed at Mason. "You there. Hiding in the shrubs at the side of the house. Come on out. I watched you both on camera since you left your car down the road." James Campbell moved to the edge of the porch. From his position by the side of the house, Mason could barely make out the brown corduroy pants and the checked shirt in the porch light. "You want to come up to the front porch here to join your partner and explain what's going on?"

Mason stepped out from behind the bush and started for the porch. It was likely Sarah wasn't here yet. But it also presented great possibilities. If Mr. Campbell had that kind of security detail, they'd be able to watch from inside the house as Sarah approached. The arrest would be simple. They could drive away and be done with her before morning.

Mason grinned as he ascended the Campbell's front steps. It was going to be a fine evening after all.

Chapter 40

Something bit into her side. Something pulled her arm. She was being dragged. The rough concrete floor scraped her skin near her right hip. Her shoulder, which took the brunt of the hit on the basement floor when she stumbled from the stairs, felt like it had been set on fire.

She tried to pull away from her captor, but the effort was weak. The man mumbled something like *meddling* or *bitch* to himself as he tightened his grip. She twisted just enough to stop the floor from scraping her hip.

She shook her head, but it didn't make things any clearer. Did she have a concussion? How often had she been hit— even shot in the head—and came out of it quickly? Maybe that was the problem: a head can only take so many hits before the skull decides it's had enough.

The man released her arm suddenly. A groan escaped her lips. She tried to curl into a ball to see if she would feel the gun in her waistband. She did. It was still there. The handcuffs were tucked snuggly by her leg, still clinging to her belt loop. He hadn't searched her nor relieved her of the weapon. That would cost him.

She slipped a hand along her side as the man busied himself with something behind her.

"Sarah Roberts," he said. "We meet again."

Thirio. Her hand hesitated a moment. That voice. From the grocery store.

"You know," he continued, "I don't hate you." He moved behind her and adjusted something. "I don't like you, but I don't hate you." His voice strained as he dragged something across the floor. She moved her hand again. This time her fingertips made contact with the butt of the weapon. "In fact, I don't *like* anyone. Wait!" He raised his voice. Her hand stopped as it settled over the weapon. "Tonight is called My Denouement. So I would like to formally welcome you to witness the final act."

The very second she squeezed the butt of the weapon and began to withdraw it from her waistband, he gripped under her shoulders and yanked her upward. The gun tumbled from her hand, bounced once on the concrete floor, and was kicked aside when she scrambled to regain balance.

"Shit," she stammered, then grunted with the strain of being manhandled.

He let go of her when she was almost upright. A brief moment of panic swept over her as she fell backward, but then she landed safely on a plush armchair.

He stepped in close and jammed his face an inch from hers. "Don't move," he shouted. "You're sitting on a bomb."

Sarah gasped and reached under her legs to feel around

the cushion.

He eased away about a foot from her. "It's like in a minefield. A landmine. Your ass depressed the Belleville spring. Stand, and you release the firing pin that was forced down into the detonator when your ass activated the mine. One second later, my Bouncing Betty rises to its glorious conclusion." He stood up and shone the light on his face. "Well, I think you get the picture."

The cobwebs in her head dissipated rather quickly. "Bouncing Betty?" she asked, leaning back on the chair and trying not to move her butt.

"They're referred to as a Bouncing Betty. It's simple. The ignitor sets off a propelling charge. This lifts the mine out of the chair about a meter high. The main charge then ignites, causing severe damage to the chest and head of anyone close by." He slapped his hands together, apparently not thinking about what would happen to him if Sarah fainted and slipped off the chair. "My Bouncing Betty is an anti-personnel mine, modified in several ways, one of which is fragmentation."

Sweat had beaded on her forehead and ran down the center of her back. How the hell was she supposed to walk away from this if she couldn't even get off the chair?

"I'll bite," she said. Better to keep him talking so she could keep thinking. "Fragmentation?"

"Think shrapnel. I've added shards of metal and glass to this lovely piece of art under your pretty little ass, so when it launches into the air, it shoots out that shit and injures people at a distance of two hundred meters. Basically kills everyone around." He raised his arms outward and twisted his upper body back and forth. "Look around. We're in a basement. The windows will be blown out, but the basement interior will take most of the fragmentation." With one index finger raised to make a point, he continued, "But whosoever happens to be in the basement will never make it upstairs."

"Thirio?" Sarah whispered.

He stopped the histrionics and stood to his full height. "What?"

"Do you want to die?"

"Of course I do." He grinned.

Insanity had many names and many faces. If Sarah could ever compile a picture book of smiles from all the madmen she'd dealt with in her lifetime, Thirio's grin would look the most insane. Even Charles Manson smiling would look like a loving father watching his children play in the park on a Sunday afternoon compared to Thirio's level of insanity.

"But I don't want to die yet," Thirio added, that incessant finger raised to make a point. "Not yet. Must have the Campbells here first." He stuttered something under his breath. "Did you bring someone with you?"

Sarah didn't answer him. After several heartbeats, Thirio peered at her sideways. He grinned that I'm-insane-and-I-love-it smile again. A body shiver jolted her. She tensed and waited for the bomb to propel upward, but nothing happened.

"I saw that," he whispered as if it was their little secret. "Don't worry. You're what, a hundred and twenty pounds wet?"

"You should never ask a girl her weight, but I'm one hundred thirty-one. Wet."

"Right. Well, for this device to kill us both, you must take all your weight off it." He held up his cell phone. On the screen, a window appeared with six slots where a code could be added. "I have set several seconds' delay in case I accidentally triggered the device while working on it. The code entered into this phone sends a signal to cancel the explosion." He lowered the phone and slipped it into his pocket. "It acts like a delay element burning for a moment, then igniting. In this case, the code deactivates the burning phase and renders the bomb a dud, momentarily." He rolled his hand in circles. "That only happens once, though. The next person who sits on the donut-shaped Belleville spring will die instantly upon standing."

"Type in the six-digit code," Sarah said, her voice cool, even. She blinked sweat from her right eye, glaring at him. Her moist hands gripped the armrests of the chair.

"Now, why would I do that?" he asked. "You don't want to die, Sarah. I get it. But I do." That raised finger again was maddening. "So don't get up from the chair until I return."

"Where are you going?"

"To have the Campbell family join us down here."

"Then what?"

"Then I want your soul."

"My soul?" She frowned. "What the fuck are you talking about?"

"I want your soul before I die. Offer that to me, and I'll let you live."

"How do you propose I offer you my soul?"

Thirio moved to the right, dangerously close to the fallen gun, pivoted, and walked to her left. As he paced, he wagged that damned finger.

"When I return with the Campbell family, I will type in the code and deactivate the mine. You will stand from the chair and have your life. Then you will persuade Mr. James Campbell—or force him—it makes no difference to me to have a seat in the chair. Once you've completed that, you are free to leave. Mr. Campbell and I will have a talk about all the bad things he's done in his life. This isn't atonement. This is a gift to Lucifer, my God. Don't worry. You'll have plenty of time to leave the building. I have much to say to the asshole Campbell patriarch." Thirio skipped two steps, spun around, and hopped once. "Don't you think this is a damned good idea?" He laughed like Sheri Moon Zombie laughed in *The Devil's Rejects*, that high-pitched giggle. "Get it? *Damned* good idea?"

"You want me to be complicit in murder so I can live, which forfeits my soul to you?"

"Correct."

"And how exactly do you propose to take my soul when you will be dead and I will be alive?" She pulled her hands closer to her chest. Not a word from Vivian came in Sarah's time of need. For some reason, the pattern had been to see someone from the other side, and Vivian got blocked afterward for what seemed like forever.

"Sarah," he whispered. "You fail to see my objective. I'm surprised by that."

"Isn't your objective to randomly kill as many people as you can without regard? To hurt, poison, and maim as many people as possible until caught. Basically, your objective has been to be an asshole who's fucked in the head and deserves nothing better than a plush-lined coffin under six feet of dirt."

"Oh, Sarah." He smiled wickedly. "You and I will make quite a pair when we arrive home to our master."

"I don't have a master. Only the mad do. It's called delusion, and they follow that until it takes them to a rubber room or a coffin."

"No, Sarah, you've got a master. He's the prettiest angel. Man, wait until you see his wings. They're glorious." Thirio thrust out his arms and flapped his hands. "Lucifer, my Lord, is who I'm collecting souls for. And the Campbell family are the last souls, other than yours, that I'm here to take."

"Sorry to burst that bubble, but there's no such thing as the devil. He's what we decide he is. The pain and suffering we cause each other on this plane. You're delusional, just like the rest of the insane people ranting about religion and then killing others because they won't conform. Trust me. I have the information from a qualified source. There is no Lucifer. He's a fable perpetrated on people before the days of a regular police force. Organized religion isn't needed in our world anymore. That's why it's fighting to stick around. You're a dying breed whether you're Christian, atheist, agnostic, or a Satanist."

Her hands were on the chair's armrests now, elbows thrust outward. She was ready and hoped her idea would work. If it didn't, she would be shredded by Thirio's fragmentation device.

"Thirio's not even my real name." He spoke as if he hadn't heard a word she said. "My Christian name," he slapped his hands together and guffawed. "Isn't that a riot? Christian name?" He turned back to her. "My given name was Leonard Martin. But when I killed myself—well, my twin brother, actually—I renamed myself Thirio. Do you want to know why, Sarah?"

"No, I don't." She was almost ready.

"Thirio is the Greek word for beast. That's what I am, am I not? A beast?"

"I'd agree. You're a beast."

"I'm a beast and want to hasten my arrival in Hell."

"How about without the Campbells?" Sarah asked. "You could die right now."

He stopped moving and glared at her. His eyes lowered to her legs, then back to her face. "You wouldn't stand up. You'd die, too."

She shrugged. "Do I care?"

He stepped closer. "Sarah, stay seated."

"And if I don't?"

He moved even closer. "But you have to. No one wants to die, and this isn't over. I need the Campbells in here first."

"I want to die, Thirio," she said, her voice gravelly and hoarse.

"Wait." He moved within distance.

Sarah jerked upward, trying to keep a modicum of weight on the device below the seat of her pants.

Thirio acted as she suspected he would. His hands rammed down on her shoulders to force her back into the chair. Deftly, with years of practice in close-quarters combat, Sarah snatched the handcuffs off her belt loop, flipped one of the cuffs up, and jammed it onto Thirio's wrist. The cuff's loop closed, flipped around itself, and came back down over his wrist, locking it in place. By the time it clicked, she was already affixing the other cuff to her wrist. In seconds, they were cuffed together.

Thirio gasped and tried to pull away but only succeeded in yanking Sarah's arm upward.

"Go ahead," she screamed. "Pull me right off this chair. We'll see who wants to die then."

"Oh, Sarah," he cried. "Why did you do this? You've ruined everything."

"Punch in the deactivation code on that phone, and we'll both go to my car, where I've got the keys."

He shook his head back and forth. "No, no, no. Can't do that."

He raised his index finger and was about to say more when she yanked him toward her. He teetered off balance, then dropped to one knee in front of her. She drove her left hand, open-palmed, into the tip of his nose. Thirio's head shot back. Before he fell, she slipped her fingers into his hair, yanked his head downward, and shot her knee up at the same time. Head met knee, and then his face jerked away from her.

He fell to the floor beside the chair, pulling on her cuffed wrist until her arm dangled off the side of the chair. His eyes rolled back in his head, and Thirio's lights dimmed. Until Vivian appeared, Sarah would sit on the plush armchair and wait. Vivian would know the deactivation code.

She had better know the code. Or Sarah would die in an armchair. Not a very fitting way to go.

Chapter 41

Mason stayed by the front door. "Who else is in the house, Mr. Campbell?" he asked.

Calder had provided James Campbell with his police ID as he moved deeper into the foyer to inspect the kitchen to the right and the living room to the left. Calder turned back to Mason as Campbell watched the two of them.

"You want to explain this intrusion," Mr. Campbell said. "Am I to believe that I have prowlers on my property? Is that why you two approached in stealth? Or are you the prowlers?"

"There is no cause for alarm," Mason said. "Yet," he added. He wished his voice was less nasally and more authoritative. "We are hunting a suspect in a series of murders."

Calder shot him a hard glance, his face skewed in confusion. When Campbell turned to Calder, his face relaxed instantly.

"Hunting a suspect?" Campbell said. "As in one?"

Mason moved closer to Campbell. "Show us your security screens. Where do you monitor your property from?" If Sarah were already inside the house, she would have tasked Campbell to get rid of them. Mason waited for Campbell's response to gauge whether or not Sarah was there.

"Gentlemen, it's late." Campbell waved his hands toward the door. "I bid you farewell. I must head to bed soon."

Mason edged up intimidatingly close to Campbell. "You need to understand this fugitive is quite dangerous, and we have reason to believe she was heading to this address. Or is she already here?"

James Campbell took a step back and bumped the wall.

"There is no woman here." He spat the words. "I'm alone."

"If you would be so kind as to show us your surveillance room," Mason said. "Then we'll be on our way."

Campbell's lips compressed into a white slash. He opened his mouth to say something, then closed it again. Mason and Calder shared a look. Sarah had to be inside the house. Campbell was stalling to concoct a plan to get them out of the house.

Finally, Campbell released a heavy sigh, then gave an I-give-up gesture.

"Follow me," Campbell said, then stomped away.

Mason and Calder stepped in behind him, shoulder to shoulder, slowing at each doorway before crossing it. If Sarah lurked behind a door, neither one wanted to be surprised by her.

"After this one courtesy, I want you both to leave."

"We will," Calder said. "We'll watch for the fugitive from outside the house."

"The fugitive, the fugitive," Campbell rambled on in front of them. "Who is this sought-after female? That Sarah Roberts girl?" Mason and Calder stopped. Campbell slowed, then stopped outside a small door that led to a darkened room. "What, you don't think I watch the news? Sarah Roberts saved a lot of people from the coffee shop bomb. It was all over the news. I remember what happened to that double-dealing cop when Sarah was here the last time. Everyone knows."

Mason was too stunned to respond. Calder stepped forward. "The security room, sir."

"In here." Campbell pointed to the darkened room.

"After you," Calder said.

Campbell disappeared inside, and Calder followed him. Mason stood in the doorway where he could watch what the old man was showing his partner but still keep an eye on the corridor in case Sarah popped out of a doorway.

"These twelve screens access our three quad camera systems," Campbell explained. "Every square inch of the house's perimeter is monitored for motion. If a camera is off, there's no motion. Detectors are set to roughly fifty pounds so rabbits, small coyotes, and rodents don't activate the system."

Campbell glanced back at Mason, a cold expression on his face.

"You two showed up on this camera," he pointed, "when the car stopped. As you both approached the house, this camera and this one triggered your movements and recorded everything. Time and date stamped it as well."

"Erasable?" Mason asked.

"Everything's erasable," Campbell responded. "As you can see, no fugitive has been within one-hundred meters of my property this evening except you two."

The suggestion that Mason and Calder were fugitives wasn't lost on Mason. James Campbell was an old man from another era. He was not just well-known in the city; he was something of a celebrity. The kind of man with lawyers on call and the money to spend years in court without worry. Basically, he felt above the law because he could slime his way out of anything. A car accident gone awry? A large cheque could make it go away. A criminal lawsuit? Nothing a team of lawyers and a smear campaign wouldn't remedy. In other words, he was the kind of man Mason detested. He vowed to himself when this was over that he would make a point of harassing Mr. Campbell for several years. The man deserved humble pie, and who better to serve it to him than his friendly RCMP officer?

Mason was convinced that Campbell had a preconceived notion of who they were because of Sarah Roberts. She had to be in the house. Who else could fill his noggin with such bullshit about what happened with Barry Ashford.

Mason believed Sarah was close. He just needed to be more persuasive with Mr. Campbell.

"Where is she?" He asked from the doorway. "Once we know, we will remove her from the premises, and you can go on with your evening as if we weren't here." *And erase any digital evidence of our presence*, Mason thought but didn't say.

"Where is whom?" Campbell asked. He stood ramrod

straight and glared hard at Mason. "I presume you're referring to the supposed fugitive."

"Just tell us where she is, Campbell. Asking more than once makes you an accomplice in her actions. Aiding and abetting won't bode well for the family name."

"Excuse me, young man," Campbell bellowed, his voice amplified by the small room. "I am not aiding or abetting anyone, and I resent the notion and the charge of such lunacy. I don't have time for this. Please leave my home." He started forward. "I've done as you asked. Now get out."

Mason didn't budge from the doorway. "Stand where you are, Campbell."

The man froze one foot in front of Mason. "What is the meaning of this?"

"Yeah, Mason," Calder whispered from the security console area. "What's up?"

"Sarah is in this house, and Mr. Campbell wants us to leave." He focused on Campbell's eyes, studying the man closely. "Is it sanctuary you're offering her? Or do the young woman's attributes enamor you?"

"All right," Campbell roared. "That's enough. Out. Or I'll have my lawyers remove that filthy badge of yours—"

"Don't threaten me," Mason out-shouted Campbell. The violence of his rage irritated the nose injury. His eyes watered from the pain. "Remain in the room and calm down. No one is leaving."

"How dare you," Campbell said, his cheeks flush with redness. He looked at Calder. "You're going to let this man order me around?"

Calder shrugged nonchalantly as if this was a daily activity. Mason knew he would never challenge him.

Calder spoke next. "My partner and I have it on good authority, from multiple sources, that Sarah Roberts is either here or on her way to this location. If what you're saying is correct and she is not here, you have nothing to worry about. We wait, monitor your cameras and watch for her. But if she's already here, Mr. Campbell, hiding in this house right now." Calder looked down and shook his head. "Well, dealing with Mason will be the least of your worries."

"You're going to threaten me in my house, too? You're both finished when I'm done with you."

Old men like Campbell were a nuisance. They'd lived their lives, served their purpose. It was a new generation now, and James Campbell could die and take his old boys club with him. He was something even the world knew was to be discarded.

"Sit the fuck down," Mason bellowed. "And shut up. I'm tired of your yapping mouth." Mason moved into the room, forcing Campbell back toward the chair by the console.

Spry for an old man, he grabbed the elbow of Mason's cast, pushed it upward, and slipped around him, heading for the door. The pain in his broken arm shot through his shoulder and fired rockets off in his head. Even his knees wanted to give up holding him upright, but he fought the urge to drop. With his good hand, he clamped onto Campbell's collar. His hand tightened into a vise grip and yanked downward. Mr. Campbell lost his balance and stumbled back, but Mason had pulled too hard for Campbell to stay on his feet. The old man hit the floor with his buttocks first, then his shoulders. The air whooshed out of him along with a low-grade moan, the kind that signaled defeat and despair. Sprawled out on the floor, the old man stared wide-eyed up at the ceiling, breathing in and out in quick gasps.

"What the hell did you do that for?" Calder asked, kneeling to check on Campbell.

Mason stepped over the prone body of the old man and stood by the dozen security cameras. "Because he's helping Sarah, and he assaulted me." He tapped several keys to move the cameras and familiarize himself with the system. "Self-defense, Calder. Self-defense."

Calder rose to his feet and stood beside him. "You better hope you're right."

"Oh, I'm right, my friend, I'm right." He tapped several keys again. "Help me bring up the last two hours on this thing. I want to see when Sarah approached the house and where she entered. Then we'll have our proof."

Calder took a seat and got to work. Mason turned around to look at Campbell on the floor. The man's eyes were closed, and his mouth formed a circle as he breathed rapidly.

"You should've tried to help us, old man, instead of fucking around. We're the RCMP. How come people don't get it? We're here to help."

"Uh, Mason," Calder said.

"What?"

"I think we've got a problem."

Mason spun around and stared at the camera Calder was pointing at. Two unmarked cruisers and two police SUVs had just pulled up behind their vehicle. The vehicles paused a moment, window to window, then one cruiser and the two SUVs moved out of camera range, headlights extinguished.

"What's up the street?" Mason asked.

"It's a dead end. The Martin Family Winery is the next stop, then that's it."

He looked at Calder. "Could Sarah be up there?"

Calder shrugged. "No idea."

They watched as men slipped out of the unmarked cruiser by their car and disappeared from view.

"Did we lock the front door?" Mason asked.

Calder shook his head.

"Shit," Mason said and ran out of the room.

Chapter 42

Lee stopped behind a car parked on the side of the road. The other vehicles slowed in response to his stopping.

"That's Mason and Calder's car, isn't it?" Lee asked.

Gossett nodded. "I can confirm that, sir."

Lee radioed the other vehicles and told them to carry on toward the Martin Winery, park out of sight, then double back and surround the Campbell house. Possible rogue officers inside the house.

The other vehicles disappeared up the road in the dark, their headlights off.

"Stay low," Lee said. "I'll take the lead. Gossett, move to the right of the house. Parkman, move to the left. Flank the front. Then follow my lead. Got it?"

"Yes, sir," Gossett barked under his breath.

"Gun?" Parkman asked.

Lee reached over the seat and dangled one in front of

him. "Don't kill anyone with it unless you have to."

"Awww." Parkman grabbed the gun, then checked the chamber. "You're no fun." He pulled the door open a few feet, then slipped out. Gossett moved around him in a crouch, then ran across the road toward the darkness in the bushes that led to the front. Parkman followed with Sarah on his mind. What would her boyfriend Aaron say if something happened to her? Scratch that—how could Parkman live with himself if something happened to her?

At the side of the house, he lost sight of Gossett. Oh, to be young, strong, and agile again. Lee strode to the front windows, which were lit up by an overhead chandelier just inside the foyer. He cupped his hands and peeked inside.

"All clear," he whispered loud enough for Parkman to hear.

Parkman adjusted himself to have a better view of Lee and the door as his friend started up the front steps. Lee hesitated, taking one last look to either side, then rapped on the door.

They waited. No one came to answer.

Parkman looked behind him, toward the street, then back at Lee. Where was everybody? If Mason and Calder were inside, why wasn't someone coming to the door?

A flashing light caught Parkman's eye. He glanced upward and stared at the black dome of a camera by the roof's edge, a tiny green light blinking on its rim. The camera moved as he watched it. He followed the roof's edge along the eavestrough and spotted three more cameras. Someone was inside the house watching their every move.

"Lee?" he shouted loud enough to be heard.

"Shh," Lee whispered back, a finger in front of his lips.

Parkman moved out of hiding and pointed above Lee's head to the roof's edge sixteen feet up. "They already know we're here."

Lee looked up, stomped his feet in exasperation, then hammered on the front door.

"Officer Tom Mason," Lee shouted at the door. "Officer Jeff Calder. Open up. This is the police."

Chapter 43

"Mason," Calder said, cracking his knuckles. "Decision time. It isn't too late to walk away from this."

Mason spun on him and glared the smug look off Calder's face. "Your head is so far up your ass you have no idea what's going on, do you?"

"What?" Calder stammered.

"Those officers were at my hospital room to hold me on attempted murder charges. Lee thinks we're after this little pet psychic of his, and he would be right. When this is over, we'll have an inquest, and we'll tell our story, and Sarah won't be around to tell hers. That's how this ends. Until then, it's always too late to walk away from this. It was too late the moment you *helped* me get out of that hospital."

Calder stopped cracking his knuckles. His eyes wandered from Mr. Campbell on the floor, then back to Mason. "What now?"

"We leave through the rear door before Lee's friends surround the house. If Sarah's somewhere in this house, we'll have to come for her another day because it'll take too long to search the place. If she isn't here, we leave via the forest road at the back of this property and continue hunting her until we find her."

Lee smashed the front door again. "Open up," Lee shouted through the door, muffled.

Calder exited the room and turned toward the back of the house. Mason stepped over Campbell and followed him along the corridor. He only hoped they weren't too late and the house wasn't surrounded yet. Sarah would win if they were stopped now; he could never allow that.

He pulled his weapon as he stepped onto the Campbell's back porch. The safety was off as he hit the grass, running toward the row of bushes, Calder slightly ahead of him.

As Mason rounded a row of hedges in the almost complete darkness, something moved to his right. He dropped low, swung his gun around, and fired at what looked like Sarah Roberts. The person who startled him was no more than three feet away. That was close enough in the dim light from the moon to see the person's hair jerk upward as the bullet exited the back of their head. The ground under Mason's feet trembled slightly as the body one meter away thudded to the ground.

"What the fuck?" Calder hissed, his voice high, girly-like as it escaped his mouth.

"I got her, man," Mason breathed. "Sarah Roberts is fuckin' dead. It's over, Calder." He dropped to his knees beside the corpse. "Finally."

Chapter 44

Thirio—née Leonard—mumbled something to himself as he came to. While he was passed out at her feet, Sarah had retrieved the cell phone from his pocket. For whatever reason, the phone had no signal. She couldn't call for help, text anyone, or even get it off the screen where six missing digits waited to be entered. The gun sat on the basement floor just out of reach. The BAE vest over her vital organs warmed her like a sauna in the basement. Her face ached and throbbed where she'd been kicked earlier, and her wrist had numbed where it was now attached to Thirio.

Something like a firecracker popped outside. Did someone fire a gun? The sound came once, then faded and didn't repeat.

She leaned over the edge of the chair and looked down at Thirio in the faint gleam from the penlight left unattended two feet in front of her.

"Wake up, asshole," she said. "We need to talk."

"Huh?" he mumbled.

"What's the code?" she whispered. "Tell me the code. We need to get out of here."

"Fuck you."

"Tell me about the Campbells. Why do you hate them so much?" She watched the small basement window where the moon gave it a rectangular shape.

"Feud. Longstanding."

"What kind of feud?"

"The kind where you fight. Dense much?"

"Fuck you. I mean, what caused it?"

"Originally? Or now?"

"Both." Her eyes didn't leave the window. Someone was out there; she was sure of it.

"Originally, a land dispute. In the winery business, land is gold. Grapevines are gold." He swiveled beside the chair until he was sitting cross-legged. Thirio rubbed his head where Sarah had clocked him. "This sucks, Sarah. Why'd you hit me? Now we both die, and it's all been for nothing. I *have* to kill James Campbell." He held up their cuffed wrists. "You've ruined everything."

"Why the current feud? You didn't finish."

"Because they killed my Julia."

The discarded penlight offered enough glow for her to see his face easily. "Julia? Who's that? Your sister?"

"We were going to get married."

"What happened?" She would stall him until Vivian showed up with the six digits for the phone. *Come on, Vivian. Where are you?*

"They killed her at her bridal party."

That sparked Sarah's interest. She faced him. "How'd they do that?"

"By crashing it. The girls had gone downtown, and we headed to a pub for a final round of shots. A couple of Campbell's sons were driving downtown and saw Julia. They recognized her. It was raining that night. At the red light, the Campbells sat in their car and waited for Julia and her girlfriends to walk by. When Julia was in front of their car, Harris Campbell hit the gas, then immediately hit the brake. The car hopped forward several feet. Dwayne, his brother, said it was meant only to scare the girls. A prank. A joke."

"How does that kill someone?"

"The car went close enough to bump Julia. She fell down and hit her head. She never woke up."

"So it was an accident." Sarah leaned forward in the chair to look down at Thirio. "That caused you to bomb innocent people and spread poison on vegetables in grocery stores? That's quite a leap from a family feud."

"There's no leap." He tugged on the cuff, examined its link, then released it. "The feud has been going on too long. What Dwayne and Harris did wasn't a joke. Someone had to end it."

"And you thought killing innocents would end it?" Sarah asked, her voice rising as she spoke. "That's a stretch even I can't connect."

"The bombs were random, but they would lead back here. When this house blew with that bomb under you, James Campbell was supposed to die with it. Over there," Thirio pointed off into the darkness to another part of the basement, "is a workbench and table where I've left all the bomb-making materials. Everything would link back to the

Campbells, and it would be over. Their name would be ruined and their businesses destroyed. My family would win in Julia's honor."

"You don't sound like a Satanist when you talk about Julia. You loved once. Satanism isn't synonymous with love."

He fixed her with a cold stare. "Sure, I'll admit that I loved once. But if I have a heart anymore, it's as black as tar and as empty as a nun's dried-up snatch."

"You've never been good with similes, have you?"

"Fuck you, Sarah, and unlock these things." He pulled on the cuffs again. "You're a renegade. You're a maverick. Too fucked for your own good. How are you not dead yet?"

"There's a little *go fuck yourself* in everything I do. Keeps me breathing." She adjusted herself as the BAE vest started to dig into her right side. "Who'd you kill first? How'd it make you feel?"

"I killed my brother." He swallowed as if the thought of it bothered him. "It made me feel really good. Now, open these damn things." He raised his cuffed hand.

"Why kill your brother?"

"Because he wanted to stop me. Once I talked to my one true god, Lucifer, the plan was revealed to me. With my brother dead, I could disappear and exact my revenge plan. Killing him was my test. Kill my own flesh, and I could kill anyone I wanted without remorse. It worked."

She frowned. "That doesn't make sense. Why not just disappear? Why'd your brother have to die?"

"He was my identical twin. When the family performed the positive ID at the morgue, they'd think it was me. Helps a man disappear."

"Skeptically, I have to ask why they wouldn't be looking for him?"

"Wait a second. I thought you were some kind of psychic. How come you don't know any of this, and yet you showed up here?"

"I'm not psychic. My dead sister tells me things once in a while. That's it. Sometimes those things are about bad people like you." She smiled crookedly. "That's how I showed up here. She gave me the name Trumpeter Road. So tell me, why wouldn't everyone be looking for the twin brother?"

"Because he left a decade ago and has been living in Italy. For many years, he was incommunicado. When he called to come to attend the funeral, he spoke only to me. I picked him up at the airport. He helped me for several hours, and I told him what I wanted to do. When he told me I couldn't complete the plan, I killed him and dumped his body. It was genius. Everything worked flawlessly until now." He pulled the cuffs, his hand in the air. "Unlock this, and let me finish what I started."

"I'll make you a deal." Sarah held up the cell phone. "Give me the six-digit deactivation code. I'll stand up and unlock the cuffs. Then you do what you have to do, and I'll do what I have to do."

"No way. You're fast. You're strong. I can't fight you. I'll never let you out of that chair." His face scrunched up. "Wait a second. Earlier, you said the cuff's keys were in your car."

"I lied." She sat back and let her head rest on the chair. "Then we die together."

"No," he yelled.

"Then give me the six-digit code."

"Never."

"Who's the sharpshooter?"

"Sharpshooter?" he asked. A smirk widened his mouth, showing teeth. "Oh, you mean the glassy-winged sharpshooters."

"The what?"

"Little bugs that fuck up a winery by spreading a disease in the vines."

Sarah sat up and focused on him. There was no *sniper* in her future. She hadn't needed the BAE vest after all. She sure wished the messages could evolve over time to be a tad more specific.

"What kind of disease?" she asked.

"It's called Pierce's Disease. The sharpshooter feeds on the vegetation at the winery. They inject the bacterium, which blocks the movement of water. It kills the vine. Once it's in your winery, you're toast. They can't cure Pierce's Disease."

"And you've brought these bugs here to Kelowna?"

"I brought them to the Campbell Winery. They've been busy since Julia's death. The Campbells will be ruined soon enough." He had a smug look on his face. The kind that Sarah would love to smack off. "The sharpshooter spreads the disease at an aggressive rate. They're quite the voracious little eaters."

"You really are a horrible person, aren't you?"

The privileged-kid attitude, the spoiled boy turned man, was Thirio's consummate makeup. He wasn't better off in life. He wasn't contributing to his family business by attacking the Campbells. He was wreaking havoc on his family's neighbors, supposedly doing it in the name of Satan to justify the behavior.

The time for talking was over. An idea came to her

regarding the dead man who had been haunting her ever since she arrived in Kelowna. Each time he showed up, his arm gestured wildly as if attempting to communicate something to her. A number. Nine, five, six, two, or something like that.

She stared at the cell phone. "What happens when the code is entered?"

"Don't worry about it. I'll never give it up."

She forcibly yanked the cuffs toward her. He was jerked out of his cross-legged position and had to grab the edge of the chair to avoid smashing into it with his face.

"Just tell me what happens. It won't matter if you never tell me the code."

"You'll hear an audible click as the ignitor is released and placed back where it belongs." He took a deep breath and tried to massage his wrist. "It'll only happen once, though. Once you stand up, if you were to apply pressure to the top of the landmine again, there's no code." He looked into her eyes. "Kaboom."

"Last question. And don't even try to lie. Your life depends on it."

He frowned and pursed his lips, then nodded.

"Is it six digits, or can it be five or four?"

"Six digits. Nothing less. I swear."

Sarah distinctly remembered the old man gesturing out four digits, not six. She allowed her cuffed arm to relax. Thirio sat back down beside the chair.

"What next?" he asked.

"I will type the code into the phone in a few minutes."

"How's that?" His voice cracked. Thirio seemed nervous. "You can't guess at that sort of thing. I have a three-try limit programmed into it."

She looked at him in the semi-darkness. "Only three tries?"

He nodded.

"Then I better make sure I do it right."

Vivian hadn't made an appearance yet. Sarah wasn't going to wait all night. The dead man had shown her the numbers—she was sure of it. The first number had been a nine. She typed the nine, then snuck a look at Thirio. He gasped. The look in his eyes told her she was right. Then she typed a five. Thirio's mouth opened.

"How could you possibly …" his voice trailed off.

"I just can't recall if it's a six and then a two or a two and then a six." Sarah closed her eyes momentarily and stared at the dead man gesturing in her mind's eye. In the future, she would pay more attention when dead people showed up and gestured wildly.

She decided on six, then two. If she was wrong, she had more tries. After typing in the six, followed by the two, she was stumped. At no time did she see the dead man gesture other numbers. His hand would make a violent gesture to signal he was done, then restart on the nine.

"What are the last two digits?" Sarah asked.

"Never," Thirio said. He shook his head and stared down at the basement floor. "I can't. Not in Julia's honor." He looked back up. "You're psychic. You figure it out."

"Maybe there are only four numbers."

He shrugged noncommittally.

She hit the enter key to accept the four numbers. The screen flipped to the empty six spots again. Nothing else happened.

"Two more tries," he said. "Then we're dead."

"And you're not going to help me?" she asked, certain of his answer.

"You've thwarted me along the way, and now you're taking away my final act, my triumph. Why would I help you?"

"Fine."

She typed in nine, five, then changed the position of the six and the two. Thirio mouthed the word *wow*. That confirmed it. She'd nailed the first four numbers. But what were the last two? Maybe there were only four, after all.

She hit enter and listened for the audible click Thirio said would happen.

Nothing.

"With one try left, I will remind you that the code has six digits. Hitting enter with only the first four is a waste of your chances. You have only one more chance, and I'm certain you'll never figure it out."

She retyped the first four numbers. Nine, five, two, six, then closed her eyes and focused on the old man again. What numbers were the last two? What had he done before starting at the nine again? Thirio had said *digits* and not *numbers*. Were the last two entries something other than a number?

She scanned the row of numbers along the top, then stared at each option below the numbers. Backslash, semi-colon, colon, parenthesis, the dollar sign, and so on. What did that old man do with the last two gestures? Whatever the last two items were, they were the same because the man had jerked his arm sideways. Could he have been doing a hyphen or a dash? That was all that made sense. The dash.

Sarah typed the dash key, then hit it again.

"No," Thirio said. Desperation had entered his voice. "Don't."

Sarah hit enter. A small vibration emanated from under her. Something clicked. Her heart doubled its beating in her chest. Did she just trigger the bomb and was seconds away from dying? Or did she deactivate it? Only one way to find out.

Sarah pushed off and rose from the comfy plush armchair.

Chapter 45

"Did you hear that?" Lee asked.

Parkman nodded. "Gunshot. Back of the house."

Lee turned to his right. "Gossett, circle around back and see if the rear door is open."

A muffled, *sir*, came from the side of the house.

Lee knocked on the front door again, then stepped to the side. "Open up. Police. Last chance. I will blow the lock off."

Parkman peeked inside the front window. "Can't see anyone."

"Someone's in there." Lee knocked again.

"Wait," Parkman said. "There's a shadow at the end of the corridor." He watched as Officer Gossett stepped into view. "It's Gossett," Parkman told Lee.

Gossett paused by an open doorway, then cautiously continued toward the front door, his gun clutched in both hands. Parkman hopped up on the concrete porch as Gossett neared the door. The lock clicked, and the door swung inward.

"All clear, sir. Old man on the floor behind that door." Gossett pointed. "I haven't cleared the upstairs yet."

Lee stepped inside the house, his own weapon held down low by his right thigh. Parkman did the same.

"Clear the upstairs. Then get back down here. We'll tend to the man."

"Yes, sir." Gossett hit the stairs running, ascending two at a time. The man was in stealth mode and made nary a sound as he bolted up the stairs, stunning for a man of his size.

Lee started along the corridor toward the room Gossett had pointed at. Parkman hadn't been this active with other officers in a long time. It was usually Aaron, Sarah, or even Darwin leading the way, and it wasn't as safe or organized. Those friends of his were usually more reckless.

At the opening of the room, Lee stepped in and flicked on the light.

"Shit." He dropped to his knees and searched for a pulse while Parkman stayed at the door, watching the hallway.

"Anything?" he asked.

"Faint, but he's still with us." Lee yanked out his cell phone and called an ambulance. Once he gave them the address, he patted the man down.

"There's no blood," Parkman said.

"There's no bullet wound," Lee said.

Parkman met Lee's gaze. "Then who got shot a minute ago?"

Lee diverted his attention back to Campbell. "Hang in there, buddy. Help's on the way." He got to his feet and joined Parkman at the door. "We have to clear this house before emergency services arrive."

"Then let's do it."

Gossett came bounding down the stairs. "Clear upstairs, sir."

"Stay by the front door. Watch for the ambulance. Direct them to Mr. Campbell here the moment they arrive."

"Yes, sir." Gossett dutifully moved to the edge of the vast living room window and stared out into the street. Parkman knew the man would remain a statue until the ambulance's flashing lights announced their arrival—he was that disciplined.

Lee moved toward the rear of the house, where the door stood wide open. At the door, he flicked on the outside lights. Parkman followed his lead and moved onto the back porch.

A row of hedges lined the rear of the house. Beyond them lay darkness. Lee kept his back to the house and moved to the right. Parkman moved to the left. When Parkman got to the corner of the house, he stuck his head around and looked up toward the road. When he turned back around, he saw a pair of black boots upended on the grass behind the row of hedges.

"Psst." Parkman hoped Lee would hear him. "Over here," he whispered.

Lee ran toward him. As he neared, Parkman pointed. "There's your gunshot victim."

Lee approached the boots, his own weapon extended in front of him. When he neared the fallen man, he lowered his weapon and stomped the ground.

Parkman's eyes adjusted to the darker area until he saw the face of the victim. It was one of Lee's men. He had ordered them to drive closer to the Martin Winery next door, park, and circle back to surround the Campbell house. They had done as ordered, but one of their men had been ambushed.

"For fuck's sake," Lee muttered.

Someone was running toward them. Lee hopped behind the bushes, and Parkman followed his lead. A siren squealed in the distance—the approaching ambulance.

One of Lee's men materialized out of the darkness a moment later. All three men jolted, then lowered their weapons.

"Two men, sir. Shot Watkins here, then ran that way. I tried to see if I could revive him. I'm sorry, sir."

"You said two men?" Lee asked.

The cop nodded.

"Recognize them?"

"Too dark, sir."

Parkman couldn't tell in the darkness if the man was lying. He could be telling the truth, or he didn't want to say that he saw Mason and Calder shoot his fellow officer.

"Which way?" Lee asked.

The cop pointed.

"I take lead," Lee said. "You stay here with Watkins. Parkman, cover me. Stay close, but whatever you do, don't shoot me in the ass."

Lee bent low and started for the bushes. Parkman followed close behind but didn't know how he would be able to locate the blue spruce in the dark. According to Sarah's note in his travel bag, he was supposed to hide behind the blue spruce. That was a vital part of the note. He knew Mason and Calder were back there somewhere. They had murdered one of their own in cold blood. He had to assume when that bomb went off, Mason and Calder would die—as Sarah said they would—and he needed to have Lee and himself sequestered behind a blue spruce.

It would be better to have more light because he hated running blindly in the dark after two raging, murderous rogue cops. And there was a bomb to consider.

"Fuck my life," he mumbled under his breath.

Lee didn't seem to hear him. The darkness swallowed them as they ran.

Chapter 46

SARAH STOOD OVER THE chair, looking back down at it. She yanked Thirio to his feet.

"Now, we take a walk to the cop shop," she said.

"Abandon all hope, ye who enter," he muttered, staring at the ground.

"What's that? Something spooky to scare me?" She leaned down to get a look at his face. Thirio's eyes were closed. "Oh wait, that's from *Dante's Inferno*, isn't it?"

He raised his head and glared at her, his eyes roving her face, studying her. Alone in the basement of the abandoned guesthouse at this late hour, he had the potential to freak her out. But she was tired, sore, and angry. The longer they took to leave, the more pissed off she would get.

Sarah started for the stairs, her cuffed arm trailing behind her. Thirio reefed on the cuffed arm within two steps, yanking her backward. The force nearly tore her shoulder out of its socket. Sarah emitted a small screech of pain.

Before she could regain her footing, he had dropped to the floor, dragging her with him. Maybe it wasn't such a smart idea to cuff themselves together.

Braced for the fall, she lifted her free arm and ceased her descent, protecting her face. Two words shot through her mind in that second. *The gun!* She had forgotten it in delight after being released from the chair's landmine.

Thirio must have seen it. That was why he wrenched her back to the ground. Before she could yank her arm back and regain control of the situation, Thirio gripped the weapon and rammed the tip under Sarah's neck.

They froze like that, mid-motion.

"My deal still sticks," he said. "We go and get the Campbells together now, cuffed as it were, and you help bring them here. Then you leave. Nothing has to change."

She breathed through her mouth, scenarios racing through her mind. Could she be fast enough? Would she be able to twist out of the way in time? How many bullets were left in the gun? Was the safety off?

Thirio pushed the tip of the gun deeper into her flesh. She had to lean away, but her cuffed arm restricted movement greatly.

"Or I could do it myself and kill you now. When they discover Campbell's remains among the bits and pieces of the bomb-making materials, they will also find your DNA. Your death would be blamed on the Campbell family." She felt his shrug as the tip of the gun tilted up slightly, then back down. "Maybe that's the better solution."

He forced her downward until Sarah's cheek rested on the cold basement floor. Angling his body up and away from her, Sarah's cuffed arm twisted backward, he placed a foot on the side of her neck. Something akin to a raw panic enveloped her. Even mild squirming did nothing to relieve the pressure on her arm. The way things stood, she was virtually immobile.

Vivian? You're going to let me die here?

"See you in Hell, Sarah Roberts."

Someone ran by the window. Thudding footsteps startled Thirio. Then someone else approached the house.

"In here," a man whispered just outside the basement window. A door opened upstairs.

Thirio leaned close to Sarah's face and put a finger before his lips.

Panting softly, she eased her free hand into her pocket and brought out the handcuff key. Raising her free arm as high as possible, she let the key dangle in the soft light. It caught Thirio's attention. He snatched it from her and opened the cuff from his wrist. Leaving her cuff fixed to her, he crawled on top of her and used his body weight to hold her down as if they were lovers and he was mounting her from behind. His ragged breathing caressed the back of her neck. Then his mouth was beside her ear.

"Smart girl," he whispered in her ear. "I'm assuming by removing the cuff, you're interested in taking my deal?"

She tried to nod. Anything to get him off her.

"It's too late, Sarah. You missed your chance. Your deal is with the devil now."

Two pairs of footsteps moved on the floor above. They traversed toward the back of the house. She was pretty sure it was Mason and Calder.

Thirio pushed up and sat on her lower back. Sarah placed

her hands on the floor beside her chest, took a deep breath, then shoved upward and snapped her head back violently. She connected with something hard, heard a snapping sound, then Thirio was falling. She twisted around as Thirio groaned, his hands racing to cover the wound. His balance off kilter, Sarah continued to twist under him and pushed him off. His nose gushed blood over his mouth.

"You bitch." It sounded like he spoke through several layers of cloth.

Sarah coiled her body inward, bringing her knees to her chest, then kicked out. The soles of her shoes connected with his chest. Thirio was knocked back and was lost to the darkness of the basement.

The thought of a bullet entering her body any second made her desperate. Scrambling to her feet, she dove toward where Thirio had disappeared but hit the ground on her elbows and knees. Thirio was gone. He'd moved away to a darker section of the basement. She swiveled on her side, kicking the air all around her, but hit nothing.

The small rectangular basement window disappeared momentarily as someone crawled into it, extinguishing the moonlight.

Thirio.

By the time she got to her feet, he'd reached the apex, rolled onto the grass, stuck his arm back inside the window, and began firing the weapon. Bullets zinged by. Chunks of concrete burst forth and showered her right forearm. Sarah ducked away from the window, covering her ears and offering up her back. On the last report, something smacked into her lower right side, knocking her off balance. She grunted and dropped to the ground.

"What was that?" a man shouted upstairs, loud enough for her to hear him.

Sarah jumped to her feet and winced at the pain in her side but was grateful Vivian made her wear a vest by keeping the sharpshooter message brief and ran for the stairs. She couldn't let the Satanist escape. He would disappear for good until he started killing randomly again.

The BAE vest had worked as promised. It had stopped the bullet and hadn't localized the injury. The force had been spread throughout the area of impact. Like a hard bodycheck into the boards in a hockey game, she would be bruised, but nothing that would incapacitate her. Especially not on the adrenaline high she was riding.

A large body filled the opening when she was two steps away from the top of the stairs. Mason held a weapon. He tried to aim it at her, but Sarah barreled into him, hugged him close, pinning his cast tight to her chest, spun in a half circle while he grunted and tried to extricate himself from her, then released him. Mason teetered momentarily at the top of the stairs, arms pinwheeling, then stepped backward into open space and fell. Before he reached the bottom, Sarah was running for the open front door.

Calder had to be close, but she couldn't waste time looking for him. Not while Thirio was running away. The thumping of Mason's body going down the stairs, coupled with his shouts of pain, diminished as she launched off the porch and ran toward the back of the property where Thirio's truck was parked.

The gun had been emptied. Thirio was unarmed. There would be no weapons between them this time. Thirio wasn't a born fighter. All she had to do was catch up to him, and he would be hers again.

The handcuff snapped back and forth on her wrist as she ran. The open cuff side cut into her flesh. The pain spurred her on as she ran through the darkness.

A message had said that Mason and Calder might die in Thirio's last explosion. It didn't make sense when Sarah was sitting in the chair, but it did now. She didn't want to be anywhere near the guesthouse when that bomb blew. She hoped Parkman got the note she left him in his luggage so he, too, could be far enough away.

The thought of Thirio disappearing in the night made Sarah run harder like the hounds of Hell were nipping at her ankles.

Chapter 47

AFTER A BOUT OF rapid gunfire in the distance up ahead that made Parkman and Lee hit the ground, they got back to their feet and continued moving forward. A building came up on their left. Parkman edged closer to Lee and tugged on his arm.

"Lee," he whispered. "This is insane. We can't see anything. I think we need to steer clear of that place."

It was nearly too dark to see Lee turn toward him. Parkman felt the man move his way while his hand clutched Lee's arm.

"Why's that?" Lee asked.

"Something Sarah said."

"What did she say?"

The moon had slipped halfway behind a cloud, leaving them partially blinded.

"In the note she left me," Parkman said.

"The one you read to me in the car?" Lee asked.

"Yeah."

"It didn't say anything about this building out here." Lee pulled away slightly. "Unless you didn't read the entire thing."

"I didn't."

"What else did it say, Parkman?"

The tone Lee used told Parkman he wasn't interested in half-truths or misguided information. Lee wanted to know what Parkman knew, and he wanted to know it now.

Parkman retrieved the note from his pocket and handed it to Lee, who used his cell phone to read it. After several tense moments, Lee handed the note back to Parkman.

"Destroy that."

"What?" Parkman stumbled and then righted himself. The note said Mason and Calder would likely die, which would be Mason's doing.

"Save everyone a fucking headache. Destroy that note. As far as I'm concerned, I didn't read it."

"What about the blue spruce?"

"The blue spruce you're referring to is the only one on the Campbell Winery property."

Parkman frowned in the dark as the moon eased out from behind its shroud of clouds. "How would you know something like that?" he asked.

"There's only one blue spruce because it used to be the tip of the property line between the two wineries up here. The Martin Winery lost two-hundred meters of land in the eighties after a long court battle with the Campbells, effectively putting the single blue spruce solely on the Campbell Winery property. The court case was dubbed the

Blue Spruce Territory Battle in the local media." Lee started toward the guesthouse. "As far as I can remember, it's about one hundred meters from their guesthouse toward the back of the property. Something like that—"

A figure jumped from the front porch of the guesthouse and ran off in the distance. They were too far back to see who it was.

"That wasn't Calder or Mason," Lee said. "I think that was Sarah."

"Might've been Sarah," Parkman agreed. "Running from the house like that." He stopped. "It might tell us something. Think we should find that blue spruce now?"

Lee skirted the house, offering it a wide berth as he led Parkman toward the fabled blue spruce. A man's voice emanated from the guesthouse. Then another. One of the men yelled something.

Parkman hoped they'd find the blue spruce before it was too late.

Blindly, he followed Lee wondering how everything got so fucked up that he was looking for a tree in a winery in the middle of the night while waiting for a house to blow up.

"Fuck my life," he mumbled to himself again.

Chapter 48

OFFICER TOM MASON HELD his broken arm close and rocked back and forth on the basement floor. He swore to himself that Sarah Roberts would be dead before daybreak if he had to take her out into the street and shoot her in the face. Throwing him down the stairs amounted to attempted murder. Even touching a police officer was assault, let alone grabbing one and shoving him down a flight of stairs.

Calder made it down to him and whispered something.

"What?" Mason shouted. "Whispering does no good." He breathed in, trying to manage the pain. "I need help here."

"I know, I know. Just hold on. I'll call an ambulance."

"No, get me up. I just need a minute. Then we go after that whore."

"Anything broken?" Calder asked, his hands touching Mason's legs.

"Get off me. Fuck! Everything's fine."

"You're hurt."

"Yeah, I'm hurt. Bruised and sore. Nothing new is broken."

Calder got so close his arm touched Mason's cheek, then brushed his broken nose.

Mason screamed at the pain. Water cleansed his eyes. Lightheaded, he rolled to his side, hugging his cast close. He would kill Sarah. Then he would shoot her in the mouth, the eyes, the ears. Anywhere she had a hole, he would fill it with lead. He would chainsaw her body if he could afford the time, slicing her into tiny pieces until she was no more. Then dump her body into the fish of the Okanagan Lake so no one would ever see or hear of Sarah Roberts again. He would do all that, but not until he caught his breath.

"Calder, help me to that chair."

"Listen, Mason. I think we might have taken this too far. I mean, that looked like one of our emergency task force guys back there."

"Fuck off and help me up."

Calder placed his hands under Mason's arms. "You ready?"

"Just do it."

Calder lifted, and a new set of aches and pains rippled through Mason's body. He gritted his teeth to keep from shouting out. He had hurt women before. In fact, he reveled in hurting the weaker sex. Beating, punching, even tying them up, and whipping a few of his ex-girlfriends. They claimed to want it. He was the man to deliver it. But he'd never had a woman cause him so much pain in all his life. Was this karma? Was this about making things right?

As Calder half dragged him, half helped him walk to the

chair, Mason realized what mattered. Pain mattered. Not receiving it, giving it. Instead of killing Sarah quickly, he would take and hold her for a while. How long would suffice?

Calder gently set Mason in the armchair. As he settled down, something under his butt clicked.

"You hear that?" Calder asked.

"An old spring is loose. It's nothing. The building's abandoned. Of course, the furniture won't be first class."

"True enough," Calder said, always agreeing with him.

Mason eased back in the chair and moaned. He would tie Sarah up. Naked would work. She could shit and piss in a bucket. He would use wipes to keep her clean and barely feed her to make her skinny over time, like every woman should be. Then, when he was done hurting her—six months, maybe a year—he would release her, and as she ran, he would cut her down in the street like the criminal she was.

Through the pain and the aches in his body, he could still smile. The thought of Sarah's torture elated him.

"Oh, joy," he whispered. "Oh, bliss."

Calder moved over to the window and peeked outside.

"I think someone's out there," Calder whispered. "I heard thumps, like someone running. Maybe more than one person."

"Of course," Mason said. "Sarah just left. She's still around, frightened that we'll come after her."

Calder moved away from the window and stopped beside Mason. "No," he whispered in Mason's ear. "Someone else. Like three or four people. Maybe more."

"Then we better leave so we can catch Sarah on our own." Mason tried to stand but stopped when Calder spoke.

"I think I'm done," Calder said.

Mason eased back into the chair. "Done? What are you talking about?"

"You hurt Campbell, then killed someone by the hedges."

"Calder. If you keep it together long enough to get through this, it'll be a miracle." He grabbed Calder's sleeve and pulled him close. "We are decorated police officers. Everything can be covered up."

"Are you sure about that?"

"Fuck off and listen. That man was an intruder. We told Campbell we were there because we heard from multiple sources that a fugitive was coming to his house tonight. We convened in his security room, where he was overcome. I tried to help him, but he fell. Then we heard something outside and went to investigate. We're fucking cops, idiot. That's what we do. That guy tried to jump us. My gun went off. Even if he is who you think he is, all that holds up in court if you go along with it."

"I will. I will. It's just …"

"Just what?"

"I didn't sign on for this."

He let Calder's arm go. "Neither did I, Calder, neither did I."

Calder moved back to the window and peeked out. "I think the coast is clear."

"Then let's go finish this and be done with it. After that, we can get on with our lives."

"Yeah," Calder said. "That sounds good."

Although bruised and sore, Mason used his one good arm to push off the chair and get to his feet.

Something snapped behind him. Movement brushed up

his back. He turned around in the dark, thinking someone had gotten the jump on him, when his face felt punched in a hundred different places. It all happened so fast. There was virtually no pain. His mind understood something had exploded, but he didn't understand what. He fell to the floor, but part of his body remained standing. Another part of his body moved across the room. Calder had emitted a short scream, cut off by whatever had punched Mason.

His consciousness wavered, his vision all but gone.

What the hell happened? Nothing responded to his thoughts or his mind's direction. He wasn't even breathing anymore. Was he alive? His brain worked a moment more, contemplating his fate and rushing to nightmarish conclusions, then it shut down.

The basement's darkness enveloped Mason's consciousness, and all thoughts of pain, whether inflicted or received, ceased forever.

Chapter 49

Sarah crested a small rise by the road, then dropped to her hands and knees. Thirio's truck hadn't moved. She collected her breath and took a moment to scan the area. Where would Thirio go if not to his truck? She stared across the open area at the truck, which was close enough to Upper Mission Drive to be illuminated by streetlights. A darkness moved inside the cab. Virtually motionless, Thirio sat with his head down on the top of the steering wheel.

What was he waiting for? Thirio probably assumed he had shot her, or she was held up by the men upstairs in the guesthouse. If Thirio thought for a second that she was still in pursuit, he would have hightailed it out of there.

But why wait so close to the winery?

Sarah crawled down the embankment. In a wide arc, staying to the outer rim of the streetlights, she came around the back of the truck. Crouched low, not ten feet from the rear of Thirio's vehicle, she picked up a large rock, cradled it in the crook of her arm, and advanced the last few feet.

A large explosion rattled the night. Someone had ignited the anti-personnel landmine in the chair. It had to be Mason or Calder.

Thirio's truck turned on. The brake lights lit up as he put the vehicle in gear. He'd been waiting for the explosion, and now he was leaving. He thought Sarah and the men who had been upstairs were dead.

Sarah lurched forward, took three large steps, planted both her feet, and hopped sideways, rolling her body over the side of the truck's bed as the truck shot forward. She landed inside on her sore shoulder, rolled into the wheel well on the other side, and stopped, the handcuff clanging against the truck's side.

She grabbed the cuff with her free hand and held it tight. Through the rectangular back window, she watched Thirio's head. He didn't look back at her. He likely dismissed the thudding sounds as road bumps. The truck dipped into two more potholes before hitting the paved section of the road. The pickup turned to the right and shot down the street, escaping the carnage behind them.

The rock had bounced to the back tailgate, where it was wedged in the corner.

Thirio took another turn, then another, each one going too fast. With gravity being what it was in the back of the truck, she couldn't get to the rock, let alone get to her feet and attack him in any way.

A red light. She would have to wait for him to stop. With precious little time at a red light, she would already want the rock in her hand. Twisting sideways, the vest cutting into her hips, she tried to slide along the bed to the rock. Thirio turned another corner too fast, the tires squealing as they fought for purchase. Sarah slid sideways and banged her head on the other side of the bed. A wooden pole rubbed against her bad shoulder. Thirio revved the engine, the wind in Sarah's ears as loud as the din of a concert hall. She grabbed the wooden pole and pulled it toward herself.

The pitchfork.

The rock forgotten, Sarah turned her body so that her feet were planted against the rear of the cab. She lay on her back looking toward the cab's rectangular window, the pitchfork in her hands, the offending tines aimed at Thirio's head. At this speed, hitting him now would also spell disaster for her. She had to wait until he slowed enough that she could still walk away from it when they crashed.

The streets were mostly empty at this late hour—or early hour, depending on perspective. Thirio drifted in and out of lanes, ran yellow lights, and kept moving at a good clip. She had no idea why he was driving so fast when no one was on his tail. Streetlight after streetlight whizzed by. An apartment building with little light on the upper floors passed by on her right. Staring up at the now cloudless sky at this hour under any other circumstances could be deemed romantic, but this was anything but.

The engine revs slowed. The brakes were applied. Her weight pushed toward the cab, putting pressure on the soles of her feet. She allowed her knees to bend as the truck slowed even more. Then Thirio stopped completely. Sarah sat up, pulled the pitchfork back, and shoved it forward with every ounce of strength she could muster.

The tines rebounded off the glass. The garden tool

vibrated, dangerously close to bouncing out of her hand.

Thirio jerked around and gawked at her, his eyes wide, mouth agape.

Sarah slammed the pitchfork into the glass again.

Nothing.

She rolled backward, hit the tailgate, and stopped. Thirio slammed the accelerator to the floor. The work truck squealed away from the intersection. Immediately, he swerved back and forth, tossing Sarah from side to side. She hit the wheel well, bounced away, hit the other side, and bounced off again.

She dove for the large rock in a final lunge, clasped it, and yanked it with her as she careened off the side again. In Thirio's wild antics to make her feel like she was in a washing machine, he almost lost control of the truck. It bounded up onto a curb, sideswiped a parked car in a driveway, veered to the left, and hit the rear of a large SUV.

Sarah jerked around, raised the rock, and cast it forward, aiming for the spot the tines had struck.

The glass shattered inward, showering Thirio's shoulders. He grunted something, tried to put the truck in reverse, and smashed the gas pedal down, but the pickup remained where it was.

Sarah retrieved the pitchfork, stood up in the bed, and was thrown into the back of the cab as Thirio unglued the truck from the SUV. The wind knocked from her lungs, and Sarah gasped for air like a landed fish as she slipped to the floor of the truck bed.

Survival taught her many things over the years. One was never to let go of the weapon that may save her life, even if she was taking debilitating blows. And another was never to stop fighting until your heart stopped. Ignore the pain; ignore the injuries. She could deal with those things later as long as she made sure there was a later.

Her breath came through in fits and starts, squeaking in and out. Sarah brought the pitchfork around and shoved it through the broken window.

One of the tines pierced his right shoulder, shoving him forward onto the steering wheel. Thirio shouted louder than the wind in her ears as the truck shot left, tilted sideways, and almost tipped over before it hit a parked moving van head-on and stopped dead.

The lights went out for Sarah when her head smacked the cab's roof.

The night got suddenly darker.

Chapter 50

PARKMAN GOT OFF THE ground and gave his body a once over to make sure he wasn't injured in the blast. Over fifty yards from the huge blue spruce tree Parkman and Lee took shelter behind, the building had been mostly destroyed. There was an initial blast in the basement, the lower windows registering a short burst of light. Then a larger blast shot out part of the side wall, and the house collapsed in on itself. Chunks of wood and crumbled brick flew dozens of feet in the air, with several pieces of the building landing within yards of their hiding place.

"You good?" Parkman asked.

"Yeah," Lee said as he patted himself down. "Remind me to thank Sarah. We would have never been this far from the house without her telling us to do so."

"She's got a way about her, that girl."

Lee started toward the main house, where the

ambulance's flashing lights lit up the circular fountain. Parkman hurried to catch up.

"What now?" he asked.

"We go find Sarah and locate the perp she's after."

That was what he wanted to hear. Parkman quietly followed Lee to the front of the house, where his phone vibrated in his pocket. Thinking it would be Sarah, he answered it before it vibrated a second time.

"Hello?"

"Parkman, it's Aaron."

"Oh man, am I glad to hear your voice." Parkman moved away from the front of the house, headed toward Lee's cruiser. Lee had run up the porch steps and disappeared inside the house. "How are things back in Toronto?"

"When are you guys finished there?" Aaron asked, ignoring Parkman's question.

"I can't imagine we'll be too much longer. After tonight, I think everything will be wrapped—"

"Parkman, listen to me."

"I'm listening."

"We've got a problem," Aaron whispered.

Parkman wasn't sure he heard him right. "A what? A problem?"

"Can you put Sarah on?"

"She's not here."

"Do you know where she is?"

"Well." He rubbed the back of his head. "That's a little tricky. She's kinda tied up at the moment."

"I have to go," Aaron whispered again. "I'll call back later today. Try to have Sarah with you."

The call disconnected.

Parkman held the phone out and looked at it as if it offended him.

"What was that all about?" he said to himself.

Toronto was three hours ahead of Kelowna. The sun would be rising where Aaron was. What could be wrong? Parkman wasn't sure Sarah would be interested in racing back to Toronto to deal with more issues. The girl needed a break.

Lee strode out the front door of the Campbell house, jumped off the porch, and jogged across the lawn toward Parkman.

"What's the hurry?" Parkman asked.

"Reports of a pickup truck driving erratically through the city. It smashed into another vehicle down on Gordon Drive." Lee made it to the car and dropped into the front seat. Parkman hopped in the back and slammed the door.

"You think it's our guy?"

"Yeah," Lee said. He started the car and made a U-turn. "Work truck matches the description given to us from the neighbor of that Durowitz fellow who was killed in Vernon." Lee flicked on the siren and lights. Parkman held the door handle as his friend drove erratically.

They had seen someone run from the house before they took cover behind the tree. They had thought it was Sarah. It made sense that she would keep fighting, keep moving forward until the perp was apprehended or dead.

"It's gotta be him," Lee said. "Maybe he was fighting with Sarah, and he crashed."

"You're probably right." Parkman slapped his knee and wished Lee would drive faster. He couldn't help but feel the need to be there for Sarah. "You're probably right."

Chapter 51

SHE BLINKED AWAKE, GASPED, and got up too quickly. Her head spun for a moment. Thirio was still pinned behind the wheel. The front of his truck hissed, and steam rose skyward where it met the side of the moving truck.

She had to have been unconscious for less than a minute.

"Gonna have to have my head examined when this is over," she muttered to herself.

Adrenaline retreating, she rolled over the side of the pickup and landed on the ground with a grunt. Everything seemed sore. Her shoulders, her legs, her abdomen. In her back, where the bullet had hit, told her that painkillers were in her future—her near future.

She tried to open Thirio's door, but it wouldn't budge. The frame had bent enough in the accident that it was stuck. She walked around the back of the truck, grabbed the passenger door handle, and yanked on it. The door opened on the first try.

Exhaustion overwhelmed her. She needed a sixteen-hour sleep when this was over. That and a bottle of whiskey.

She crawled inside the cab, clutched the pitchfork, and yanked it out of Thirio's shoulder. He jerked his head up and screeched like a fifteen-year-old girl. Sarah balled up her fist and drove it into the side of his head.

"Just shut up," she yelled. "Fucking baby. It's only a pitchfork."

She grabbed his shirt and started hauling him out of the cab. At the door, she climbed out and pulled him the rest of the way. Thirio slipped off the seat and hit the concrete with a thud and a grunt. Before he could move, Sarah lunged back inside the cab, seized the handle of the garden tool, and pulled it loose from the truck.

Thirio rolled onto his back, holding his wounded shoulder where blood already covered his hand. Sarah stood over his head, the pitchfork in hand, then brought it down before Thirio could move out of the way.

Two of the tines penetrated his shoulder wound in almost the exact same holes and made a loud metallic sound when the tines struck concrete.

Thirio screamed. Sarah dropped to her knees and held a hand over his mouth.

"You don't get the pleasure of screaming," she rasped in his face. "All the people you killed or tried to kill. The innocent lives you stole because you lost your mind. Couldn't you lose your mind and wander off into the forest somewhere? Why do people lose their minds and have to murder others?"

She released his mouth. Thirio sucked air like he was

trying to eat it.

Sirens approached. Her job was done. It was over. Kelowna's homegrown terrorist had been neutralized. She placed a foot on his chest and held the pitchfork handle as if she held a sword and had beaten her enemy in battle.

When the headlights of the first unmarked cruiser arrived and covered them with high beams, Sarah turned to look down at her captive.

Thirio had blacked out. She watched his chest rise, then fall, and wondered why she hadn't killed him when she had the chance. Was she getting soft? Did she care too much? This guy wouldn't rehabilitate, and if he was ever released one day, who could be sure he wouldn't re-offend? The recidivism rate was too high to have not considered ending his life.

Wiping the slate clean wasn't always the right answer, though. Accountability was. Making Thirio accountable in the eyes of the law, allowing the families and the people he hurt to watch his court process and see him sentenced for his crimes may offer closure for them. Maybe for some solace.

Death wasn't always the answer, even though it was her preferred ideology.

She would watch Thirio's progress. She would monitor what happened to him going forward. And if he ever became a free man one day, she would come for him. She would know the public was safe if he was locked up and pinned down.

Some people should die. She knew that. But others should live so they could suffer like the rest of humanity. Isn't that what life was, an endurance of suffering? Some weakened under pressure, and others thrived. When the suffering ended, you died. You went home when there was nothing left to learn on this plane. That was how it worked. The world, according to Vivian.

Car doors opened and closed. Police officers ran toward them. The musical tone of a friend's voice warmed her.

"Sarah?" Parkman said. He wrapped his arms around her, and she fell into him, thoroughly spent. "It's so good to see you."

He led her away from Thirio, an arm around her shoulders, as officers attended to the unconscious man with the pitchfork in his shoulder.

"What happened?" Parkman asked.

"It's a long story," she said. "But first, I need a shot of something strong. Do that, and I'll fill in all the blanks."

"You're on." He squeezed her shoulder.

She pulled away from the squeeze, pain flaring in that shoulder, and let a small whimper ease from her mouth.

"Oh, sorry," Parkman said, releasing her.

"It's okay. You couldn't have known how sore that shoulder is."

They walked to Lee's cruiser in silence.

Neither one touched the other.

Chapter 52

Lee's office hadn't changed since she visited last, except a lamp in the corner lay shattered on the floor. Sarah lounged on the small couch against the wall with a coffee in her hands and watched Lee manage call after call while Parkman ate a turkey sandwich. The three of them had discussed the case after Sarah gave her statement to Lee's handpicked RCMP officers.

Now was the time for goodbyes. Their job done, Sarah and Parkman were to board a direct flight out of Kelowna headed for Toronto in a few hours. Lee had requested they come to his office to meet several people before leaving the city, a city Sarah had little desire to return to.

Officers Tom Mason and Jeff Calder were both confirmed dead in the landmine explosion in the basement of the Campbell Family Winery guesthouse. The father of the family, James Campbell, had had a minor heart attack and was resting in the hospital. He was due to make a full recovery.

Leonard Martin—aka Thirio—had been arraigned on multiple charges of first-degree murder—premeditated—including the murders of two peace officers, Mason and Calder. He was still under police guard at the hospital, where pitchfork wounds to his shoulder were being tended.

The glassy-winged sharpshooters had become a non-threat. All the bugs Thirio had brought to the Campbell Winery had died within the first week with virtually no damage to the vines.

Lee set the phone down and turned to Sarah. "Julie informs me we have an unexpected visitor."

"Who?" she asked.

"That realtor you met, Trever Florko."

"Do you know what he wants?"

The office door opened.

"Ask him yourself," Lee said as he stood from behind his desk.

Trever entered the room, leaving the door open. He looked from Parkman, who was wiping his mouth and getting up from his chair, to Lee and finally to Sarah. He wore an expensive-looking suit jacket and cream-colored slacks. The beard was as neat and trim as before. It was like he had a barber measure every hair and ensure the beard was perfect every day before leaving the house.

After locking eyes with Sarah, he sauntered over to her, his right hand extended.

"You did a great job out there," Florko said.

Sarah rose from the couch and shook his hand. "I didn't expect to see you after, you know." She exchanged a glance with Parkman. "After kidnapping you for one city block."

"I had to come. After I dropped you off on Dayton Street, I was visited by those two officers who died." He drifted off and looked down at his shoes for a moment. "I don't know." He shrugged, then looked back at her. "After reading the news, I can see none of this had anything to do with me, and as far as I can tell, I did the right thing by helping you."

She placed a hand on his shoulder. "You did do the right thing. And I have no issue with you telling those cops where I'd gone. They pursued me. What happened to them was their doing. It had nothing to do with you or me. In fact," she touched her side and winced, "if you hadn't directed me to that army surplus store, I would probably be dead right now. Or recuperating in a hospital with a bullet wound. So thanks for that, and thanks for coming so I could say it to you personally."

They shook hands again. Trever nodded at Lee, shook his hand, talked to Parkman briefly, then left.

"That wasn't so bad," Sarah said. "Decent guy. Seems honorable."

The buzzer on Lee's desk lit up. "Yes, Julie."

"Mrs. Brooke Martin here to see you."

"Send her in."

"Martin?" Sarah said. "As in Leonard Martin's mother?"

Lee nodded. "The one and only."

"Be nice," Parkman warned.

"Aren't I always?"

He glared at her briefly.

The door opened, and Thirio's mother stepped inside the office tentatively. She held a folded Kleenex in her hand. The peach-colored dress she wore seemed to be in a brighter mood than she was. The woman stopped three feet inside the office and took a deep breath. No one spoke.

Mrs. Martin took another deep breath, fidgeted with a fingernail, then said, "I didn't raise him like that—" her choked voice cut off. With the Kleenex over her mouth, she said, "I'm so sorry for the pain my boy caused everyone."

Her plea, the obvious pain she was enduring, meant something to Sarah. Sometimes people don't turn out the way you expect. Sometimes it had nothing to do with parenting or upbringing.

Sometimes people were just fucked, to begin with.

Sarah trudged over and wrapped an arm around her shoulder. Brooke Martin, a Satanist's mother, wept in Sarah's arms as Sarah cooed to her and waited for the sobs to abate.

When Sarah turned back to Parkman and Lee, two people had joined them. Sarah jolted at the sight of them, but Brooke barely seemed to notice her sudden jerk. In the early hours of the day, Sarah had talked briefly with Vivian as she caught some sleep and then dictated her statement. She understood much more now. When Sarah died in Denmark, the sisters made a pact. Sarah would be able to foretell things about the future through emotions. Sarah would also be able to *know* things as if she'd known them for years. Vivian could add to Sarah's memory stores at will. Their connection would be forever stronger, with Vivian closer to her consciousness than ever.

At the time, Vivian didn't know or understand that opening this avenue as wide as they did brought Sarah that much closer to the other side. She could hear her sister but not see her. With other entities, she could see them but not really hear them. The old man had to use his hands to give her the cell phone code because he knew she couldn't hear him.

That old man stood beside Parkman now.

A woman in her forties stood behind Lee. She watched Lee with sorrow in her eyes. As Sarah studied the woman, certain things became clear, things she needed to tell Lee.

Mrs. Martin collected herself, took another deep breath, and faced Sarah.

"I'm sorry." She turned to Lee and Parkman. "Leonard killed his brother, my son. I will try to find forgiveness, but that's a long way off."

Mrs. Martin pulled a cell phone out of her burgundy purse suspended from her shoulder. She opened it and flipped through the photos.

"Sarah, I want to show you Leonard as a young boy." She stopped at a photo where a boy about three or four was playing with a large yellow Tonka truck. "When he was young, he was sweet and innocent. The perfect little boy." She flipped through more pictures until she stopped on one with Leonard and his brother.

"Wow, how could you tell the twins apart?" Sarah asked.

"As their mother, that wasn't so hard." She flipped through other pictures.

"Stop," Sarah said. "Go back two photos." Brooke swiped sideways. "Who is that?" Sarah asked, staring at a photo of the old man who stood in the room beside Parkman.

"That man was my brother," Brooke said. "Leonard's uncle."

"Sarah?" Parkman got up from his chair. "You look like you've seen a ghost."

Sarah faced the man—Thirio's uncle—as he tipped his

head her way, gestured that he was washing his hands, then turned and strode through the wall of Lee's office, head bowed.

Thirio's uncle had come to save her life. Thirio's uncle helped save her from his own nephew. Sarah wrapped her arms around Mrs. Martin to avoid having Parkman and Lee see her face.

"I'm sure Lucas Martin was a good man." Sarah pulled back from Brooke. "Your brother loved those boys."

"He sure did." She slipped her phone away and turned toward the open door. "I know my apology won't mean much after all that Leonard's done, but I wanted to do it anyway."

"It means something to me," Sarah said. Parkman stood beside her.

"I'm curious." Brooke turned back at the door. "Did Leonard ever talk to you about his family?"

"Our time together was a little more chaotic. Family didn't come up."

"I've heard about you, Sarah. Read what Google offered. I'm grateful you didn't kill my son when you could've. Even after all he's done, I'm a mother first. But let me ask you something." She wiped the tip of her nose with the Kleenex. "How did you know my brother's name?"

Sarah blinked, then refocused. "It's what I do. I know things. Your trip to Google would have told you that about me."

"I guess so." She backed into the corridor. "I'm just not a believer in all things psychic."

Sarah smiled wide. There wasn't much else to say. She'd heard the woman, listened to her, and offered empathy. Her visit wasn't a complete waste, though. There was a breakthrough moment. Sarah now understood who the old man had been and why he'd hung around since she arrived in Kelowna.

Mrs. Martin moved down the corridor, leaving Lee's office door open. Sarah took a second to collect herself, closed the door, then faced the sad woman behind Lee's chair.

It was easy to see the family resemblance to Lee. Uncanny, really. The nose, the eyes, and even Lee's forehead looked the same.

"What?" Lee asked. He glanced over his shoulder, then back at Sarah. "What are you seeing?"

The woman met Sarah's eyes, then raised her hands. She held a different kind of fruit in each one.

"I need paper and a pen," Sarah mumbled.

Lee scrambled on his desk until he had what Sarah needed. Parkman grabbed it and delivered it to Sarah.

"You okay, Sarah?" Parkman asked.

She nodded. "Just give me a second, guys." Sarah moved back to the couch as if in a daze, watching the woman decipher what she was trying to communicate.

After Sarah had written several things down, the woman stopped her antics and stared at Lee again.

Sarah eased back into the couch and sighed. "Lee, have you been in touch with your son, Nick?" she asked.

"No," Lee said. "I tried." He snuck a look at Parkman, who was no help, then continued. "Talked to his wife, though."

"Any plans to try again?"

"I thought it had to do with the case."

"Originally. But ultimately, it was about family."

"Parkman, what's she talking about?"

Sarah raised her hand. "He won't be of any help. Yes, Nick had a picture of Thirio because of work Thirio had screwed them out of weeks ago. But there's something greater here, and it has to do with your health."

Lee touched his chest and guffawed. "My health? What the hell are you talking about?"

"Your son is terminal, Lee. I'm sorry to say it like this, but here's the truth as I know it, and I don't have much time to be gentle. Your son is dying, and his family will need you. You already know some of this, Lee. You must be there for Nick's wife and your son's two young daughters."

"Okay," he said, his voice subdued. "Okay. I'll call him. I'll reconnect. I'll do what I can."

"But that's not all."

"What? What else is there?"

"The woman behind you."

Lee turned around. Parkman stared at Sarah, his eyes boring a hole in her.

"I think she's your mother. Her name starts with the letter D. Dana, Danielle, Daphne, something like that."

"Daphne." Lee stared back at Sarah, the color draining from his cheeks.

"I keep seeing an image. It's weird, though."

"What image?"

"A cat in a cradle."

Lee's mouth dropped open. "Cat's in the cradle. That's the song Nick used to quote when he was younger. I was always so busy with the force. Couldn't be home all the time. My son would say I would regret it one day, and then when I was older, he wouldn't have time for me. Cat's in the cradle is a private joke between Nick and me that blossomed into something more serious."

"When you call Nick, you're supposed to say that to him. Say you'll fix it."

"Okay, I will. I will."

Sarah referred to the notes she'd jotted down. "Do you have pain in your side?"

Lee nodded.

"You thought it was sugar? Then alcohol?"

He nodded again.

Sarah looked at her notes, trailing the words with her finger. "It's salt."

"Salt?" Parkman said. "Wow, who would've known?"

"Lee, your kidneys are having a hard time expelling the salt in your diet because you eat a lot of fast food with this job which is loaded with salt. The reason your kidneys are being taxed is because of your high blood pressure."

"How did you know about …" he let his voice trail off.

"I've written down kiwis and bananas for potassium, which your arteries will love. Daily moderate exercise. I've been told that some dark chocolate and a little red wine will do wonders for the blood pressure. Lose ten pounds, your mother says. It'll reduce your blood pressure numbers by ten points." She got up from the couch and walked over to his desk. "Look, your mother is trying to save your life so you can have more time with Nick's family." She placed the pad on the desk face up so Lee could see everything she'd written. "Heart attack is expected within months if you don't take these measures." She placed both hands flat on the desk and leaned closer to him. "You've got many years left, Officer Stephen Lee, but the stress and food of this job has taken its toll. Retire. Do it now before this place kills you. Eat better and exercise. And go spend time with your family. It's over for you here. Besides, you deserve this."

Parkman walked around the desk and patted Lee on the back as the veteran police officer began to weep silently. "Listen to her, my old friend. She knows what she's talking about."

Lee wiped his eyes and read what Sarah had written down. He nodded. "I can't believe it. My mother told you all this?"

"I'm not a doctor. I don't diagnose people. She came because she loves you and wants you to stay here longer. Check out some of this with your doctor, but it all sounds right to me."

He set his hand on the paper. "I will make changes and get in touch with my son. I was already thinking about retiring."

Parkman's cell phone rang. He grabbed it and read the screen.

"Aaron," he said and handed the phone to Sarah.

"Hey," she said.

"You coming home?" he asked. His voice was off somewhat.

"Yeah. We've got a flight in," she turned to Lee's office clock, "just over two hours."

"I'll pick you up."

"What's going on?" She looked at Parkman. "Should I be concerned?"

"Nothing we can't handle."

"Aaron. What happened?"

"Two Italian guys visited us. It's nothing, really. I just

didn't like the way they asked for you."

"Asked for me?"

"They entered the new dojo we're building and ordered us to locate you. Call you, find you. We told them to fuck off. They came back again today."

"And?"

"There were five of them."

Something told her it was worse than she expected. "And?"

"They were armed."

That was worse. "Shit. They tell you what they want?"

"Just to talk to you."

"Bullshit. I have no beef with the Italians that I know about."

"Look, don't worry about it. Just come home. When's your flight coming in?"

She told him. "I'll see you then."

Aaron clicked off without saying goodbye or his usual words of love, which was unlike him.

"Parkman, I'm worried. Aaron's pretty freaked out."

"It's probably nothing. Fill me in on the plane."

They started for the door.

"Wait," Lee said, bounding out of his chair. He wrapped his arms around Sarah when he got to her. "Thank you."

"Just put in the work. Fix yourself. Buy a fucking Fitbit or an Apple watch or something. But deal with it. That'll be thanks enough."

He let her go and hugged Parkman.

Ten minutes later, they were racing toward the Kelowna airport along Harvey Avenue. As Sarah explained her new ability to Parkman, she retracted her earlier statements about being freaked out by it.

"We're all freaked out when things are unclear," she said. "Now I know who these people are and what they're trying to do."

"Why do you think the Italians are looking for you?"

"I'll meet with them, find out what they want. Then deal with it. I'm sure it's nothing."

Parkman stared out the window. She stared out hers, thinking about all the Italians she'd known in the past. Maybe it had something to do with the time she spent in Italy.

Before they reached the airport, Vivian showed up and whispered two words into Sarah's consciousness.

The Chase.

Whatever the Italians wanted, it had to do with *The Chase.*

A chill ran through Sarah. Even though those two words alone meant nothing significant to her, she did not like their sound.

The Chase gave her an ominous feeling of danger and regret, loss and struggle, which seemed to be what made up her life nowadays.

Would it ever end? she asked herself.

Afterword

DEAR READER,

I'm glad you're still here. It's been a long run, this being book eighteen in Sarah's life. I love what's planned for *The Chase* (book 19) and *The Betrayal* (book 20). I plan to release both of those titles in 2017. *The Terror* is over for now, the threat neutralized, but it is only the beginning of Sarah's new abilities. Since the beginning of this series, I've endeavored to evolve Sarah as a character, maturing her and changing her based on events in her life. She's definitely not the same girl from *The Crypt* (book 3) or even *The Vigilante* (book 7).

In *The Terror*, I wanted to take Sarah back to her roots. I wanted to have her on her own, that maverick kick-ass girl we all came to love in *Dark Visions* and *The Warning*. The Sarah that does it her way, with supporting characters in the background. If this was your cup of tea, then my plan worked. If this wasn't, and you prefer Sarah surrounded by her supporting cast, you're in luck: Sarah returns in *The Chase* (book 19) with almost everyone I can gather. In no particular order, you'll see Darwin Kostas, Bruno, Drake Bellamy (aka John Whitman), Spencer, Aaron, Daniel, Benjamin, Alex, Parkman, Buck Schaffer (aka Casper), and a whole lot more.

In *The Terror*, I wanted to touch on bullying. Mason is a bully. He hits women freely, bosses his fellow officers around, and does what he wants without much regard for anyone. I wrote him in because I hate bullies. Most of us have dealt with bullies in our past or at least seen their destructive effect on others. I dealt with a few bullies in grade school. It wasn't until around grade seven that I learned that bullies were basically cowards. That understanding comes complete with a free black eye if you're not careful how you express that knowledge, but I learned quickly how to handle them, and by grade nine, bullies were a thing of the past for me.

My sensei years ago always taught us to walk away. His mantra was *never fight.* Then he went on to teach us how to fight—ninety percent self-defense, ten percent aggression—although I got the message. I learned a lot from that man, and now Aaron emulates him. Aaron is as good as my sensei. I still wear the scars on my knuckles from the board breaking and the intense workouts my sensei put us through. What I don't wear anymore is the fear of a bully. That's their issue, not mine, and I don't take it on. Sarah seems to be able to deal with the Tom Masons of the world as I would (without murdering them—that part's fiction), with confidence, bold statements, and action. And a serious deficiency of fear.

I don't claim to have all the answers on bullying. Sometimes a bully isn't a coward. Sometimes they're an asshole who loves to fight. As a rule, I've navigated the bully terrain my way and found moderate to confident success. I hope you do, too, if ever faced with an idiot and a fist.

Satanism is an interesting belief system. I say this because, as Sarah believes, I do, too, that there is no such thing as a devil. A God of love would never create a being in his image and then delegate an ultimatum like believe in me, or you'll burn in a lake of fire. If that's love, then what's hate? I might alienate several religious people here—to those people, let me just say that I respect your right to believe in whatever you've decided to believe. Extend that courtesy to me as well. Doesn't that go along with the nonjudgmental nature of religion?

As I've mentioned in previous Afterwords, I've spent several years studying various world religions but had not studied Satanism. I met a man in my retail business in my mid-twenties. He always dressed in black and wore a 1920s-era black hat. Curious, I asked him why the black garb. With a quirky smile, he told me that he was a Satanist. His parents were ultra-religious fanatics, he explained, which drove him nuts. Not sure how that works, but shouldn't religions endear people to them with promises of wonderment in the afterlife? Yet it seems I have met so many people (since the days of my twenties) who have turned from religion if they were raised in it.

A few more quick points. The part about the Abbotsford RCMP investigating the Kelowna detachment in chapter 34 was true. That is still happening at the time of this publication. By adding that bit, I showed Officer Lee's frustration with the state of his force. Along with that, the investigation into the man who died who had been in need of medical attention and the ensuing investigation afterward in Kelowna was also true. In addition, the Kelowna taxi cab intimidation story was pulled from the local newspaper. Lastly, the Hell's Angels are in a legal battle over one of their houses on Ellis Street in Kelowna as the government is trying to seize their property. HA is actively fighting the seizure, as mentioned in the novel. All of that is true and still happening at the time of publication in Kelowna, which was once ranked with the highest crime rate in Canada per capita.

Regarding police officers. As I did at the end of book ten, The Antagonist, I need to point out that I don't have an issue with cops. In fact, it's the opposite. I love and respect what they do. What I hate are power-tripping cops. Or bad cops, which make for good fiction.

Here's a quick story about cops:

When I was eighteen, my girlfriend of over a year broke up with me. She walked away without telling me a reason why. To this day, I still don't know what happened all those years ago (but it doesn't matter now). Two weeks after the breakup, I was hanging out with a few of my friends, staying busy, keeping my mind off things, when I saw her and three other people—two guys and another girl—in the park across the road. Thinking she might want to talk and tell me what happened, I left my pack of friends, crossed the road, and called out her name in a friendly manner. The foursome got up and started walking in the other direction.

I pleaded for her to stop and give me a minute of her time. These are the days before cell phones or texting—even email. When you wanted to talk to someone, you could call their house, but if they were perpetually never home, bumping into them at the park offered a person a chance to talk. After several minutes of walking behind the foursome, keeping pace at a safe distance, I gave up and rejoined my friends on the other side of the street. It was pointless, I explained to them. She didn't want to clear things up or talk to me again. With no closure, I was ready to move on. She had her reasons, and she wasn't willing to share them. It is what it is …

Fifteen minutes later, a police cruiser pulled into the parking area where I was hanging out with my friends. The officer exited his car, strode up to us, and barked out my name. Panicked, I stood and identified myself.

At this time, I thought something had happened to my parents or family member.

I was wrong.

It turned out my ex-girlfriend had called the cops on me and laid a complaint of harassment. I was manhandled into the back of the cruiser and told that my future dreams of being a police officer were over. (I had applied to be a cop and was currently working as a patrol officer with a local security company.) The cop charged me with something called "Watch and Beset," a crime under a subsection in the Canadian Criminal Code titled "Harassment."

I hired a lawyer and one year later ended up in court. The charges were dropped as the case was frivolous, and the complainant never appeared in court. I walked out a free man with no criminal record and a few thousand dollars lighter.

In conclusion, I'm not a bad guy. I've never hit a woman and abhor men who do. I was not following that foursome threateningly, nor did I pose a threat. This was a girl who used the system, in my opinion. The cop was overzealous and unnecessarily mean. I never lost my job at the security company because of the charge, and the only reason I didn't get the job at the police department was that I had broken my back and was deemed unfit for the force during a routine physical. I understand, in today's world, following someone can be a scary ordeal. But in 1988, in a wide-open park, one boy following four people, only asking to have an audience for several minutes, isn't a crime. As far as I know, it still isn't.

The reason I added this story was because of the cop's behavior. I still remember sitting in the back of that cruiser, the Plexiglas jammed against my knees, wondering what my family would say to me. Wondering what my future would look like without law enforcement, as my father had spent so many years as a decorated police officer with Ontario Provincial Police and the Toronto Metro Police. The cop yelled at me, berated me, and made me feel quite small. It didn't fit the deed. He kept me locked in that back seat in front of a convenience store where all my friends gathered to ensure there was a certain level of embarrassment. Either way, it all resulted in nothing, and the cop's threats of no future were empty.

Anyway, on to a brighter topic. I'd like to give special thanks to the people who helped complete this novel. I appreciate being able to use Stephen Lee's name, as well as Corey Hallagan, Nan Hammock, Mark Gossett, Trever Florko, and Julie Deighton. An extra special shout-out goes to John and Lori DeBeau, who you met in the hospital scene in Vernon with Sarah. John is suffering from Lewy Body

Dementia. That part is not fiction. They've got a large family, and like anyone else in their situation, they're moving forward in life with this hanging over them, being as strong as they can be for each other. I wanted to highlight what real people and families struggle with daily. Sometimes life is stranger than fiction, and sometimes fiction can bring light to that life.

Be well, John and Lori DeBeau. Sending my best to you and your family.

On that note, it's time to wrap up and prepare for *The Chase*, book nineteen in the Sarah Series. I simply cannot wait for *The Chase* because it'll set up the twentieth novel, *The Betrayal*, which will bring down the house. I'm messed up over these novels because of what's coming. I hope you all find them to your liking.

Thank you, Dear Reader, for coming along on this journey with me. It's been a good run. I'm loving every minute of it, and there's still so much more to come.

Until then, be well, and care for yourselves and each other. Spread love, not hate, and read, read, read.

Sending my love, as always,

Jonas Saul

P.S. For those who love my true stories, here's one more about what I deem bad cops—at least in the sense of cops harassing the public.

On a cool fall day in October 1986, I was walking on a busy street in Calgary, Alberta, headed downtown to the Greyhound station, where I had placed my luggage in a locker the night before. I was sixteen years old and was heading home to my parents after spending time with my sister. I had a ticket in my pocket for a 48-hour ride from Calgary to Toronto.

As I passed a side street, I witnessed two men sitting in a nondescript brown vehicle on the side street. The men seemed to be watching me. I looked away, saw the busy street—multiple cars whizzed by me going both ways—and realized that those two guys were cops in an undercover car monitoring traffic.

I looked back at them just before they were lost from sight and smiled at how well they were hidden from view. It was genius, really. I mean, these guys could see all the traffic without a single driver seeing them until it was too late.

In 1986 I had hair past my shoulders and always wore my red and black lumber jacket. Who doesn't think they're cool at sixteen years of age?

Anyway, I guess those cops didn't like how I looked at them—and I assure you I didn't have a disrespectful bone in my body toward police officers in those days. Shit, man, I was in Bible study at sixteen!

The undercover cruiser turned on, the wheels screeched, and the car lurched into the road, swung around in front of me, and jerked to a halt. The passenger cop jumped out, flipped open his ID, said his name out loud to this stunned kid (yeah, I'll admit it, I was freaked out), and ordered me into the back seat.

I complied.

Once in the back seat, they asked me who I was, what I was up to, and where I was going. When I told them I was heading to the bus station, they asked what my destination was. I produced my ticket. I was grilled on why I was running from Calgary. Who did I burn? What mess was I leaving behind? Nothing I said seemed on the level to these guys.

Finally, the driver got the car going again and headed downtown. The entire way, they warned me that my luggage had better be in the locker I told them it would be in.

At the Greyhound bus station, these two officers escorted me inside, one on each arm (they left bruises), to the delight of dozens of travelers who got a free show. They made me open my locker and produce my luggage. Once my bag was on the floor, one of the cops unzipped it and rummaged through everything, upturning my neatly folded clothes and ruining the packing job that I'd spent time organizing. He claimed he was looking for the drugs I had stashed away, which they never found, as I've abstained from them my entire life.

Once that was complete, my bag was left open in disarray on the bus station floor, clothes haphazardly strewn everywhere, the two officers got up, patted my shoulder, offered me a warning of some kind, and walked out of the station.

I collected my things and continued my travels to Toronto. When I got home and opened my bag, I discovered what the cop had done. When my attention was diverted to the bus depot in Calgary, the officer located my expensive cologne, unscrewed the cap, then gently placed it back in the zipped pouch. After I jammed my clothes back inside and closed the main zipper of the luggage, I didn't touch my bag again until I left the bus in Toronto. During the 48-hour ride, the cologne emptied all over my bag, soiling my clothes and costing me an expensive bottle for a sixteen-year-old.

I had done nothing wrong. Is it a crime to look at cops?

Is it a crime to think their plan of watching traffic was brilliant? These were two overzealous police officers out having fun at my expense, and this isn't the first and only time it happened.

I have another half a dozen times I've experienced something like this with officers of the law. To write about them, all would need several more chapters. I'm a law-abiding citizen with no criminal record. I would hate to see how certain cops treat people who are actually breaking the law. We've all seen some of that on YouTube.

In summation, not all cops are like this, and I spend considerable time sending good karma their way whenever I can.

I thought I'd offer my experiences to explain why I'm so passionate about bad cops and how destructive their behavior can be.

Until next time, be well, and kiss your loved ones goodnight.

Jonas Saul

December 28, 2016, Addendum: The Abbotsford RCMP has announced the investigation into the Kelowna RCMP is over. They found no evidence to continue the investigation.

About Jonas Saul

Jonas Saul is the bestselling author of the Sarah Roberts Series—more than two million sold!—and has written and published over sixty thrillers. After acquiring an agent, he signed several deals in Los Angeles, with MadRiver Pictures optioning his Sarah Roberts Series— over forty books!—(currently in development).

Jonas has often outranked Stephen King and Dean

Koontz on Amazon over the past decade. He's regularly invited to be a guest speaker, teacher, or workshop presenter at international writing conferences and film festivals worldwide. He hosts an annual writer's retreat in Greece, where he currently lives. He focuses his teaching on how to get tension and emotion in every scene, on every page, how he made it as a creator/writer, the path to success in this business, and the pitfalls to avoid. He also hosts a reading retreat in Greece with guest authors, yoga retreats, and hiking retreats. Visit the Imagine Greece Retreats website at www.imaginegreeceretreats.com, or email him directly to discuss an opportunity to join one of the retreats at jonas@imaginegreeceretreats.com.

Jonas is also a professional freelance editor. He works for several publishers and does private editing for clients, with many testimonials on his website at www.imaginepress.org, which details each author's response to Jonas's editing skills. Email Jonas directly for an editing quote at editor@imaginepress.org.

To book Jonas for a speaking engagement at a writer's conference/festival, to have him on your jury at a film festival, or even to say hello, email Jonas directly at jonassaul@icloud.com.

For updates on releases, hit the "Follow" button on Amazon or Bookbub, and join Jonas on Facebook, where he's most active.

Contact Jonas Saul

Linktree: Find me here

Email: jonassaul@icloud.com

www.ingramcontent.com/pod-product-compliance
Lightning Source LLC
Chambersburg PA
CBHW031847310726
48972CB00005B/1443